WHEN WE FELL

ELENA AITKEN

Also by Elena Aitken

Timber Creek

When We Left

When We Were Us

When We Began

When We Fell

Women's Fiction

All We Never Knew

Ever After

Choosing Happily Ever After

Needing Happily Ever After

Wanting Happily Ever After

Fighting Happily Ever After

We Wish You A Happily Ever After

Keeping Happily Ever After

Finding Happily Ever After

Seeking Happily Ever After

Cherishing Happily Ever After

Ever After: Volume One (Books 1-4)

Castle Mountain Lodge

Unexpected Gifts

Hidden Gifts

The Springs Series

The Springs Complete Collection - Books 1-10

The McCormicks

Love in the Moment

Only for a Moment

One more Moment

In this Moment

From this Moment

Bears of Grizzly Ridge

His to Protect

His to Seduce

His to Claim

Hers to Take

His to Defend

His to Tame

His to Seek

Bears of Grizzly Ridge: Books 1-4

Destination Paradise

Shelter by the Sea

Escape to the Sun

Stand Alone Stories

All We Never Knew

Drawing Free

Sugar Crash

Composing Myself

Betty & Veronica

The Escape Collection

Vegas

Nothing Stays in Vegas

Return to Vegas

Halfway Series

Halfway to Nowhere

Halfway in Between

Halfway to Christmas

Chapter One

THE SECOND DREW ROSS opened the garage door, she wished she hadn't. When the door rolled up, the only thing staring back at her were boxes. Piles and piles of boxes.

"Awesome." Drew rolled her eyes and put her hands on her hips but there was no help for it. If she was going to find her son's baseball glove, there was only one thing to do.

Start opening boxes.

"Here goes nothing," she said aloud before taking a step into the garage. Her long, dark hair was twisted up on the top of her head in a messy bun and she'd managed to find a bandanna that she'd tied around that. Dressed in an old t-shirt and a pair of cut-offs, she at least looked as if she was prepared to do a little organizing and cleaning.

Which was good, because she certainly didn't feel ready to face the lifetime of stuff the cardboard boxes and rubber totes held. Not that she had a choice.

Austin was going to start Little League, and he needed a glove. He was just barely five. He needed stability. He needed everything to be as normal as possible.

He *needed* his glove.

That was the thought that propelled Drew forward and into the garage full of boxes and memories.

She held her breath and opened the flap of the first one. It wasn't labeled. Most of them weren't. When she and Eric had decided to pack up their entire lives and move back to Timber Creek so he could live out his last few months in their hometown, there hadn't been much time to pack up properly or label anything. In fact, it would be a miracle if half of their things weren't broken and smashed inside those boxes.

Not that she cared all that much anymore.

Drew did most of the packing herself, with Eric helping out as much as he could. He was already so weak, even then, that he spent most of his time resting in a chair, keeping her company and trying to make her laugh while she threw things in boxes so they could uproot their entire lives that were about to be shattered completely.

"You might want to wrap that in bubble wrap," he'd said when she picked up his overstuffed trout pillow. He'd owned it for years and for reasons Drew could never understand, insisted on keeping it on the living room couch.

Drew paused, the pillow in her hand. "Seriously?"

He nodded, a grin on his handsome, but way too pale face. "Deadly. It's very special."

"I was actually thinking maybe we could donate this." She held the printed pillow up. "I mean…really?"

"No way." Her husband of eight years pushed himself to his feet and made his way over to her. He took the trout out of her hands and kissed it before turning and using it to kiss her. "This is my most prized possession." He laughed and before she could protest, wrapped his arms around her, and pulled her into him.

There were times when, if she didn't look close, Drew could forget that cancer was ravaging his body, and just for a minute she could pretend that it was just an ordinary day.

When he pressed his lips to hers, and dipped her backward, just a little, it was one of those times.

Maybe the doctors were wrong and as soon as they got home to Timber Creek, Eric would finally beat the cancer and they'd live to be old and gray together.

The memory washed over Drew as she stood with the box open in front of her, surrounded by their memories.

The doctors hadn't been wrong. She was the one who was wrong. Being home in Timber Creek hadn't saved Eric. It had been almost nine months since he'd been gone. Nine months that Drew had to adjust to the idea of a new future.

For the most part, she was succeeding. With the help of her friends and family, she was starting to live again. More and more each day, it got a little easier to breathe without wanting to cry, kiss their son—who looked so much like his father—without thinking of all the things Eric would miss out on, and just get through the day without having a total meltdown.

Yes. Most days were easier.

But most days she didn't have to go through their boxes.

Drew wiped a tear from her cheek and shook her head. "Come on, Drew. You've got this. They're just boxes." She scanned the garage again, a new determination steeling her resolve. "And one of them has Austin's glove in it."

She took a deep breath, held it and opened the first box.

The rush of air came out in a laugh as she realized she was looking at the very same trout pillow she'd just been remembering. She should have thrown it in the donation pile before they'd left Nevada. After all, it was completely ridiculous. She lifted it out and held it in her hands for a moment before putting it aside.

Maybe she should have donated it, but Drew was glad she hadn't. It was ugly and ridiculous but it had been Eric's. She had no idea what she was going to do with it, but for the time being, it was going to have to live in the garage. She had more pressing issues than redecorating the house. Although the time would come where she would have to go through the boxes and actually do something with them, it was not on that particular warm day in the middle of May.

Drew shoved the fish back in the box and reached for another one.

Nothing but photo albums and old books she'd never read again.

Next.

Mercilessly, as if each box that turned up without the glove fueled her toward the next, Drew reached for box after box. She dug through the contents, sometimes pulling them out to the floor around her, before shoving it to the side and reaching for the next as if the contents of each container didn't hold the intense power to hurt her.

They did.

But she refused to let the pain in. Not today.

She had to find the glove.

After too much fruitless searching, Drew finally stood and wiped her arm across her brow.

"Come on." She groaned and stretched her back side to side. "It has to be here." She straightened up and looked at the stack in front of her. It was the highest pile of boxes, mostly Rubbermaid totes that were leaning against the back wall. The glove had to be in there. She was running out of options. Austin's first practice was that night and— "Dammit." There wasn't much help for it—she was going to have to get to the top of that pile.

She didn't have a ladder, so she moved a few of the larger boxes to the bottom of the stack, put her foot on the lip of a tote and hoisted herself up. For just a moment, it looked as though it would work. Her hands brushed along the top box, the one she was aiming for, and then…the entire stack wobbled to the right and then swayed to the left. And in the split second before the entire tower of totes fell with her still clinging to the side, instead of panicking, all Drew could do was laugh.

BEN ROSS LIFTED the last of the oversized planters out of his truck bed and hauled it to the brick patio at the back of the Log and Jam. He set it with the others he'd just unloaded and used the edge of his t-shirt to wipe the sweat from his face. It was only the end of May, but it was already hot for the mountain town of Timber Creek, a fact that boded well for the new patio he'd just finished constructing behind his pub.

He'd opened the Log and Jam almost ten years ago and it had quickly become the favorite place for locals to hang out. The problem, at least as far as Ben was concerned, was that the cozy timber-framed interior, decorated with local logging antiques, was cozy and perfect during the snowy winter months, but during the all-too-short mountain summer months, he just wanted to be outside.

And if he wanted to be outside, then his customers likely wanted the same thing, which was why he'd spent the last six weeks getting permits and loans and then finally, building the huge outdoor patio at the Log and Jam.

Ben leaned back against the log wall of the building and surveyed his work. It had been a huge job and one that had taken a whole lot of collaborative effort from his friends and people in the community, but it was almost done.

He'd taken the empty space next to his building, which had served as overflow parking, and had created a combination of decking and brick-laid patio space. Because the weather could be unpredictable in the mountains, he'd covered half of the space with a huge timber-framed open-sided roof, which not only served as shelter in case of inclement weather, but also held his lighting and industrial space heaters, which would be perfect on cool evenings and extend his patio time well into the fall months.

He'd been able to leave most of the trees around the space, which gave it a feeling of privacy and intimacy, but he'd been told by almost all of his female staff members that planters full of bright flowers were an absolute must. Which was why he'd just spent the last few hours unloading the massive ones he'd bought in Seattle and hauled back earlier that morning.

Soil and plants could wait though, because as much as he'd like to finally see the space ready to go, Ben had other matters he had to take care of that afternoon.

He left the patio and entered his pub through the side door.

"Something smells amazing," he called into the kitchen at Michael, his head chef. "What's the special today?"

Michael appeared a moment later from the swinging door. He wiped his hands on his apron. "Roasted chicken club sandwich with a loaded baked potato soup. Want some?"

He hadn't had a chance to grab anything to eat, and Ben's stomach rumbled. But a quick glance at the clock over the bar told him that as much as he'd love to sit and enjoy a meal, he didn't have time.

"Maybe later," he said. "I'll be back for the evening shift, but I have to run right now."

"I can't promise a sandwich," Michael said. "But I'll save you a bowl of soup."

Ben laughed. Even as the boss, he didn't seem to have any pull when it came to enjoying the amazing food Michael created. Ever since he'd started working at the Log and Jam, the pub had become one of the most popular lunch destinations in town, and the dinner crowd was picking up too. Business was booming. Which was a good thing, considering the loan he'd just taken out in order to make the patio happen in time for the summer season.

But he couldn't think about that right now. It would only

stress him out and there was nothing he could do about it. Sometimes you needed to spend money to make money, and the pub business wasn't any different. The patio would pay off; he knew it would.

Ten minutes later, Ben was across town in the childhood bedroom he'd shared with his older brother. It never failed to hit him how much things hadn't changed inside this room, with the matching twin beds, various posters tacked to the walls— mostly cars because their mom wouldn't let them put up anything that might be considered *too provocative*. Good thing she didn't know about the *Playboy* Eric had stolen from a friend's dad when he was thirteen.

Ben chuckled a little at the memory of how Eric had given him the contraband magazine two years later when he'd turned thirteen. He'd treated it very seriously, as if it were a rite of passage for his little brother. Things had been different then. They'd been close when they were young. Inseparable. Ben's chest ached with the familiar pain of loss that had dulled, but not disappeared in the months since his brother passed.

He didn't think it would ever go away completely. *How do you fill the hole your brother leaves behind?* It was a question he couldn't even begin to answer.

The idea of searching for the box where he'd hid that magazine crossed Ben's mind. No doubt it was still under his bed where he'd left it all those years ago. But he shook it off. That's not what he'd come to find.

"What are you looking for, Ben?" His mother's voice from the doorway startled him out of his memories and Ben turned around to see Sylvia Ross, a dishtowel in her hands, watching him.

"Sorry, Mom. I didn't think you were home." Ben crossed the room and gave his mother a quick hug and kiss on the cheek.

She looked tired. Older. She'd aged at least ten years since

Eric had died. It wasn't easy to lose a brother; Ben couldn't even imagine how hard it had been for his mom to lose her oldest child.

"You look good, Mom."

She gave him a look that made it clear she knew he was lying, but she managed a smile anyway. "I've been sleeping a little better these days."

"It'll come, Mom. Maybe you should go see the doctor about some sleeping pills. You really do need to take care of yourself."

She shook her head and waved the dishtowel to dismiss the idea. "The best medicine for me is seeing you. Can I get you a cup of tea?"

Ben instantly felt guilty. He knew he wasn't spending enough time with his parents. But there was only so much time in the day, and...well... "I'm sorry, Mom. Not right now. I came to grab something. But I'll come for dinner tomorrow," he added when his mother's face fell.

"I'll make roast chicken." Her face once more lifted, but Ben's guilt didn't disappear. "And I'll see if Drew and Austin would like to come by as well. There'll be plenty for everyone."

"It sounds perfect." Ben made a quick mental note about making sure the bar was staffed properly for the following night. He wouldn't let his mom down.

"What is it exactly that you are looking for?" Sylvia asked as Ben got down on his hands and knees and started rooting around Eric's old bed.

"I'm hoping that you still haven't cleaned under here," he teased.

"If you're talking about that dirty magazine, I got rid of it years ago."

"What?" Ben lifted his head so quickly, it made a sharp, hard contact with the bed frame. "Ouch." He turned around, his hand on his head to see his mother grinning at him.

"Don't tell me I don't clean under there."

He couldn't help but laugh as he resumed his search. A moment later, it was Ben's turn to smile as his hand landed on the item he'd been hoping to find.

"Got it." He held the item up over his head in triumph. "I'm glad you're so sentimental, Mom. Because I know one little boy who I'm hoping will be pretty excited to see this when he gets home from school."

"Oh, Ben." Sylvia put her hand to her mouth and bit her bottom lip. "I didn't even think...you're so thoughtful."

He shrugged. "Anything for him, Mom. Anything." He gave his mother a kiss on the cheek. "Don't cry, Mom. Please."

Sylvia wiped her tears, but Ben was sure she'd be crying again the moment he left. He knew in his heart that it would have broken Eric's heart to see his mother still so torn up about his death, but she'd always been an emotional woman. Strong, but emotional. She was healing; it was just taking her a bit longer.

"I'll be fine." She waved him away. "You get going and I'll see you tomorrow."

Ben left his mother at the front door, and made the quick drive down the street. Not even five minutes later, he was parked in front of the low-rise bungalow where he'd spent more time in the last nine months than his own house.

SHE MAY HAVE BEEN LAUGHING as she fell from the boxes, but Drew definitely wasn't laughing a second later as she toppled to the ground. Fortunately for her, she landed in one of two oversized cardboard boxes where she'd packed a variety of throw pillows that Eric had always complained were more of a pain in the ass than decorative.

At the moment, considering her somewhat soft landing that

could have been a lot worse, Drew couldn't think of anything negative at all to say about the blue and yellow throw cushions she'd bought a few years earlier to brighten up their living room, despite the way Eric used to toss them to the floor whenever he wanted to watch television.

"It's a good thing I wasn't very good at donating much of anything." She laughed and rubbed her hip that had connected with something a little less soft that must have been hiding under the pillows.

"Jesus Christ! Drew?"

She tried to swing her head around toward the voice, and the front of the garage, but Drew was somewhat stuck in the box. Like a turtle on the back of their shell. The image made her laugh again.

"Are you okay?"

She leaned her head farther backward, stretching until she could make out the image of her savior. Her eyes landed first on the work boots before traveling up to the muscular legs clad in worn denim, the narrow waist, untucked t-shirt and finally familiar dark hair and green eyes. Her laughter caught in her throat as she sucked in a sharp breath.

Eric.

Drew froze in place, not that she could move very much anyway, as her eyes focused on the upside-down man.

She blinked once and then again.

No. It wasn't Eric. Of course.

"Drew? Are you okay?"

Ben.

A second later, Ben stood over her, his face twisted in a frown. "What the hell? Did you..." He glanced up and took in what was left of the precariously stacked totes. "Were you *climbing* that?"

She opened her mouth to answer, but ended up closing it again and shaking her head in an effort to clear the image of

Eric—her late husband and Ben's older brother—from her mind. It wasn't even that they looked anything alike. Eric had been fair and slighter in stature—even before he got sick—than Ben, who had dark features and a much more muscular build. But every once in a while, Drew was struck by some similarity. Something Ben said, those deep eyes, or the way he stood, or... something else.

Just like Eric.

"I'm fine," she said after a moment. "But I seem to be a little stuck."

Ben reached for her arms and lifted her easily out of the box and set her upright on her feet as if she were a doll. "Were you seriously climbing up that stack of totes?" he asked again.

She tilted her head in answer and raised an eyebrow.

"What the hell, Drew? You could have killed yourself."

"But I didn't."

"I don't think that's the point."

She took a step toward some of the totes that had toppled down with her and winced in pain, her hand flying to her hip. Whatever she'd landed on was definitely not a throw pillow.

"You okay?"

"I really am." Ben was sweet and had been nothing but amazing since they'd come home and then especially after Eric had passed. She didn't know what she would have done without him over the last few months and the way he'd taken care of her and Austin and made sure she was eating properly, getting out of the house, and of course taking care of some of the random jobs around the house. Along with Amber, one of her best friends, Ben had been an absolute rock over the last few months. But as amazing as the care and attention was, more and more Drew had been looking for opportunities to stand on her own two feet without depending on anyone else.

Even if she should have asked for help.

Ben was still looking at her with disbelief on his face.

"Really," she said. "I'm okay. I just landed a little funny. I'll probably have a bruise is all."

Fortunately, Ben didn't press the issue but instead put his hands on his own hips and looked around the disaster of a garage. "What are you looking for anyway?"

She sighed. She'd been looking all afternoon and still hadn't found Austin's glove. "Austin starts Little League tonight," she said. "Eric bought him a glove last summer and they'd tossed the ball around a little bit in the backyard before…well, before we moved. I need to find it."

A shadow passed over Ben's face but it was gone as quick as it came. "Okay then," he said. "We'll find it." He grabbed one of the totes that was now laying on its side. "I assume you were reaching for these?"

She nodded as relief washed over her. Something about Ben's presence, despite her desire for independence, was comforting and strong and just made her feel as though everything was going to be okay. For the first time in hours, Drew actually felt as if they would in fact find the glove in time for Austin's practice.

With Ben's help, they sorted through the last few bins and in the second to last one, finally found what they were looking for.

Drew held it up triumphantly. "Thank you so much."

He shrugged the way he always did, brushing off how helpful he was. "You know I would have helped you from the beginning, right? I mean, I know you're perfectly capable of looking through boxes," he said quickly before she could object. "But sometimes these things are made a little easier with two sets of hands. Especially considering…" He waved his arms around.

Drew knew he was referring to how hard it probably was to go through all of their things, or, more specifically, Eric's things.

"It was fine." It wasn't totally a lie. It hadn't been nearly as hard as she'd expected it might be. "What are you doing here, anyway? Don't you have a patio to put together?"

"I do." He grinned and gestured outside. "Come on," he said. "Let's get out of here."

Drew laughed and shook her head. "I can't go to the Log and Jam right now. I have to go get Austin from school right away and an early dinner and—what's that?"

Ben stood on her driveway, proudly holding a wooden baseball bat in his hands. He gave her a sideways look.

"I mean, I know what it is." She smacked his arm. "But *what* is it? As in…where did it come from?"

"I went by Mom and Dad's earlier. By the way, Mom wants you to come for dinner tomorrow."

Drew nodded. Absolutely they'd go for dinner. Spending time with Sylvia and Mitch had been good for everyone after Eric died. She'd even noticed Sylvia crying less and less.

"This was Eric's bat when he was a kid," Ben continued. "I think he got some sort of record number of home runs or something with it. It was under his bed, just where he'd left it."

Heat rushed to her face. "It was…" She reached for the bat. "It was Eric's?"

Ben nodded. "He never let me use it. Well, except that one time. But that was different." He shook his head and his smile was back. "It was his lucky bat and I'm absolutely positive he'd want Austin to have it."

Drew took the bat from him and held it in her own hands. It was way too big for Austin. At least it would be for a few years, but without a doubt it was an incredibly special gift. "Ben, this is perfect. He'll love it. Thank you."

To Drew's surprise, she wasn't going to cry. The tears threatened, but then they were gone. It was getting easier and easier to control the sadness that still washed over her with a regularity that was exhausting.

Chapter Two

"BUT ARE you *sure* I'll hit the ball?" Austin stood next to the car, his glove that Drew had rescued only hours earlier in his hand. They'd arrived at the ball diamond almost twenty minutes earlier, but Austin had yet to make it out of the parking lot.

"Yes, you'll hit it," Drew said. "I mean...you might not get it right away...but—"

"Mom!"

Drew took another glance over at the group of kids starting to gather by the dugout. They were going to be late. She crouched in front of her suddenly anxious son. It wasn't like Austin to get worked up about little things. At least, it hadn't been like Austin. But at five years old, maybe the first day of Little League wasn't such a little thing.

Especially considering his father should have been there.

Drew pushed away the thought, the way she tried to most of the time. There was nothing she could do about Eric. She took a deep breath and tried again to soothe her son's concerns.

"I'm just saying that sometimes it takes a little practice to

hit the ball, but before long you're going to be amazing at it."
He tilted his head and looked doubtful. "And you know what
else?" He waited, his eyes wide. "You're not the only one. All
of the kids on your team are going to have to learn, just like
you."

That piqued his interest. "So none of us will be able to hit
the ball?"

She didn't mean to, but she laughed a little.

"Mom!"

"I'm sorry. I'm sorry. Yes, I'm sure you'll all be able to hit
the ball, Austin."

"Of course you'll be able to hit the ball."

Drew jumped up at the voice and turned to see Ben in the
parking lot, a large duffel bag slung over his shoulder. He'd
changed out of his work jeans and t-shirt and was now wearing
athletic pants, a fresh shirt, and a Mariner's ballcap. He looked
almost like...a coach.

Without missing a beat, Ben crouched in front of Austin.
"You're all going to hit the ball, and right away, too. Because
we use this thing called a T." He looked up at Drew and
grinned. "It's T-Ball."

Even if Austin had no idea what that meant, it seemed to
satisfy him. If Uncle Ben was saying it, it must be okay. "Why
don't you go join the rest of the team? I'll be over in a minute."
Ben tapped the brim of Austin's cap and he was on his way.

Drew watched him run over to the rest of the kids before
she looked to Ben. "What do you mean, 'we use a T'?"

Ben laughed. "Oh, it's this rubber thing that we stick the
ball on and——"

"I know what a T is." She cut him off. "I meant, what do
you mean by *we*?" She crossed her arms over her chest and
waited for the answer she already knew was coming.

"I'm one of the coaches of Austin's team." He lifted the
duffel bag in a sort of shrug. "I just found out. Sort of."

Drew cocked an eyebrow and couldn't help but grin. "What do you mean, sort of?"

"I told Evan the Log and Jam would sponsor the team this year. You know—jerseys, caps, jackets, that kind of thing."

"Jackets?" Drew tried and failed to keep the chuckle out of her voice. "I hardly think that five- and six-year-olds need jackets for a Little League team."

Ben laughed. "I know, I know. But I couldn't help it. They're going to look so awesome."

Together, they started walking toward the group of kids at the diamond. "That doesn't tell me how you ended up as a coach."

"That's my fault." Evan Anderson, their good friend and new husband of one of Drew's best friends, Cam, joined them. He put his arm around Drew's shoulders and squeezed. "One of the dads was supposed to help me out but he had to take overtime shifts or something, so...I needed an extra set of hands."

"And he convinced me to help," Ben added.

Drew looked between the men and smiled. "Well, it looks like the kids are going to have some great coaches. How long have you been doing this, Evan?"

"This is my fourth year as the coach of the Timber Creek Trout."

"The Trout?" Drew couldn't help it; she burst out laughing. "That's a...that's a pretty tough name."

"Hey." Evan shrugged. "The kids voted. I wanted the Timber Wolves, but...trout are pretty awesome, too."

"They sure are."

Still chuckling, Evan shook his head. "I better go tame the trout and get started with our first practice. You ready, Assistant Coach Ben?"

"Absolutely."

With a wave to Drew, Evan took off, but Ben lingered.

When Evan was out of earshot, he turned to Drew. The smile he'd worn a moment earlier faded. "You're okay with this, right, Drew? I mean, I don't want to—"

"Yes." She interrupted him. "Of course I'm okay with it. And I think Austin will love having you coach. It's special, Ben. Really."

He nodded. His smile returned and for a moment he looked as though he were going to say something more, but then he turned and joined the rest of the team. Drew watched as Ben was quickly surrounded. He gave all the kids high fives and soon both coaches had them warming up with jumping jacks.

"Hey. Come sit." Drew turned to see Cam calling her from the bleachers. She took one more look at Austin, who was doing some sort of half jumping jack, half lunge. She shook her head and laughed before joining her friend.

"Oh my goodness, he's so cute," Drew said as she climbed up the bleachers and sat next to her friend, her eyes on the baby in Cam's arms. "Let me have him." She reached out for Cam and Evan's young son, Theo, and was immediately satisfied by the weight of him in her hands. "I can't believe how big he's getting. I feel like I haven't seen him in forever."

"It was last week." Cam laughed. "But I know what you mean. He's almost two months already. Isn't that crazy?"

"So crazy. I remember when Austin was this small." Drew traced Theo's chubby cheek with her finger. Austin had been such a content baby. He'd always been perfectly happy to hang out with her in his snugly or bouncy chair while she cooked. He'd hardly ever fussed. Her gaze lifted and she found him on the field tossing a ball to another boy. Not much had changed. He was still a resilient, happy little boy. She knew he missed his dad, but he seemed to be taking it all in stride.

As she watched, Ben went over to the boys and showed them how to hold the ball properly.

He was so amazing with the kids. It was becoming a very common thought, but Drew had no idea what she would have done if Ben hadn't stepped up and helped her out so much after Eric passed. In the months immediately following, Drew had mostly been in shock. Despite all the time she had to prepare for the inevitable, it had still been much harder than she could have anticipated. She knew she'd leaned on Ben too much in those early days. But she couldn't help but do anything else.

Now though...

"Hey." Cam touched her arm and brought her back to the present. "I lost you in thought there for a moment," she said. "You okay?"

Drew nodded and turned her attention back to baby Theo. "I am. I was just remembering Austin when he was this age."

"And..."

"And I was thinking of Eric," she admitted. "But only sort of." She twisted a little until she was looking at Cam. "I was actually thinking of Ben." Her friend's face twisted in question, so she continued. "Well, mostly just how great he's been with Austin, and me of course. But also...how I probably shouldn't depend on him so much anymore, you know?"

Cam nodded, but Drew could still see the question in her eyes. "I'm sure Ben is helping you out because he wants to, Drew. And it's okay to accept that help. You've had a huge life-changing event. We know you don't *need* the help."

Drew nodded distractedly. Obviously Cam meant well. They all did. But Drew was getting sick of everyone cutting her so much slack. She wasn't some china doll that was going to break. Sure, she'd had some rough spots; that was to be expected. But she was okay. It had been almost nine months. And over a year before that preparing for it. She'd more than proved that she could handle herself.

She looked back out to the field. This time her gaze landed

on Ben. They'd been close friends since grade school. There'd been a time once she'd even had a crush on him. A big one. But that had been a lifetime ago, before she'd started dating Ben's older brother and everything had changed between them.

Ben was a great guy. He deserved everything life had to offer him. Drew watched him and the easy way he had with the kids.

He deserved that.

What he didn't deserve was to be stuck babysitting his dead brother's family.

It was time to put an end to it.

"I THINK that went pretty well, don't you?" From behind the bar at the Log and Jam, Ben poured two draft beers before sliding one over to Evan, who sat on a stool.

He took the beer and drank deeply before answering. "It went about as well as can be expected for a first practice. The first few are always like herding cats. But they'll get it and by the end of the season, the Timber Creek Trouts will be scoring home runs. Wait and see."

Ben laughed. "I sure hope so. They're cute kids."

"They are. And in a few years, I'll have my very own trout out there with them. That'll be pretty awesome."

Ben took a deep drink of his beer. He was happy for his best friend. It had been way too long since he'd seen that smile on Evan's face. In fact, up until about a year ago, it had been about fifteen years. Since Cam left after high school.

But she'd come back.

Cam and Evan had been high school sweethearts and everyone had been positive they were going to get married. But things never seemed to work out the way you expected them to when you're seventeen and one misunderstanding had turned into a bigger one. It had taken fifteen years and Cam moving back to town with her teenage daughter for the two of them to find their way back to each other and finally figure out that they'd loved each other all along.

Now they were married with a baby and as far as Ben could tell, his best friend had never been happier.

If he wasn't so bloody happy for them, he'd be jealous. *Really* jealous.

He'd managed to convince himself for a long time that he didn't want or need all that. There'd only been one woman he'd loved and when that hadn't worked out, well, it just didn't seem like something he needed in his life.

"It will be awesome." Ben forced himself to focus on the conversation. "Theo is pretty friggin' cute. Thank God he takes after his mom." He laughed and ducked as Evan threw a paper coaster at him. "Seriously, though," he said. "It's awesome to see everyone so happy. And so many babies." He rolled his eyes, but he meant what he'd said. It was great to see all his friends so happy.

Besides Cam and Evan, their other good friends Christy and Mark, who'd been married practically since high school, had just come through a hard time of their own and were now the proud parents of an adopted baby girl, Mya. Amber, was another of Drew's best friends and she'd moved back home after Eric died and had been a massive help with Drew and Austin in those early months. No one had any idea that she was battling the aftermath of an addiction that had almost claimed her life. But now she, too, had found love, although no baby. Yet. And as genuinely happy as Ben was for all his friends, he was also starting to feel a bit...

"Maybe time for you to have a baby, too?" Evan was joking of course, but the idea hit closer to home with Ben than his friend realized.

"Not for me." Ben took his friend's empty beer mug and refilled it before handing it back. "I think I'm good being the crazy uncle who spoils the crap out of Austin."

"That's not a bad gig." Evan agreed. "But...it's not really the—"

"Don't say it's not the same," Ben warned him. "I know it's not the same thing as having a kid of my own. But that's not going to happen. At least not any time soon. I'd need to have a girlfriend at the very least. Besides, Austin needs me. So does Drew."

Evan gave him a look and Ben knew without asking what his friend was thinking.

He shook his head. "You're wrong."

Evan smirked. "I didn't say anything."

"You didn't have to." Ben filled his own now empty beer mug. "I know you, and I know what you were going to say and you're wrong."

"Okay, tough guy." Evan put his mug on the bar. "If you know so much, tell me. What was I going to say?"

There was no point playing games with Evan, so Ben took another swallow of beer and said, "You were going to tell me that I'm getting too close to Drew."

"Was I?"

Ben swallowed hard before saying anything else. Even if Evan *wasn't* going to say that, he didn't have to. Ben knew it was a fact. He'd avoided Drew for years. Ever since he'd played the key role in getting them together in high school. He'd kept his distance because it was the only thing he could do without going totally crazy. That had been easier when Drew and Eric had lived in Nevada for all those years. And definitely before he'd sworn to his brother on his death bed that he'd look out for his family.

It was much harder to keep his distance now.

"You were," Ben said after a moment. "And if you weren't, I was." He shook his head and took a deep drink of his beer.

It was a few moments before he realized his friend was silently watching him. He raised his eyebrows in question.

"I was just going to say that maybe..." Evan took a breath and continued, "I know it's been incredibly hard for these last few months. I mean, I know losing Eric hit you harder than you—"

"I'm fine."

"You and I both know that's not true."

Ben considered arguing with him further, but what was the point? Evan was right. Losing Eric the way he had, after so long being estranged, it was...well, it just wasn't fair. For the first few months after he died, Ben had tortured himself with the *what-if* game. *What if he'd reached out years ago? What if he'd never had feelings for Drew? What if he'd mended their relationship instead of letting their distance grow?*

It had driven him crazy because he couldn't go back in time and change things. Those years were lost forever and he regretted every minute he'd lost with Eric, but also with Austin when he was a baby. Nothing was worth missing time with the ones you loved. There was no argument too great. No reason important enough to justify that kind of distance.

It was just too bad it took him so long to realize it. And it had been at the expense of his relationship with Eric.

Ironically, it had been Eric himself who'd helped Ben through those rough first few months. Or more specifically, his words to him in the weeks leading up to his passing.

"Don't sweat it, little brother. What's done is done," Eric had said when Ben once again expressed his regret for all the time they'd wasted. "It wasn't just you. I could have called. I could have brought the family home more. I could have done a lot of things. But I didn't. And here we are."

"But, we could have—"

"Yeah," Eric interrupted. "We could have done a lot of things. But what I don't want to do now is live in a past we can't change. And I don't want you to either. Remember that when I'm gone. There's no going back. Just forward." He paused to catch his breath. More and more in those later days, it exhausted Eric just to talk. "We do the best we can at the time, and when we know better, we can do better. Now we know better." He managed a grin. "So I expect you to do better."

Ben shook his head and chuckled. "Man, when did you get so damn smart? Because the Eric I remember was a dumb ass."

He remembered the smile Eric had given him—his usual cocky grin, shrouded by a deep sadness. "Facing the end does that to a man, Ben. And I mean it. Don't live in a past you can't change. Not for me. Promise."

Ben chuckled in an effort to brush it off, but Eric would not be deterred. "I mean it, Ben. Promise me."

His laughter had died on his lips and he had looked into his brother's now dulled eyes, and made the promise.

It was those words, and that promise, that finally sank in months later. It didn't make it any easier to know Eric was gone, and it didn't lessen the ache of his absence, but he'd promised, so he was trying. Just like he was trying to keep other promises he'd made.

"Okay," Ben confessed to Evan after a moment. "I'm not fine *fine*. But it's coming. And I think with Drew, well…"

"It can't be easy."

"Hell no." Ben shook his head and scrubbed a hand over his face. "But it is what it is."

"You shouldn't be too hard on yourself, Ben. It's only natural if you're getting close to Drew. Everything you guys have been through together and the way—"

"No." Ben cut him off because whatever Evan was saying,

it was *not* okay that he was getting close to Drew. The feelings he'd had for her years ago were nothing more than a childhood crush. It wasn't real. Besides, that had been years ago. A lot had changed and she was his brother's wife. It wasn't like that and it couldn't be like that. Ever. "It's not like that," he said aloud. "But maybe you're right," he said. Evan looked confused, but Ben kept talking. "Maybe I should start getting out more. I mean, Drew is doing better and Austin is busy with school and the Trouts now." He grinned a little, remembering his nephew holding his father's old, much too large for him bat only a few hours ago. "Maybe it is time that I start entertaining other things."

Evan shook his head. "I'm not sure what that means."

Ben drained the rest of his beer and smiled triumphantly at his friend. "Maybe I should finally start dating."

And stop living in the past I can't have or change.

Chapter Three

DREW WALKED around the ring one more time. Her feet slogged through the mud and she was once again glad she'd thought to wear her rain boots out to the ranch. Amber had warned her that things were still a little muddy out at Taking the Reins, and with the rain the night before, *a little* muddy was an understatement.

Not that she minded. Not really. She just liked being with the horses.

"And you don't seem to mind a little mud," she said to the horse. "Do you, Peanut?"

The horse made a snuffing noise in response and she chuckled before stopping so she could stroke the horse's flank and talk a little more. When she'd first started coming to Taking the Reins, Logan Myers, the owner and equine therapist, told her that the horses would be able to sense what was going on with her emotionally, even if she couldn't, and the best way to work through it was simply to talk to the horses.

So that's what she did.

It felt a little strange at first, but it didn't take long for Drew to open up to Peanut. She was a good listener and had never once tried to interrupt her to tell her that she'd get over it or that the pain of her loss would fade and pretty soon she wouldn't even be able to remember how sad she'd once been.

It's not that the people who actually did tell her those things didn't mean well. They did. She knew that. But it didn't change the fact that talking to the horses was just so much better.

"You're a good girl." She stroked Peanut's mane. "Thank you for listening." Although Drew would have liked to spend more time with Peanut, she'd already been there for almost an hour and Peanut was a busy horse. Logan's horse therapy program, although still pretty new, was growing in popularity and the horses were in high demand.

Drew was also very aware that she was only there because she was Amber's best friend. Logan refused to take money from her in exchange for her sessions with Peanut, claiming a *best friend rate*. Not that she didn't appreciate it, she did, but she was going to keep insisting that she should pay. Logan was a great guy, and she couldn't be happier for Amber that she'd met someone so incredible with such a huge heart. But that huge heart wasn't going to make them any money, and she'd never forgive herself if Taking the Reins wasn't the roaring success it should be.

Amber and Logan had invested so much time and money into building up the stables and a small treatment center where they could host out-of-town patients. Drew knew that their success wasn't going to hinge on her payments, or lack thereof, but still…she wanted to contribute.

She led Peanut back toward the stables, where Amber was waiting for her. "How did it go today?"

"Fantastic as usual." She gave Peanut one more pat on the flank before handing Amber the reins. "She's just such a good listener."

"Careful." Amber laughed. "Or your best friend will get jealous."

"You know that no one, or no horse," Drew added with a smile, "will ever replace you, Amber. Thank you again for this. I had no idea that talking to an animal could be so therapeutic. I really think she's helping me heal so much faster."

"I know exactly what you mean." Amber led Peanut into her stall. She gave her an apple and together the friends walked out into the spring sunshine. "You are doing amazing with everything," Amber said. "How are you feeling?"

"I still miss him." Drew kicked at a clump of dirt with her boot. "But...not as much as I did. Does that make sense?"

Amber nodded. "It does." She put her hand on Drew's shoulder. "And how's Sylvia? I ran into Eric's dad at the store the other day and suggested that maybe they both come and make a visit to the horses."

"Oh, I don't think so." Drew shook her head. "Mitch is actually doing really well, I think. He misses him of course, but he's pretty pragmatic, you know? It's like, he just kind of accepted it."

"Some people are really good at handling this type of thing." Amber nodded thoughtfully. "And Sylvia?"

Drew bit her bottom lip and shook her head a little. "It's harder for her. I think she's getting there, but I don't think equine therapy is a thing for her. She did join a grief group, though." Drew didn't add how her mother-in-law had been trying to get her to go to a meeting. It's not that she didn't think it would be helpful, but she truly didn't think she needed it. Besides, the horses *were* a thing for her. "She's been going for a bit and I think it's really helping. I know everyone copes in different ways," Drew continued. "But sometimes it's just... well, I'm just glad to see Sylvia doing better."

"I'm so glad to hear it, too." Amber put her hand on Drew's shoulder and added, "And it's okay, you know?"

As usual, her best friend could see right through her and she'd heard loud and clear what Drew hadn't even said. Drew nodded but didn't look up.

"It's okay that you feel good, Drew. You don't have to miss him with the same intensity that you did right after he died. That's not only okay, it's normal. You're *supposed* to feel okay."

Drew nodded and finally looked up at Amber's kind smile. "I know," she said, and meant it. "Eric wouldn't want me all sad anyway. He actually told me so. It just still feels...well, it's just hard to put it into words." She fell silent for a moment, but she wasn't lost in grief the way she once would have been. It was getting easier and easier for her to think of her husband and feel happy for the time they did have instead of sad for what they'd lost.

"Well, I think you're doing amazing." Amber put her arm around her and together they walked through the yard. "And Austin...I hear he's going to the World Series of T-Ball with the Timber Creek Trout."

Drew laughed. "I don't know about that. But he is loving it and it's so awesome to see him out there with the other kids. Evan and Ben are the best coaches too. You'll have to come to a game."

"Of course. You tell me where and when, and Logan and I will be there to cheer on the Trout."

Drew laughed again at the silly team name, and she was still laughing and smiling thirty minutes later as she pulled into her driveway.

With Austin at school, the house used to feel empty and quiet. Almost sad. She'd tried to avoid it, but this time as she walked into the living room and took in the stark white walls, the empty side tables, the mantel over the fireplace that was still left bare, she realized for the first time that the house didn't feel sad because it was empty of life—both Austin's while he was gone for the day and Eric's because he was...just gone.

The house felt sad because even after living in it for a year since they'd moved back to Timber Creek, she still hadn't decorated. In fact, all of the things that made their house special and *theirs* were still in those stacks of boxes in the garage.

When they'd moved, everything had been in such a rush. When Eric was first diagnosed with pancreatic cancer, he'd thrown himself into every treatment the doctors offered him. Eric was unwaveringly optimistic, so much so that at first they didn't even tell family and friends back home what was going on. In fact, they waited until the diagnosis became terminal before they said anything, something Drew still felt badly about. But then again, they had been just so *sure* that he'd be okay.

And when he wasn't…well, when that piece of information had finally sunk into their realities, they packed up and moved back to Timber Creek so Eric could spend those final days among family and friends. And that's what had been important. Not the house or unpacking. In fact, Drew hadn't even given much thought to where she'd live after…well, *after*.

She'd contemplated moving back to Nevada, but it had been a brief thought and now, there was no way she could leave Timber Creek and the people there. No. She'd be staying. Which meant she needed to do something about her house.

Drew put her hands on her hips and surveyed the space again before walking room by room through the rest of the little house. The only room that had any kind of personality in it was Austin's, and that was only because like most little boys, everything he owned was spread across the carpeted floor. As for the rest…it was long past time she did something about it.

Without bothering to change clothes, Drew turned and went right back outside to start bringing in boxes and finally, truly unpack.

"EVERYTHING LOOKS GREAT, Ben. Are we ready to open up?" Annie, Ben's new manager at the Log and Jam, stood at the edge of the patio they'd just finished setting up and grinned. "It's going to be a beautiful evening and I bet we can fill the tables out here."

Ben surveyed the space. They'd just finished putting out the umbrellas as the tables and chairs he'd ordered had just arrived. They really were almost ready to go. Even the patio heaters had been set up and tested so when the sun went down and it got a little cool, his guests wouldn't have to move inside. The brick fireplace at the far end of the patio would also provide much-needed heat on those colder nights, too, and it looked amazing. But something was still missing.

"I still need to get some plants," he told Annie. The planters he'd brought back from the city a few days earlier still sat empty and Ben knew that once they were filled with plants and flowers, it would really bring the space alive. "But yes, we should open soon. In fact, let's aim for Friday night. That's two days away. Long enough to sort out the details and then we can have kind of a grand opening." As he spoke, the idea started to fully formulate in his head. "Yes," he said, more to himself. "We'll have a few drink specials and maybe we can see about Timber Heart playing a few songs."

Across from him, Annie shook her head and laughed. "You want to see if the most popular band in town is free with less than forty-eight hours' notice?"

He realized the request sounded insane, and it might have been, too, if he wasn't friends with the lead singer of the band and if he also didn't happen to know that Christy was in town, and the band wasn't already booked for a gig—a fact he only knew because he'd run into her husband, Mark, at Daisy's Diner earlier that day. "Don't worry about the band," he told

Annie. "I'll reach out to Christy. Can I leave you in charge of coming up with a few patio-style specials that we can offer?"

"No problem, boss." Annie gave him a mock salute. "I'll work on it now before the lunch rush starts."

"Perfect." Having good staff in place over the last few years had given Ben more freedom with the pub then he'd ever had. There was a time, not too long ago, when he would have had to spend every last minute at the Log and Jam, overseeing everything. It had been an exhausting time as he'd worked to turn what had once been Bud's, an old run-down bar, into his pride and joy. Setting everything up and getting established had been hard. But it had all been worth it, and more and more he was discovering that everything ran fine without him. Especially with Annie around. "I'll head out and get some plants and things right now."

Annie laughed and shook her head. "Are you sure you don't want me to go?"

"Why? You don't think I can handle a few plants?"

"It's not that. It's just...okay." She nodded. "I don't think you can handle a few plants. Picking planter flowers can be harder than you might think. You'll want something tall and something that will cascade over the edges. Some will need to be shade flowers, but the ones over there," she pointed to some of the planters, "those will need to be sun tolerant. It's actually quite a lot of work."

Ben shrugged. "How hard could it be? Really?"

Annie tilted her head. "If you want, I can—"

"Don't worry about it." He waved her away. "It can't possibly be that hard. I'll run over and get some things."

Ten minutes later, Ben stood in Petal Pushers, the local flower shop, his eyes glazed over. He stared at a variety of cut flowers and potted plants, none of which looked like they'd be suitable for his planters. Tentatively, he stepped forward and reached out to a rose.

White.

Just like the ones that had been at Eric's memorial. Just like the ones they'd each held and placed one by one in front of his picture.

Ben's breath caught in his throat, his breath gone momentarily from his lungs.

"Can I help you with something?"

He exhaled hard and dropped the rose he'd been holding at the sound of the voice. He spun around to see a young blonde woman holding something that resembled a fern in one hand, and a pair of scissors in the other.

"I'm looking for something for my planters." He bent to pick up the rose. "I'm not sure if—"

"No." She shook her head. "That's not for a planter. That's for a vase."

Or a funeral, he thought, but instead asked out loud, "What's the difference?"

She laughed and Ben couldn't help but smile along with her, the memories of the roses and the memorial fading with the sound. The woman stepped past him and gestured to the buckets of flowers where he'd found the rose. "Well, this one is cut already, so you could put it in a vase of water, but if you put it in a planter, well…"

"I see." He nodded, feeling more than a little out of his depth. "So, could you suggest something for my planters? I'm afraid I really don't have a clue where to start here."

"You don't say?" She winked at him, put her scissors down and extended her hand. "I'm Calla," she introduced herself. "I don't think we've ever met, but you're Ben Ross, right?"

He nodded and smiled. "I am. How did you—"

"I've been to the Log and Jam." She shrugged. "And… well…I'm sorry about your brother."

He nodded. "Thank you. He was a great man."

She smiled kindly, and Ben appreciated that she didn't

further the discussion. "If you come out back with me, I'm sure we can find something for your planters." She led the way through the store, out to the back where long greenhouse tents were set up. There were huge pots of flowers and trees, and more plants and flowers than Ben considered possible.

"Wow." He rubbed a hand through his dark hair and pulled at the roots a little. "I have no idea where to start."

"Don't worry," Calla said. "That's my job. Tell me about your space and the size of the planters you're trying to fill and I'll make sure you have everything you need."

Over an hour later, Ben was pretty sure he had more than he needed. They'd filled the back of his truck with a variety of different plants and bright, beautiful flowers. There were bags of soil and fertilizer and Calla had even sketched out planting diagrams so Ben would know exactly where to plant each thing. He was still very much overwhelmed, but at least now he had some semblance of a plan.

"I still think it's too much," he said again to Calla as he handed her his credit card. "And I don't know if I'll be able to make it look as good as you seem to think it will, but—"

"They're going to look great," she assured him. "And if you're really not sure what to do, I don't mind coming by. I could give you a hand, if you'd like. It is a pretty big job."

"You'd do that?"

He watched while she finished running his credit card and handed him the slip to sign. She was younger than him, to be sure. But she was cute and funny and he'd had a much better time picking plants than he could have imagined he would.

"Of course." She winked. "I had fun helping you, and I can tell you'll need all the help you can get actually getting everything planted."

Was she flirting with him?

He had no idea. But he did know that she was right. He

would need all the help he could get. "I'd actually really appreciate that."

"Great. Tomorrow morning work for you?" She beamed at him. "I don't open up till eleven tomorrow, so I can be there by eight. It should be enough time to get it all done."

"Sounds great. I'll see you then." He took his receipt from her. There was a little flicker of pride in his belly. He was doing just what he told Evan he was going to do; he'd just made a date. Even if it had felt wrong in a way he couldn't begin to describe.

Chapter Four

IT HAD TAKEN Drew the better part of the afternoon, and the rest of the evening after she picked up Austin from school, but she'd made huge progress. Austin had been delighted to unpack the boxes for her. He said it was like Christmas but better because he'd missed all of their stuff.

With his help, they managed to drag a number of boxes into the house so she could properly sort through her things. She'd hammered in nails and hung up pictures, put out vases and other mementos, and also repacked a number of boxes full of items to donate.

There was still a lot of work to do, but the house was finally starting to look like a home. The cushions brought in a splash of color, and although the walls were still a stark white, it would be an easy fix with a can of paint or some fun, bold drapes. She'd even put the trout pillow on the couch, just the way Eric would have liked.

After she tucked Austin into bed, Drew poured herself a glass of wine and contemplated how she should spend the rest of her evening. She'd earned herself a little relaxing on the couch in front of the television, but something stopped her from zoning out with Netflix. She was on such a roll that maybe she might just have enough energy to tackle one particular room that she'd been avoiding for too long.

Before she could change her mind, Drew took her glass of wine and walked down the short hall to the door that had remained closed for the last few months. To her surprise, the usual hurt and feeling of foreboding as she put her hand on the door handle wasn't there. And when she stepped through the door into the room where Eric had spent his last few weeks, she was remarkably okay.

Maybe it was true that time healed all things.

Or maybe it was because the room was mostly empty. The hospital bed they'd rented had long since been returned, so the only pieces of furniture were a few chairs, a bookshelf, and the bedside table that had been covered in Eric's pills and medicines. If she was being truthful, that was the part of the room she'd been avoiding.

The pills and medicines had long since been disposed of but it was what was inside the table that made Drew's stomach clench. But she couldn't avoid it forever. She took a sip of her wine and before she could talk herself out of it, crossed the room, opened the door and pulled out Eric's notebook.

When they were still in Nevada, Eric had started writing in the notebook during all his long wait times at the hospital while he was undergoing his treatments. He'd read a lot as well, but it was writing in the notebook that had helped him get through the long days. Drew had asked once what he was writing about, but Eric had only smiled, tucked the book away and told her, "Just jotting down a few thoughts, babe." His bright-green eyes were already so faded and dulled by then, but she could still see the light that shone there when he looked at her. "Lots of things going on up here these days." He tapped at his head and then pressed a finger to his lips until she kissed him.

Drew had never pressed the issue because there was no point. She'd known what Eric never bothered to say: it wouldn't be long before she could read the notebook herself.

But she hadn't. She'd known it was here all this time, and not once had she been tempted to open the drawer and take it out.

Why?

Drew could have laughed at herself. She had a million reasons she hadn't looked before. At least she had a million reasons that she could use to convince herself, but she knew the truth.

She was terrified.

She held the blue paper-covered book and pressed it to her chest.

What if Eric had written her a note? What if he'd used his last days to write down things he wanted her to know but couldn't bring himself to say? The idea that Eric had held back from her at the end made her so unbearably sad that she didn't know whether she'd be able to handle it if that's what the notebook contained.

But it could be worse.

What if Eric had used the book simply to write grocery lists, or inane things that didn't mean anything? Would she be equally as heartbroken to know that he hadn't bothered to leave her a message?

A tear slipped from her eye and down her cheek.

It was ridiculous and didn't make any sense, but Drew couldn't help the swirl of confusing thoughts that raced through her head. "This is what grief and loss does to you, I guess." She laughed at herself and shook her head before having another sip of wine.

Ultimately, she was going to have to look at the notebook and Drew knew that whatever he'd written in there, she'd be fine because the truth was, she didn't have any unfinished business with Eric.

Besides the fact that they were meant to grow old and watch Austin grow up together. But there was nothing she could do about that. But everything else—the feelings they had for each other—both Drew and Eric had made a point to talk as openly and honestly as they could during those last few months. It wasn't always easy. Far from it. But it was the best thing they could have done. Which was why Drew knew that whatever the notebook held, it would be okay.

She took another sip of wine and flipped the little book open to the first page.

* *The scent of pine in the air*
* *Birds singing outside my window*
* *Austin driving cars on the floor by my feet*

DREW READ the three lines once. And then again before she smiled. Those were all things Eric loved. Little details that made his day worth living. He'd told her that once. "It's the little things, Drew. The smallest of the small that make every day amazing." He'd tucked a strand of her long hair behind her ear. "Like looking at you, your brown eyes, your gorgeous hair and…" He leaned over and tucked his face close to her neck. "The intoxicating scent of you. These are the things that make me want to open my eyes each and every day, despite the pain."

She smiled to herself, remembering how they'd kissed after that. Tenderly. Carefully. Drew touched her finger to her lips and turned the page of the notebook, no longer afraid.

———

IT WASN'T QUITE nine o'clock when Ben knocked on Drew's door. He knew Austin would be sleeping, so he knocked quietly.

He'd almost driven right past the small bungalow, unsure whether Drew would be up herself, but when he saw the lights on inside, he pulled over. Michael had made extra broccoli and cheese soup earlier and despite the popularity for it at the dinner rush, there was extra. Ben knew it was Drew's favorite, and she so seldom was able to come by the Log and Jam because they currently didn't have any family friendly hours. Something Ben was working on changing. Funny how these things were never important until his nephew had become such a major part of his life.

He only had to wait a few minutes after knocking before Drew came to the door. She was wearing sweatpants and a t-shirt and a scarf around her hair, as if she'd been cleaning.

"I'm sorry it's so——"

"Ben? What are you——"

She laughed as they tried to speak over each other. It was such a sweet sound and one Ben had rarely heard in the last few months. Instinctively, he wanted to make it happen again.

"Come in." She stepped aside to let him into the small hall-way. "I've been busy. Come see."

Ben did as he was told and followed her down the short hallway into her kitchen. He noticed her hard work immediately. "Wow, Drew. You have been busy. What did... where...how?"

She laughed again. "I unpacked."

"Did you ever." He nodded and looked around again, noticing the brightly colored vases on top of the cabinets and the ceramic rooster tucked on one of the shelves, along with a variety of cookbooks. There was a bowl he'd never seen before on the kitchen table with some sort of decorative pinecones. But the biggest change of all was the fridge. The once plain white space was now covered with magnets and pictures. There was even some of Austin's artwork secured to the front.

"It looks like…"

"Home?"

He nodded and looked at her. She looked so pleased with herself that he couldn't help but smile right along with her. "It looks great, Drew. Really." He held up the container of soup and she took it from him with another smile.

"My favorite?"

"Of course."

She slipped it inside the fridge, turned and grabbed his hand. "You have to see the living room," she said. "Do you have a few minutes?"

Without waiting for an answer, she started to pull him toward the other room, but Ben was rooted to the spot, staring at their hands. Her touch sent a heat through him that had startled him to his core.

"Ben?" Drew had stopped and was looking at him with a slight frown. "Are you—"

"I'm fine." He shook his head and forced a smile to his face. "Sorry. Yes, of course I want to see the living room."

She dropped his hand, unaware of the effect her simple touch had on him. He stuffed his hands into the pockets of his jeans, still disconcerted by the unexpected feelings. It had been years since that had happened. Almost twenty, in fact. He didn't want to think about what it might mean.

Fortunately, he was distracted by the living room. Drew had put out throw cushions, more decorative vases, and bowls and the usual knickknacks that are found in a family home. There were candles, and family pictures on the mantel as well as an oversized mirror placed in the center. On the walls, she'd even hung some art, and more photos. Including a family picture of Ben and Eric with their parents that had been taken in high school before Eric graduated.

He couldn't help but smile as he looked around the room. His eyes landed on the couch. Or more specifically, what was on the couch. "What's this?" He crossed the room and picked up a stuffed trout pillow.

"Oh, that." Drew giggled. "I know it's kind of ugly, but it was Eric's pillow. It was the only thing he insisted on having in our house, no matter what. So, I thought—"

"It's mine."

"What?"

Ben turned the pillow around in his hands and looked to the belly of the fish, where he'd used a Sharpie when he was ten to write his initials before taking it to summer camp. "Right here." He pointed. "B.R. This was my pillow when we were kids. I wondered where it went." He grinned to himself as he remembered the way his brother would tease him about the ugly trout. "It disappeared right around graduation. I assumed that Mom must have thrown it out, but..." He trailed off as he realized that Eric had taken it with him when he'd moved out.

"If it's yours, you should have it," Drew said.

That was about the time when things had gotten really serious between Eric and Drew and they'd both moved away to school. Together. *Had Eric known how much the pillow meant to him? How much Drew had meant?*

He shook his head. *It didn't matter.* "No," he said quickly. "It belongs here." He put the pillow back. For the second time that day, a lump formed in his throat. He cleared his throat and turned around again. "It looks great, Drew. Really."

"Thank you." She had her hands on her hips and a satisfied smile on her face. "It was time." She laughed a little and corrected herself. "No, it was past time. It wasn't always easy." Her smile dimmed a little. "But it feels good to be settled here and make the space a little more...well, like home."

"So you're staying?"

It's not as if they'd ever talked about her moving back to Nevada, but she also hadn't said anything about settling in

Timber Creek either. It was almost as if her and Austin's life had only been planned up to Eric's death and after that...

"I'm staying," she said. "I don't really have anywhere else to go. I mean, Nevada was home for a long time and we had some great friends there, but it's not the same as being here and being around family. And of course, friends who feel like family. I guess I never really planned it, but yes." She nodded, her smile returning. "I'm staying here. I just need to work out the rest of the details. Like a job."

"You know, if I can help with anything, just let me know. I'm always looking for good help." He winked. "Especially with the patio opening tomorrow. I think we'll be busier than ever."

"Oh, is it ready already?"

He laughed. "It feels like it's taken forever. But yes. We should be up and running by Friday. Which is one of the reasons I came by. I'm hoping to make it a big event and I thought you might like a night out, too. Before you say no," he raised a hand to stop the objection he knew was likely to follow, "I already asked Cam if Morgan was free to babysit. I would have asked Mom, but I think it would be good for them to get out, too." He'd gone out on a limb organizing Cam's teenage daughter to watch Austin, but she was a responsible kid, and he really did want Drew to celebrate the patio, too.

Drew gave him a look, but she smiled as she shook her head. "I assume the whole gang will be there?"

"You know it." He grinned. "I even convinced Christy to get the band to play a few songs. I called her on my way over."

She laughed. "Well, that's always a good thing. I love Timber Heart." Ben knew that. Christy was one of Drew's best friends, but besides that, they were a fantastic band and despite their busy personal lives and the fact that Christy and her husband Mark had just adopted a baby, the success of the band was growing every day and a record deal was imminent. "Of course, I'd love to come by." She moved across the room to pick up a glass of wine. "Can I get you a glass? I don't usually drink alone," she added quickly, likely in an effort to ward off any concerned questions.

There had been one or two occasions in the past few months where Drew had tried to drown her feelings in alcohol. It wasn't often, and although Ben didn't think it was okay, he also wasn't worried that Drew had a problem. "You don't have to explain anything to me," he said. "And yes, I'd love a glass."

"I'll be right back." She put her own glass back on the table next to a blue notebook and disappeared into the kitchen.

Ben's eyes locked on the notebook. He recognized it. It was Eric's. He'd almost always had it in his hand during those last few months. Ben had only asked his brother once what he was writing in there. "Why so secret, big brother?" Ben said as casually as he could as Eric tucked the notebook away. "Are you writing all your deepest and darkest feelings about me?" It had been a joke, but one that he probably shouldn't have made. His relationship with his older brother had been strained for too long. They'd taken huge steps in repairing that relationship since Eric had been back in town, but they'd never be able to get the time back that they'd lost.

A fact that Ben was acutely aware of as each day went by and he watched his big brother grow weaker than the day before.

"Just making a few notes about things I don't want to forget," Eric responded. "My mind just isn't what it used to be." He'd smiled and tried to joke, but Ben could tell there was more behind what he was saying.

He looked toward the kitchen before picking up the notebook, but he hesitated before opening it. It somehow seemed like a violation of privacy, even though Eric was gone.

"You can look at it if you like." Ben turned to see Drew watching him, a glass of wine in her hand. "The notebook." She nodded to it. "You can look. I'm sure he wouldn't mind."

"Are you sure?"

Drew walked into the room and handed him the glass. "Very." Her smile was soft and Ben couldn't help but notice that she didn't look sad at all, but somehow much more at peace than he'd seen her in recent months. "I was nervous too," she added when he didn't open the notebook right away. "But I promise, he didn't write any final letters that will make you sad."

He couldn't help but chuckle. "How did you guess that's what I was worried about?" She was right though. Mostly. They'd talked through a lot in Eric's final days, but there was one thing they hadn't talked about. Not specifically. He swallowed hard and, with Drew watching, opened the book.

He was silent for a few moments while he flipped through the pages and sipped his wine.

Drew was right; he needn't have been concerned. The pages were filled with lists.

"Interesting, right?"

Ben looked up to see Drew watching him.

"I mean, it's interesting to see all of the things that were important to him in those…well, then."

"It's all you and Austin," he said. "Not that I'm surprised. The two of you were his entire life."

Drew's smile dipped. "You're in there too. And your parents."

That knowledge made Ben smile. "Have you read it all?"

"No." A few strands of hair escaped the knot on the top of her head as she shook it. "I thought I'd savor it."

It made sense. But he wasn't much of the savoring type. He flipped randomly toward the end of the book and read another list. He shook his head and read it again in an effort to process the words on the page.

"What's wrong? What's that one say?" Drew had moved from the chair to the couch where Ben was sitting.

"This one is different," he said slowly. He flipped quickly through the rest of the pages and it was easy to tell that the list he was looking at was made closer to the end of Eric's life.

"How so?" Before he could stop her, Drew snatched the book from his hands and started reading the list for herself.

SLEEP under the stars
   Catch a fish
   Run a race
   Carve initials in Bizarro Cave
   Vandalize the sidewalk
   Teach a dog fetch

DREW READ THE LIST ONCE. And then again. Ben was right: it was a very different list than the other ones. Eric's handwriting was shaky and messy, but it wasn't just the penmanship. The actual list itself was almost like...

"Are these things he wanted to do?" she asked Ben.

He shook his head and tapped his glass with his finger. "I can't think so. I mean, I know for a fact he's done all of those things."

Drew looked again to the list and the item that involved vandalism. She raised her eyebrows at Ben. "*All* of those things?"

Ben laughed. "I promise that's not as bad as you think. I mean, if it's what I'm thinking of. When we were kids, my dad caught us...well, basically being jerky little kids and he taught us a lesson."

"With vandalism?"

Ben laughed again, obviously enjoying the recollection of the memory. "Pretty much. We were talking crap about some kids at school and he didn't like it. For a few minutes, he lectured us about focusing on the positive things and all that, but then he just left. About thirty minutes later, he came back with a bucket of sidewalk chalk and marched us down to the school, where he had us write all kinds of positive things on the sidewalk outside of the school."

"I remember that." All the sidewalks, including the stairs that led to the front door, had been covered in brightly colored positive messages like, "You're beautiful." And, "Today is your day." And things similar to that. "That was you guys?"

Ben nodded. "It was. We were there for hours writing things and at first it was really hard. But as the time went on, it got easier and we actually started having fun. When we were finally done, my dad sat us down and told us how important positive messages were and how impactful negative ones could be. He made us promise to keep it a secret the next day when we got to school and not take any credit for it."

"Nobody knew who it was," Drew said.

Ben only smiled.

"Except you guys." She laughed. "Wow. That's so cool."

"It was cool. And it definitely made an impact and Dad more than made his point."

Drew nodded and looked back at the list. "So do you think this is a list of some of his favorite memories? What about the rest of these things?" She didn't say what she wanted to—that if it was a list of Eric's favorite memories, none of them were with her, and that would hurt.

Ben leaned over and read the list again. He hesitated a little, but finally said, "I don't know if they were his favorite things, but they were definitely things we did when we were kids. Maybe a little older than Austin. Maybe he was just remembering things from back then because of Austin."

A rush of sadness she hadn't felt all day crashed into her and she slumped down in the couch.

"Drew?" Ben shifted closer to her. "Don't be sad. I...well, I mean...you can be sad...but—"

"It's okay." She stopped him. "I'm okay. I just...well, I guess I don't know..." Drew closed the notebook and picked up her glass of wine.

"What if...well, it's just an idea," Ben said. "But what if it's a list of things that he did when he was a kid that he was hoping Austin would be able to experience, too?"

The idea made sense. "You're sure these are all things he did?"

Ben laughed. "Absolutely. I know that for a fact because I did them with him. We were definitely older than Austin, though. At least he was. But..." Ben's eyes took on a faraway look for a moment, as if he were remembering something. Drew didn't push him and after a moment, he said, "You know what? I think I actually *was* a few years older than Austin when Eric showed me all of these things. Or very close to it. Austin's five?"

"Yes."

Ben nodded. "I remember this one summer, when Mom and Dad were really busy and he was in charge of me. He was only about eight or nine, so that would have made me six or seven. I guess when you look back on it, it was still pretty young to be in charge of a younger sibling, but it was a different time then."

"It sure was." Drew laughed. "And he did all of these things with you?"

"Well, most of them. Some of them we did with Dad, too," Ben said. "Like the sidewalk vandalism and the camping."

Drew opened the notebook again to the list. "That's really special."

"It really was."

They sat in silence for a few moments, and it was Drew who finally spoke. "He must have remembered that summer while he made the list. It was probably pretty important to him."

"It was important to me, too." Ben looked to be a million miles away, no doubt lost in his own memories and not for the first time, Drew felt a flash of sadness for him. She'd lost a husband, but she wasn't the only one who'd experienced a profound loss. Ben had lost his big brother. He didn't talk about it much, or the way their relationship had changed when they'd finished school, but Drew knew there was a lot of hurt there. "I have an idea." Next to her, Ben jumped up so fast that Drew bounced a little with the shift of the cushions.

"You have a what?" She readjusted herself on the couch and looked up at him as he began to pace the living room.

"An idea." He stopped in front of her and looked straight into her eyes. "I'm going to carry out the list," he said. "With Austin."

She wasn't sure she'd heard him right. "What?"

He ran his hands through his hair, leaving it standing up at strange angles. It gave him the look of a madman, but the smile on his face and the excitement flashing in his eyes was contagious. "I'm going to do it," he said again. "I mean, with your permission of course. But there's a reason Eric wrote this list and you were right."

"I am?" She gave him a sidelong glance. "About what exactly?"

"It was special. That whole summer. Every single one of the things we did together. It was all special and one of my favorite summers. I want to give that to Austin." He swallowed and added, "And to Eric. And I think it would be pretty special, in a different way of course, if I could give this to them."

Tears sprang to her eyes. She hadn't cried all day, but there was no stopping the tears now. "You'd do that?"

"Oh my God, Drew." He dropped to his knees in front of

her and grabbed her hands in his. The heat from his touch rushed through her and centered her. She focused on the intensity in his eyes. "It would be my honor if you'd let me do this for them." She swallowed hard and before she could say anything, he added, "And for you."

Chapter Five

AMBER LEANED against the wooden fence and watched the action in the ring with a smile on her face. Logan was working with a new horse that had just arrived at Taking the Reins. Poppy was a dappled three-year-old with a sweet personality. Her previous owner had been an eighteen-year-old girl who'd moved to the other side of the country for college and her parents couldn't give her the time she deserved. They wanted her to go to a good home where, ideally, she would provide as much joy to others as she had to her teenage owner for the last few years.

"How's she doing?" Amber asked Logan when he led the horse to her. "Do you think she'll be ready soon?"

"I think she's ready now." Logan leaned over the fence and pressed a kiss to Amber's lips, sending a thrill through her. "In fact, I'm really excited to see how she does in the ring tomorrow. We have a new client starting. She's young and having a hard time with anxiety. I think Poppy will be perfect."

Just watching Logan's face light up when he spoke about his work made Amber's heart happy. He'd worked so hard to make Taking the Reins, his horse therapy program—now *their* program since they became partners—a success. And in only a few short months, their client roster was already bursting at the seams. It wouldn't be long before they would be able to open the lodge, which would be a residential center for clients who lived farther away to come and stay on site during their treatment. They'd broken ground as soon as they possibly could when the ground thawed in March and construction was coming along quickly.

Logan left Poppy in the care of Amber's dad, Joseph, who'd been volunteering with Logan's program since before Amber returned to Timber Creek. In fact, he was indirectly the reason for Amber and Logan meeting and falling in love.

Amber blew him a kiss. She knew he'd come by the house for a coffee before he left, and together, she and Logan walked to the construction site to meet with Harry, their project manager.

Just as he always seemed to be, Harry was standing out front of the building, staring intently at a clipboard in his hand. He looked up as soon as they walked over. "Amber. Logan. How are you today?" His face transformed into a smile, but Amber still noticed the worry that had been there a moment earlier before he knew they were looking.

"We're doing great, Harry." Logan shook his hand and Amber gave the older man a quick hug. "What did you want to see us about today?" Logan asked the question, but Amber watched the other man closely for the answer he might not offer. From the moment they'd met him, Harry had always given them the optimistic building scenario, which wasn't necessarily a bad thing, but more and more, Amber was looking for a *realistic* scenario. They had a business to run and it was proving to be very difficult to run it based on optimism.

"Well…" He scratched at the scruff on his face. "Everything is going well," he said quickly, "but there's this…well, I don't want you to worry, but—"

"Harry," Amber interrupted him. "Just tell us the situation. What the hell is going on?" Coming from the corporate world, and her past life as a hard-hitting attorney, Amber struggled at times to remember that life in Timber Creek moved at a different pace altogether and there were definitely times she got frustrated with the entire process. Logan put his hand on her arm, a signal for her to stay calm. "I'm sorry." She forced a smile. "I just know you're very busy, so if we could get to the point, that would be great."

Next to her, she could hear Logan stifle a chuckle, and she had to resist the urge to smack him.

"Of course, Amber," Harry said. "I just wasn't sure how to tell you that we've had some delays."

Amber wasn't surprised by the news; obviously, she knew something was up.

"What kind of delays?" Logan asked. "Will they put us terribly off schedule or are they minor?"

"A bit of both." Harry nodded and consulted his clipboard again. "Why don't we go inside and I can talk specifics?"

Amber and Logan grabbed hardhats from the back of Harry's truck and together they walked into what would hope-fully soon be the lodge that would house live-in residents. The main structure of the building had gone up quite quickly and that early progress had been exciting to watch, but then things had slowed down. As they walked through the large wooden-framed structure, Harry pointed out all of the places that were experiencing those slow-downs.

"My main framer has had some staffing issues with a few of his guys having family emergencies," Harry explained, "which is the main cause of delay for the rest of the construc-tion. We're almost closed in now, and as soon as he can get that finished, we'll be in a better spot for lining up the rest of the trades. He's working on getting a few guys in from the city to take over the project, but I won't know more about that until later today."

"And that's the biggest delay?" Amber walked next to the men, her eyes trailing over the partially finished walls that would be the bedroom wing of the lodge.

"That's a pretty big one, Amber." Logan had stopped walking and was watching her. "Don't you think?"

"I do." She nodded absentmindedly. "But I just want to know if that's the only delay?"

They both turned to look at Harry, who, judging by the look on his face, had more to tell them. "Well, as you can imagine, getting the construction phase complete is pretty major."

"Agreed," Logan said.

"And because we're experiencing delays with that, everything has been pushed back, causing the entire project schedule to have some major hiccups."

Amber sighed. There was once a time, not so long ago, when she would have freaked out at the lack of control she had in the situation. But that was before. She'd come a long way since those obsessive, controlling days. Although she still definitely had those tendencies, she was a lot better at controlling them. "Okay," she said after a moment. "Well, I'm sure you're doing everything you can to keep the project on track."

She didn't have to look to know that Logan would be staring at her with shock and surprise, so she didn't. "Please do keep us informed as things progress, Harry," Amber continued. "I'm confident that you are doing everything you can."

A few minutes later, when they'd finished up with Harry and were on their way back to the little cabin that they shared, Logan grabbed her hand and stopped her in her tracks. "You're pretty incredible, you know?" He wrapped his arms around her and held her tight to him. "And I have to say, I'm very impressed."

She laughed and looked him straight in the eyes. "And why are you so impressed?"

"Do you think you would have been so chill about the delays ten months ago? Hell, even six months ago."

"Things were different then." She wiggled so her body was pressed up closer to his. "*I'm* different."

Logan pressed his lips to hers and kissed her deeply. "You're incredible."

She smiled, feeling the love from him travel throughout her body. Things were different. So much so. Not only had she left her high-powered, high-stressed career behind in San Francisco, she'd traded it in for a soul-satisfying career with the man of her dreams and most importantly, a life free from an addiction that had claimed her for too long. "I love you," she said in response, and kissed him back because there was nothing else she would rather do.

Their kiss was interrupted by the chirping of Amber's cell phone and because they were both always expecting a business call or message of some sort, reluctantly, she slipped her phone from her back pocket to check it.

"It's Cam," she told Logan. "She wants to know if we're going to be at the Log and Jam tomorrow night. Do you know anything about that?"

Logan nodded. "I forgot to tell you." He shrugged. "Evan called me last night and told me that Ben was having some sort of grand opening for his new fancy patio space. I think Timber Heart is supposed to play and he was looking for a head count so they could reserve us some tables up front."

"You said yes, right?"

Logan slipped his arm around her again and nuzzled her neck before whispering in her ear. "I told him I'd have to check with you. I know it's been a busy week." He pulled back to look in her eyes. "I didn't want to assume that you'd be good with going out after so much crazy."

She loved the way he looked after her, thinking about her needs before she even had a chance to. It was sweet and not at all something Amber was used to. She'd been on her own for so long that sometimes it still took her off guard to realize that there was someone else in her life who loved her as much as he did. "That's sweet," she said. "And you're right, it has been a crazy week. But I think it'll be fun and a good way to relax, too."

"I agree. It's been awhile since we've all been together anyway." He grinned. "Tell her yes, to count us in."

Amber looked up from her phone and winked. "Already done."

Chapter Six

IT ONLY TOOK Ben about five minutes to realize he had completely underestimated how much work it was to plant as many flower pots as he had, and he still hadn't actually put anything into the dirt yet. He stepped back from the flats of plants that covered the patio, put his hands on his hips and shook his head, trying to remember what exactly Calla had said about shade plants versus sun-loving ones. *Was that one with the broad green leaves a shade plant or a sun plant?*

"No," he said to himself as he stepped toward it. "That's the one that goes in the shade." He moved over to another flat of plants, these ones with smaller leaves, and white flowers. "These ones like sun."

"You're right."

Ben jumped back at the sound of the voice. He straightened up and turned to see Calla on the patio next to him.

"Sorry to scare you." She walked over to the plants. "But you're right. These ones are for full sun." She picked one up and held it. "Am I late? We said eight, right?"

Ben nodded. "We did. I'm usually here early and I thought I might as well get a jump start on this since there seems to be a never-ending supply of flowers here." It was true, but he left out the part about how he was hoping to prove something to himself by getting some of it done before she got there.

"Well, it doesn't look like you've made a ton of progress yet." She surveyed the space. "You have a great-looking patio here, Ben. This is going to be awesome."

"Thank you." He beamed with pride and watched her for a moment. Her blonde hair was pulled back in a ponytail and dressed simply in jeans and a black t-shirt, she looked much younger than she had the day before at the store. He judged her to be somewhere in her twenties, not that he was any good at all at guessing such things. She was cute and when she smiled, her entire face lit up. "I have big plans for it." He refocused his attention on the pile of plants and bags of soil in front of him. "If we can ever get all of these in the pots."

She laughed and grabbed a pair of work gloves from her back pocket. "I promise, this won't take very long and it's going to look amazing. Trust me."

"That's exactly what I'm doing." He chuckled and hefted a bag of soil up into his arms. "I don't think I've actually grown anything before. At least, nothing that's survived."

"Well, that doesn't sound like a great track record." She winked. "But I promise you, after a little bit of time with me, I'll change all that. In fact, once you know some basics." She pointed to the bag he was holding. "Like, for example, that bag there is manure and needs to be mixed with those bags over there in equal parts so the plants get appropriate nutrients."

"Manure?" He tried to read the writing on the bag he was holding. "See?" he said after a moment. "It's a good thing you're here."

Calla took charge of the situation right away and with her instruction, Ben was mixing soil with manure and peat into all of the planters on the patio, while she moved around with surprising speed, putting plants and flowers into piles. When the sorting was all done, they worked together to plant everything using the sketches and plans that Calla created.

More than once, Ben found himself thankful for Calla and all her help. There was no way he'd be able to achieve what she was doing, let alone as fast as she was doing it. She moved with a confidence that was impressive and with good reason: she was excellent at what she did. The arrangements she created were gorgeous and even though he knew he wouldn't remember anything in a day's time, she patiently explained what each plant was called and how tall it would grow or what color of flowers he could expect from it.

What took the two of them just under two hours to accomplish would have taken him at least an entire day, and there was no way it would come out looking as amazing as it did. When they finished, Ben took a step back and dusted his hands together.

"Wow." He surveyed the patio, now complete. "This looks amazing, Calla. I can't thank you enough."

"It does look pretty damn good, doesn't it?" She crossed her arms and grinned. "Wow. Even I'm impressed, and I planned it."

Ben laughed. "Come on, I think we deserve a cold glass of lemonade, don't you?"

"Absolutely."

The pub was still closed for another hour, but Michael was in the kitchen, cooking up something that smelled mouthwatering. He barely looked up from the stove as Ben walked through the kitchen and grabbed some freshly squeezed lemonade from the fridge. "Smells good, Michael."

All Ben got was a grunt in return, which meant Michael was probably not satisfied with his current creation for some reason that was most likely completely unfounded. He chuckled at his friend and employee's perfectionism and returned to the bar, where Calla was waiting.

"What's so funny?"

"Oh, just that my master chef back there is probably trying to talk himself out of throwing out the lunch special he's just created." He poured the lemonade and handed Calla a glass.

"What? But it smells delicious."

"I know." Ben shook his head. "That's just how Michael is. Don't worry, he won't throw it out—I won't let him." He grinned and took a deep drink of the cold liquid. "And it will be delicious. It always is. He's the best chef around. I don't know how I got so lucky."

She smiled and crossed her legs, spinning on the stool so she faced him. "From what I hear, it's because you're pretty awesome to work with."

"Oh yeah?" Ben leaned over the bar, so he was looking directly into her bright-green eyes. "You've heard about me, have you?"

He was flirting with her, and to his surprise, it didn't feel awkward or strange. Well, not *too* strange.

"Enough." She winked and turned her attention to her drink. "I should probably get going. I have to open the store soon. But this has been fun."

"I can't thank you enough." Ben walked Calla through the pub to the heavy wooden doors. "The patio grand opening is tomorrow night—you have to come. I can reserve you a seat, or...two?"

She smiled. "Just one. And yes, I'd love to come."

"WELL, I don't know why you were going through Eric's things. Why not just pack them up?" Laura Frederick, Drew's mom, clicked her tongue the way she always did when she didn't agree with something Drew was doing, or saying, or about to do, or pretty much anything when it came to Drew. She meant well, and she'd been amazing with Austin in the months since Eric had died, but it didn't make their mother-daughter relationship any easier to navigate on a daily basis.

"Mom." Drew tried not to sigh. "Eric's gone. I'm his wife. Or, I..." It still didn't feel right saying that she *used* to be Eric's wife, and she hated the word widow. It reminded her of an eighty-year-old with blue hair. "At any rate," she continued. "I have every right to go through his things and besides that, I need to organize things and..."

"And what?" Her mother stared at her over the edge of her coffee mug from the other side of the kitchen. "What's going on, Drew? Are you...well, are you doing okay?"

Drew sagged a little under her mother's concern. Because despite the hard time her mom gave her, she loved her fiercely and had always wanted the best for her. Drew had never doubted that for a moment. It was just the way Laura showed her love. No matter how frustrating it could be.

"You know what?" Drew straightened her shoulders. "I am doing okay. I mean, there's definitely room for improvement, but I think getting settled was the right thing."

"I agree." Her mom put down her cup with authority. "In fact, I for one am thrilled to see you a little more settled and I assume that means you're staying in Timber Creek for a while."

Her mother had done a good job avoiding asking the question outright, something that Drew recognized must have been a feat of intense willpower.

Drew turned to the sink and rinsed out her cup to keep her mother from seeing her grin. "I think Timber Creek is the right place for us, and I've been thinking about a few different things I'd like to do for work."

"Work?" Behind her, Laura sputtered and coughed. "You're not going to work right now, are you?"

Drew crossed the floor with a glass of water and put it in front of her mom. "I was thinking—"

"It's way too early to go back to work, Drew. Didn't Eric leave you with a comfortable life insurance settlement? You need to take care of yourself and that sweet boy of yours. You have no business going back to work. Not yet. Not until the grieving period is over."

Drew bit her bottom lip, but she couldn't continue to keep quiet. Not if she planned to maintain her sanity. And she did. "Mom?" She slipped into the seat across from her mother. "You know that there is no set grieving period, right? I mean, everyone grieves differently. You can't put a timeline on these things."

Laura, the cup of water to her mouth, shook her head. "No," she said with complete certainty. "That's not true. When Doris lost her husband, she grieved for two solid years. She wouldn't even take company for a solid six months. Family only. And it wasn't until—"

"I'm not Doris."

"No." Laura pursed her lips. "You most certainly are not."

"And everyone grieves in different ways, Mom." The conversation exhausted her, and made her sad all over again. But more than anything, Drew wanted—no, needed—her mother to understand that just because she was ready to move on with her life in certain ways did not mean that she didn't miss Eric every single moment of every single day. It didn't mean that there still weren't days when it hurt simply to breathe knowing that Eric no longer could. How could she possibly explain to her mother that just because she wasn't wearing black and hiding in her room that didn't mean that she wasn't hurting deeply? Very deeply.

But more than that, that she was ready to start living again. "Maybe so, Drew. But…"

There was that tongue clucking again. Drew swallowed

hard and pushed up from the table, unable to sit across from her any longer.

"There are no buts, Mom. I'm just trying to do the best thing for Austin and myself. And right now, that's settling in and moving on. That doesn't mean we're forgetting Eric. Not even a little." She didn't often raise her voice at her mother, but when she did, it got attention.

Laura sat back in her chair, her mouth open. "Drew, I wasn't—"

"It doesn't matter." She held up a hand to ward off her mother's explanations and picked up the notebook that had started the whole discussion in the first place. "The point is, Eric made a list of things he obviously wanted to share with Austin. Things that were important to him once. Things he shared with Ben."

Her mom raised her eyebrows at the mention of Ben. It was a conversation she wasn't about to have with her mom, who thought Ben spent entirely too much time with her and Austin. She'd tried numerous times to try to explain to her mother how amazing Ben had been both while Eric was alive in those last few months and especially now. And how special it was that Austin had Ben in his life. There was just no real way for Drew to convey how much Ben's presence had meant to her. So she didn't bother trying.

"And you said Ben wanted to do those things with Austin?"

Drew nodded.

"Do you think that's a good idea?"

"I think it's a great idea." Drew didn't hesitate.

"Ben isn't Austin's father, Drew."

"Oh my God, Mom!" Drew dropped the notebook on the kitchen counter and pulled her hair back from her face before letting it drop again. "I know that. He knows that. Austin knows that. More than anyone, Austin knows it." She took a breath and worked to compose herself. "Austin's father is dead, Mom. And that's never going to change. But he does have an uncle who loves him very much and wants more than anything for him to experience all the things that he would have experienced with his father if Eric hadn't died." She swallowed hard, forcing herself not to cry. "And I, for one, think that's pretty freakin' special."

Her mom was silent for a moment. She opened her mouth and closed it again. Nodded. Swallowed hard and finally said, "Okay."

"Okay?" There had to be more. Where her mom was concerned, there was always more.

"Yes," Laura said. "Okay. I trust that you know what's best for Austin. You're a good mother, Drew." Her smile was kind and her eyes shone with love. As frustrating as she could be, she was still her mother, and she loved Drew and Austin ferociously. Drew knew that. "Austin is lucky to have you, and I know this hasn't been easy."

Drew crossed the room and dropped to a crouch in front of her mom's chair. "No," she said. "It's been horrific and sad and the hardest thing I've ever had to do in my life. But there's one thing I know for sure."

Laura took Drew's hand in hers and squeezed. "What's that?"

"I couldn't have done it without the incredible support from everyone. And I still need help, Mom. Especially where Austin is concerned. He's so young and he needs a strong male role model who can do all the things that Dad can't, and that I'll be terrible at." *Like catching a fish.* The thought made her smile. "He needs Ben, Mom. And you know what? I think Ben needs Austin, too."

Ben didn't talk about it much, but losing Eric had been hard on him, too. Very hard. Spending time with Austin was just as healing for Ben.

Her mom still looked skeptical, but to Drew's relief, didn't push the issue any further except to add, "Okay."

"Okay?" She eyed her mom skeptically.

"Yes." Her mom nodded. "Drew, all I ever want is the best for both of you, and I know you don't think I'm very good at showing it sometimes, but I really am just trying to be supportive."

Drew wanted to both scream and laugh in frustration at her mother. In the end, she shook her head and gave her mom a hug just as she heard the front door open.

"Mom! I'm home!"

Drew stood and braced herself in time to catch Austin as he ran into the room and launched himself in her arms for a hug. "Hey, buddy. Did you have a good day?"

"Totally. We did stations today and there were these blocks. Not Lego, but sort of and they connect and make these things. Not towers, but sort of. And the teacher—Grandma!" He untangled himself from Drew's arms mid-story and launched himself at Laura, who caught him. He immediately launched into his story with her, starting at the beginning and adding in new details.

"I see you're hearing all about these wonder blocks, too." Amber walked into the kitchen and handed Drew her son's backpack. "He was in such a hurry to tell you about them, he left this in the backseat."

"Thank you." Drew took the backpack and got to work unpacking the various pieces of artwork, along with the lunch kit and whatever else her son had collected during the day. "And thank you for picking him up. Somedays, I—"

"Don't even worry about it. I love spending time with him." Amber poured herself a mug of coffee from the pot and leaned back against the counter. "In fact, I was hoping Logan and I could borrow him next week."

Drew looked up from the lunch kit she was disassembling. "Borrow?"

"Well...we were going to do a photo shoot for Taking the Reins. Just some images for the website and brochures and stuff. He's so good with the horses and Logan and I were hoping that maybe..."

"Of course." Drew laughed. "As long as it's okay with Austin."

"If what's okay with me?" As soon as he heard his name, his story for his grandmother was forgotten.

Drew grinned. "You ask him, Auntie Amber."

Chapter Seven

THE WEATHER WAS perfect as Ben cranked up each of the patio umbrellas he'd set out. Thankfully they wouldn't be needed for rain, but to keep the warm spring sun out of people's eyes as they enjoyed the new space. Annie had put out small tabletop lanterns on each of the tables, lights were strung around the space, and the planters looked amazing.

He lit a fire in the stone fireplace and instructed one of the busboys to keep it stoked throughout the evening. Everything was perfect. Ben beamed with pride as he looked around the space. Just as with everything else with the Log and Jam, he believed fully that it would be a success. There'd only been one time, years earlier, when he'd doubted himself when it came to opening the pub. He'd taken out loans, borrowed from his parents, and pretty much put everything he had on the line to open the Log and Jam. He'd done his research and he knew it would be successful. Not just in his heart, but in his head, too. And the old log building where Bud's, the long since defunct bar that had once been Timber Creek's only watering hole, had been perfect. It had taken a lot of elbow grease, and a whole lot of renovations, but it had been worth it. And the community was more than ready for a new hangout place. It had been years earlier that Bud's had closed down and besides a few restaurants and a cafe, there was nowhere really for people to go and have a beer after work with friends.

Not unless you counted the End of the Road, and Ben did not. He'd gone to school with Tommy Jenkins, who'd taken over the dive bar at the edge of town about a year before Ben opened his own doors. The End of the Road was known for greasy food, watered-down drinks, and sleazy entertainment. It was not at all the type of place that Ben and his friends wanted to spend their hard-earned cash. But with no other options in town, Tommy ended up getting most of the business.

Even armed with all of his research and assurances from the townspeople, opening the doors to the Log and Jam had been the most nerve-racking experience of Ben's life. When he'd almost panicked at the last minute and pulled the plug on the idea, there was one person he'd turned to.

Eric.

Their relationship had been strained for years, but one thing had always stayed consistent. Eric was Ben's older brother, and despite the way Ben had pulled away, he knew he could count on Eric to be there for him when it really mattered.

"Ben?" He remembered the shock in Eric's voice when he'd answered the phone. "Is everything okay?"

"Yes. I'm just…" He didn't know how to ask for what he needed. Ben swallowed hard. "I'm not sure if I'm doing the right thing, Eric."

There was silence on the other end of the line for a moment before his brother spoke again. "The pub? Mom and Dad told me," he said. "I think it's a great idea. Exactly what Timber Creek needs."

"You think so?"

Eric laughed and not for the first time, Ben was struck by

how much he missed his brother. "I do," he said. "Why are you doubting yourself, little brother?"

"It's so much money." Ben shook his head and looked to the sky. "And I've borrowed from Mom and Dad. If I don't... well, it's just a lot."

"Of course it is. But nothing worth having is easy. And you know what they say about being scared."

"I didn't say I was scared."

Eric laughed. "Right. Well, if you *were* scared," he said, "I'd say that was a good thing."

"Why is that?"

"Because when you're scared or uncomfortable, you're growing. And you, little brother, are growing." There was silence on the other end for a moment before Eric added, "I'm proud of you, Ben."

"Really?" In that moment, Ben could no longer remember why he'd put so much distance between him and Eric. Whatever it was, it was time to close the gap, and—

"Really." Eric interrupted his train of thought. "And I can't wait to come and have a beer at your bar. Drew and I are going to come visit as soon as you open."

And there it was. The familiar pain in his chest. It was a sharp physical reminder of why Ben had pulled away from his relationship with his brother. A woman. But not just any woman. The one he'd been in love with ever since he could remember. It hadn't been an easy decision, and it wasn't even something he'd consciously done. His pulling back had happened gradually over the years.

Which was ironic, because he'd helped them get together all those years ago. When they were in high school, Ben and Drew had been inseparable, along with Cam and Evan, Christy and Mark, and Amber. He'd been too chicken to say anything back then, but he'd been head over heels with Drew for years. A story as old as time, because she had no idea he thought of her that way and when she'd come to him one day, giggling and blushing and asking Ben if he would *please* see if Eric was interested in her, of course he said yes. Because he would have done anything for her. Even if it meant breaking his own heart.

Never in a million years did Ben think that Eric would actually go out with her and even if he did, that it would last. But it had.

Even when Eric moved away to school, they stayed together. But it wasn't until Eric came home that summer that the rest of them had graduated and asked Drew to marry him that Ben realized what he'd always somehow known—he'd lost Drew forever. And he'd never really had her.

And then his brother, too, because it just became way too painful to be around Eric. So he'd pulled away.

The memories rocked through him and, just like they always did, left Ben unsettled as he stood and surveyed his new patio.

"Hey." The voice, followed by a slap on his back, jerked Ben all the way out of his thoughts and into the present moment. "This looks amazing, buddy." Evan stood next to him, his arms crossed as he took in all of Ben's hard work. "You did good, man."

"Thanks."

Evan turned and looked at him. "What's up? You seem off."

For a moment, Ben thought about lying and telling Evan a story about being tired or something, but there was no point. His best friend knew him better than anyone. "I was just thinking of Eric and how he'd encouraged me with the Log and Jam, even though I'd been nothing but an ass to him."

"You weren't an…" Evan switched gears, also unwilling to lie. "He was your brother and he loved you, ass and all."

Ben laughed. "True. I still wonder how I deserved it." He

shook his head, letting the familiar guilt sweep over him. "I never should have—"

"Stop it." Evan gripped Ben's forearm. "Don't do this, Ben. Just don't. You can't go back and change the past, so don't make yourself crazy."

It was true. Ben knew that. *Still...*

"Besides, you said yourself," Evan continued, "you and Eric were in a good place at the end. Right?"

Also true. They had gotten to a good place before Eric died. In a way, it almost made it harder to lose him, having rekindled their close brotherhood. It was just one more regret.

"And you know he would be so proud of you and all you've done here."

Ben took a breath. Evan was right. Eric would have been proud. Hell, he *was* proud of him. His brother had told him so on more than one occasion. "You're right." He slapped his hands together. "I know you're right and honestly, I don't know what came over me just then. I was...well, sometimes it just hits a little harder than others."

"I get that." Evan gave him a quick man hug with a slap on the back. "He'd be so proud of everything you've done for Austin and Drew, too. You know that, right?"

Ben definitely knew that. Before he'd died, Eric had made him promise that he'd look after his family. Not that he would've needed a promise; nothing could stop Ben from caring for them.

"You've been so amazing for Drew."

"Who's been amazing?" Ben's heart leapt and at the same time, he felt as if he'd been punched in the gut at the sound of her voice. "Are you talking about me?"

"You wish," Evan joked as Drew walked up. "How are you?" He laughed and gave her a quick hug.

"I'm great and so excited to see—oh, Ben..." Her hand went to her mouth as she took in the patio for the first time.

Ben couldn't help but feel a surge of pride rise through him, watching how impressed she was with the transformation he'd pulled off.

"This is…wow."

Her eyes landed on him after scanning the space and in an instant, Ben lost himself in her brown eyes, so full of wonder. The fact that he'd impressed her, even in a small way, made him happy in a way it shouldn't have. But when it came to Drew, he'd never had any luck ignoring his feelings, and somehow, despite how much he told himself he had to, he didn't see that changing any time soon.

"I'm glad you like it," he said. "And I'm really glad you could come out tonight."

"Well, you made it pretty easy on me, organizing Morgan to babysit." She laughed. "Thanks for that. And I'm sorry if I took her away from you," she said to Evan. "Where's Cam?"

Evan chuckled. "Don't worry. Morgan's a great sitter, but she's not up to the task of a newborn quite yet. I'll switch out with Cam later so she can pop in."

"Well, I'm just glad you're both here." Ben grinned. "I reserved you guys a table up front. Whenever you're ready, I'll send someone over to take drink orders, and—"

A flash of blonde hair in the door caught his attention just as Calla stepped out onto the patio. She waved at him, and he waved back.

"Looks like someone is looking for you." Evan gave him a nudge in the ribs, no doubt thrilled that Ben was giving even a little bit of attention to another woman. "Why don't you go say hi. I'll make sure Drew here gets a drink."

Ben turned to Drew.

"Go," she said. "We'll be fine. You're going to have a lot of people wanting to talk to you tonight and congratulate you on all this."

He gave her a quick hug and before he could get pulled off

in another direction, Ben went to say hello to Calla and welcome her to the celebration.

IT WAS a great night and Drew was happy she'd gone out. It hadn't been that long ago when she would have made some sort of excuse for why she couldn't join her friends at the Log and Jam, or at a dinner party, or whatever else it was that they were doing. Not that there was a need to make up an excuse considering everyone knew exactly why she was turning down the invitation, and nobody blamed her one bit.

It had been Amber who'd drug her out of the house on more than one occasion after convincing her that it was okay to go out and live her life and have fun with her friends. Amber had to remind Drew repeatedly that Eric wouldn't be upset. In fact, he would be happy she was moving on. That's all he ever wanted for her—for her life to go on.

And that's exactly what she was doing.

On the stage, Timber Heart was playing one of their new songs and everyone was tapping along with the beat. Drew lost herself in the music, until a voice in her ear grabbed her attention.

"They're pretty good, aren't they?" Ben's dad asked.

"Mitch." She turned a little in her chair. "I didn't see you there. I'm glad you both came." Drew looked past him at Sylvia at a nearby table, who was watching the band with a small smile on her face.

Mitch nodded. "It's good to get out." He leaned in a little closer. "It's really good to see her smiling."

"It is." Drew smiled, because the sight of her mother-in-law made her genuinely happy. "And I bet Ben is really pleased to see you both here as well. It means a lot to him, I'm sure."

"We're very proud of him." Mitch nodded. "He told us about the list Eric left."

Drew pressed a hand to her chest and waited for him to continue.

"I think it's pretty damn special how Ben plans to carry it out for Austin." He nodded and Drew pretended not to see the tear that glistened in his eye. "To see him step up with that boy, and you, of course." Drew nodded. "Well," Mitch continued. "It's pretty special. We're very proud."

To keep from crying, Drew opted instead to give her father-in-law a hug. She squeezed him tight. "He's a good man," she said into Mitch's ear. "I'm not sure what I'd do without him." She pulled away from the hug. "Are you going to help out, too? With the list? Ben said the vandalism was originally your idea."

She grinned, but Mitch shook his head. "No, I think this is for the two of them. And, well maybe you, too."

"Me?" Drew laughed. "I don't think so."

"You never know," he said. "You never really can tell how these things will play out."

She was pretty sure Mitch was still talking about the list, but there was a strange look on his face. Before she could ask him what it was all about, the band drew her attention and announced their last song, and Mitch excused himself.

She turned back to watch and after a moment, Drew was lost in the rhythm and once again tapping her feet to the beat. At the front of the table, closest to the stage, Mark, Christy's husband, sat, fixated on his wife. The smile on his face said it all. He completely adored her and as much as everyone loved Christy, Mark was by far her biggest fan.

Drew watched him for a moment. They'd always had such an easy love for each other, and as far as she could tell, besides their one major falling out earlier that year, the two of them never fought. Even as far back as high school, they just kind of seamlessly fit.

Not like Eric and me.

Drew felt bad as soon as she had the thought because it wasn't that they didn't fit. They did. They fit so well. And she'd loved him so completely. But there had been a time, a long time ago, before they even started dating, when she'd been so sure she was supposed to be with someone else. She'd never told anyone about her secret feelings, not even her girlfriends, and then, as kind of a test, she'd asked Ben to ask Eric out for her, and...well...she'd actually really enjoyed hanging out with him and...

None of that matters now.

And it didn't. She focused on Christy and the rest of the song. When the band was done playing, she cheered the loudest before falling into easy conversation with Cam, who was seated next to her and the rest of the group.

"I think we're going to have some good times out here this summer, don't you?" Cam smiled and lifted her sparkling water, making Drew laugh.

"I would say yes," she replied. "But with two of you being new moms, somehow I think you're overestimating your party skills."

"Maybe so," Cam agreed. "But even new moms need a break from time to time."

"You mean *especially* new moms." Drew took a sip of her wine. "Something that husband of yours must understand pretty well, since the two of you are tag teaming tonight." Evan had left after a quick toast to Ben and the new patio to give his wife a chance to get out of the house for a few hours. "You guys will need to find a babysitter so you can get out together, too. When do you think Morgan will babysit?"

Morgan was Cam's teenage daughter from her first marriage, and although the girl had gone through some hard times in recent months, she'd really come into herself and was thriving in Timber Creek. But looking after a newborn was still a big ask.

"Morgan loves her little brother and we'll definitely get her to babysit a bit when Theo is a little older, but...teenagers. She's always busy doing something. I'm not sure what Ben offered her to babysit for Austin, but she jumped at it. Maybe I shouldn't underestimate the power of money for a teenager." Cam laughed and Drew marveled at how light-hearted she was when it came to her daughter and all they'd been through. It wasn't long ago that it was a very different story. But time changed things. For everyone.

"I can't even imagine the teenage years." She shook her head and her eyes drifted around the busy patio, stopping when she found Ben, chatting with the blonde she'd seen earlier. "Hey," she said to Cam. "Do you know who that is?" She tried to point without it being too obvious.

"That's Calla." It was Christy, who'd crouched down between the two of them, who answered her. "She owns Petal Pushers, the flower shop in town. Or at least she does now. It was her dad's but he wanted to retire and since she was named after a flower, it was a good fit, I guess." Christy laughed. "I'm kidding. Sort of."

Drew shook her head in wonderment. Christy really did know everyone and everything there was to know about Timber Creek. "Do you know her?" She kept watching the woman, but more importantly, Ben, who seemed to be very interested in whatever it was she was saying to him.

"Not well," Christy said. "But it looks like Ben does."

Drew's head whipped around to stare at her friend. "What do you mean?"

"Whoa," Cam said with a laugh.

"Are they dating?" Drew ignored Cam. "Is she a good person? Or—"

"Drew." Christy raised her hands in defense of Drew's rapid-fire questions. "I really don't know anything about it."

"Someone is a little bit *too* interested, if you ask me," Cam said. "Are you maybe being a little protective over Ben? I mean, he's a big boy. He can handle himself."

Drew was instantly embarrassed. Her face flushed and she lifted her wine glass to cover the blush. Why *did* she care if Ben was talking to a woman?

"Drew?" Cam's voice had lost its teasing edge. "You are okay with Ben dating, right?"

"Why wouldn't I be?" She answered instinctively, but her stomach clenched in a tight knot that told her maybe she wasn't all that okay with it.

"I don't know." Cam watched her carefully. "You just seem a little...I don't know."

"It's fine." Drew forced a smile. "I think I was just caught a little off guard. I mean, we've been spending so much time together, and he never mentioned anything about her. So I was just wondering if...well, it doesn't matter. I'm just being a worrier, I guess."

"Well, I don't think you have anything to worry about with Ben." Christy squeezed her shoulder and rose to standing again before Drew could ask her exactly what she meant by that.

Chapter Eight

IT HAD BEEN a little over a week since Ben and Drew had discussed what Ben was now calling the Bro List, and it was finally time to get started on crossing off the items. Drew had agreed to let him pick Austin up early that Sunday morning, and he had the perfect idea for kicking things off.

He glanced in the rearview mirror at his nephew strapped into the booster seat Ben now kept in his Jeep.

Despite the early hour, Austin was wide-eyed and excited to go on the surprise adventure. "Where are we going, Uncle Ben? Mom wouldn't tell me anything except that it was you. I think she wanted to go, but I told her guys only. Right?"

Ben grinned. "Well, I don't know if it's necessarily guys only, buddy. If she wanted to come along, I think that would have been just fine, too." What Ben didn't say was that he would have enjoyed having Drew along with them, because he always enjoyed having Drew around. Ben heard Austin sigh in the backseat, so he quickly added, "But I think having a guys' day is pretty fun, too. Don't you?"

Austin perked up right away and nodded. "Are we having breakfast? I like breakfast and Mom said I didn't have time this morning. Can we have pancakes? Daisy's has the best pancakes. Is that where we're going?"

Ben laughed again. The kid's energy was off the charts. "I'll tell you what, buddy. Let's get through the first thing I have planned and then there'll be plenty of time for pancakes. Deal?"

"Deal!"

Austin continued to pepper with him questions about what they were doing until Ben finally, mercifully, pulled up to their destination. He unbuckled and grabbed his supplies from the back before opening the door for Austin, who was already unbuckled and ready to go. He jumped down from the Jeep to the curb and looked up at Ben expectantly. "Where are we?" He turned around to look and immediately looked back at Ben, disappointment all over his face. "What are we doing here? The old folks' home?"

"I promise it will all make sense in a minute." Ben was prepared for his nephew's reaction, but he was confident his attitude would change quickly. "But first, come with me. I want to tell you a quick story, okay?"

Austin nodded and took Ben's hand. They walked a short distance to a little gazebo that was situated behind the nursing home and he knelt in front of Austin. "When your dad and I were kids, there was one summer when he was in charge of me."

"Like a parent?"

Ben laughed. "Not really. More like a babysitter. Our mom and dad had to work all summer, so your dad was in charge."

"He was good at being in charge," Austin said matter-of-factly. It was such a small statement, but it made Ben's heart hurt.

"He was," Ben agreed. "Even when we were kids." He smiled at the memory of his brother bossing him around. "Anyway, the other day, your mom found a list of some of the cool things we did that summer and I think your dad would really like it if I showed you those things since he's not here to show you himself. Do you think that's a good idea?"

Austin nodded, but turned to look back at the building. "But why are we here? It's not cool."

Ben couldn't help but chuckle. "Maybe not. But what we're about to do will be cool. Are you ready?"

He nodded again, this time jumping a little on one foot.

"Okay. So one of the things your dad and I did once was write messages on the sidewalk of the school so that when all the other kids arrived, they'd be able to read really positive things and start their day off happy. Do you like it when someone says something nice to you?"

"Yeah. Of course." Austin looked confused. "But we're not at school."

"That's right, because I thought maybe we could leave messages for some people who really need them. These grandmas and grandpas sometimes don't feel the best, and they might not have people to tell them nice things every day, so what do you say we write some nice things so that when they come outside this morning to enjoy the beautiful day, they'll have something a little extra to smile about? Do you like that idea?"

Just as Ben knew he would, Austin jumped up and down and immediately started brainstorming things to write. For the next ten minutes, Ben crawled around on his hands and knees while Austin jumped around him and came up with things for him to write.

"Have a great day!"

"You're pretty."

"Today is beautiful."

"The sun is warm."

Ben scribbled as fast as he could, but Austin only seemed to be warming up. Cognizant that he was running out of time before the residents of the nursing home started to make their way out for morning coffee, he tried his best to keep up, but he was going to have to cut Austin off. "Okay, one more, buddy. We're running out of time."

"Can I help?"

The voice sent a shot of warmth through him, and still on his hands and knees, Ben turned around to see Drew watching them.

"Mom!"

"I'm sorry." She caught Austin in a hug. "I wasn't sure if I should come, but—"

"No." Ben sat up and dusted his hands off on his jeans. "I'm glad you're here. I need the help. This son of yours has a million nice things to say. Grab some chalk. I figure we have about five minutes, tops."

Without missing a beat, Drew grabbed a piece of chalk and dropped to her knees on the sidewalk across from him. Austin bounced between them, shouting out ideas until finally, Ben called it, and dragged them all out of there just as he heard the back door opening.

"ARE we going to go back and tell them we did it?" Austin shoved a piece of fluffy pancake in his mouth. "Because I—"

"Don't talk with your mouth full, please," Drew admonished him. But she couldn't help but smile. He hadn't stopped talking since they'd left the nursing home and sat down in a booth at Daisy's Diner.

"No way," Ben said. "The number-one rule of sidewalk vandalism is that we don't talk about sidewalk vandalism."

Drew snorted.

"Like a secret?"

"Exactly like a secret," Ben told Austin, with a wink in her direction. "It's a good deed, and we don't need anyone else to know we did it to feel good about it," Ben said. "And it does feel good, doesn't it?"

Austin nodded. "It does. Do you think they'll be happy, Mom?"

"I do, buddy." She ruffled his hair and sat back in the seat to sip her coffee. Drew hadn't been sure that she should barge in on their activity, and she hadn't really planned it. Curiosity was making her crazy, so she'd gone for a run, something she hadn't done in years, fitness not really being her *thing*, and when she'd turned the corner by Riverside Park, she'd seen Ben's Jeep parked at the end of the street by the Whispering Pines nursing home and she couldn't resist taking a peek. "I am sorry that I crashed your party," she said again to Ben. "I didn't really plan it."

"I see that." He raised an eyebrow at her running wear. "But I'm glad you did. I really needed your help back there with this guy. I guess I didn't take into consideration that he's not a super strong writer yet."

"Hey," Austin protested. "I'm learning."

"You are," Drew assured him. "And Uncle Ben is right—you did have a lot of ideas out there today. That's awesome. I'm so proud of you."

"How do you feel about what we did today, buddy?"

Austin bounced in his seat and grinned so wide that Drew couldn't help but laugh. "I felt..." He stared at his mother. "What?"

She shook her head. "It's not—"

"Why are you laughing?"

A tear sprang to her eye, but she didn't bother to wipe it away. "I'm laughing because you're just so amazing."

Austin's face screwed up in confusion. He looked to his uncle for help, but Ben only shrugged.

"Don't bother trying to understand women," he said as way of explanation. "But you are pretty amazing, Austin."

Austin seemed to be satisfied with the answer and went back to shoveling pancakes into his mouth. It didn't take him long to finish eating and when he was done, Drew could see the early morning start to take its toll. He sagged back into the booth and his eyes started to flutter closed. She let him tuck his feet up and put his head on her lap as he fell quickly into sleep the way only a child could do in a public place.

"He's exhausted." She stroked his hair absently while she lifted her coffee mug with the other. "Maybe it was the excitement of the morning. Do you think he understands what he did for the seniors? Really?"

Ben shrugged. "I'm not sure. But I was thinking of taking him by later to see if any of the residents were mentioning it. And since he enjoyed it so much, maybe we could do some sidewalk vandalism at the school later, or even in front of the hospital."

"That would be really sweet. And he really did seem to enjoy it. Thank you again, Ben. I can't wait to see what's next." Drew hadn't intended on inviting herself along to the next adventure, or really any of them at all, but now that she'd been there for the first one, more than anything she wanted to participate in the completion of the Bro List. And it didn't have anything to do with how easy it was to be with Ben or how when she spent time with him, her life felt almost normal. And it definitely didn't have anything to do with the strange way she'd felt when she saw Ben talking to Calla last week.

Nope. Not at all.

Wanting to tag along on the adventures was all about Austin. It had nothing to do with her.

And she'd keep telling herself that until she believed it, too.

"What's next?" Ben raised an eyebrow. "Does that mean you're going to crash that party, too?"

She blushed a little. "I am," she said. "That's okay, right?"

He chuckled. "Of course." He reached his hand across the table and put it over hers.

His touch was unexpected. The heat from his skin sent a spark shooting through her.

"Drew, I need you to know…"

Her breath caught in her throat and she had no idea why. "What?"

He took a breath and for a moment, Drew was terrified about what he might say. "That the next thing I have planned involves sleeping outside. With bugs." Ben burst into laughter and pulled his hand away right as Drew threw a sugar packet at him. He ducked it neatly and laughed. "I'm serious, Drew. I know you've never been very into the whole camping thing and…well…"

"It's fine." She swallowed hard, and picked up another sugar packet to fiddle with so she wouldn't have to look at him. It was the strangest thing, and there was no way she could explain it because she had no idea what had just happened. But for the life of her, she'd been sure Ben was going to… what? It didn't matter. "I'll go camping," she announced before she could say anything else. "Why wouldn't I?"

"Because when we were kids, you straight up told me that there was nothing less appealing than sleeping outside in the cold with the bugs and random animals." He laughed and she wanted to throw something much heavier than a sugar packet at him. "In fact," he continued, "I'm pretty sure that's a direct quote. Am I wrong?"

"Yes."

"I am?"

She crossed her arms. "Yes. You're wrong. Because I'm not that same person anymore."

"You're not?" He was teasing her, and clearly getting a great deal of joy from it. "Because you seem to be——"

"Look." She put her coffee mug down with more force than she'd meant to and instantly regretted it. "I am the same person, but at the same time, I'm not. A lot has changed." Her voice dipped and she cleared her throat quickly. "And okay, I'm still not a big outdoorsy person but I can handle it."

Ben leaned back in his seat and grinned.

"I can," she insisted.

"Of course you can."

"I mean, how hard can it be to—wait. What?" She stared at him.

"Of course you can handle it," he said again. "I mean, it's camping, Drew. It's not like I'm asking you to climb Mount Everest." He winked. "Seriously, I'd love to have you come along, and I promise to make it easy on you."

It was much later that day when Drew reflected back on what Ben had said. *Easy on her?*

No.

It wasn't going to be *easy*.

For reasons she couldn't seem to explain, not even to herself—maybe especially not to herself—camping with Ben was not going to be easy. And the scariest part about it was that she was pretty sure it had nothing to do with creepy crawly bugs or wild animals.

Chapter Nine

"LOOK OVER HERE, AUSTIN."

"And smile."

"Looks great."

The photographer and his assistant called out a variety of orders, and like a little professional, Austin posed and smiled at the camera as Drew and Amber looked on.

"He's doing amazing." Amber turned to see the love in Drew's eyes as she watched her son, who rode on the back of Peanut. "Such a natural."

"It's because of you," Drew said. "Well, you and Logan and the horses, of course."

"That's not even true."

"It is." Her friend turned on her. "Don't be so modest. Everything you and Logan have done here is amazing and you need to realize it."

Amber laughed at her friend's insistence, but the laughter dried up when she saw that her friend might cry. "Drew." She put her hand on Drew's shoulder and turned her away from the photo shoot for a moment. "What's going on? You look...I don't know. Talk to me."

Drew wiped at her eyes. "I hate crying. I feel like I've done enough of it to last a lifetime."

"But not lately." It was true. In those early months after Eric had died and Amber had moved in with her and Austin, there had understandably been lots of tears. But they'd slowed in recent months. In fact, with every day that went by, Drew seemed to be a little bit stronger than the day before. "Why the tears today?"

Drew squeezed her eyes shut and shook her head. "I've just had some feelings lately, I think. I mean…I actually don't know what I mean." She smiled, but Amber wasn't fooled. "Really, I'm fine. I must just be tired today."

"You know I don't believe that." Amber narrowed her eyes. "Drew, just tell—"

"Amber, can I get your opinion on this for a minute?"

The photographer called over to her, pulling her away from Drew. She glanced over to see the photographer standing with Charlene, the account manager she'd hired to work on their advertising campaign with them. Charlene waved her over as soon as she made eye contact. Amber looked back to Drew, who was nodding and forcing what she could tell was a fake smile.

"Go," Drew said. "I'm not going anywhere."

She pulled her friend into a quick hug. "I'll be right back."

A moment later, Charlene was firing questions at her and pointing to different places around the yard that she wanted to move the shoot to.

"The light will be better over here," she said. "And since the building isn't finished yet, we can't take any shots over there. In fact, I don't think we should even use it in the background. Not yet."

"I agree," Amber said, jumping into advertising mode at once. She'd shifted easily from her corporate lawyer job into her role with Taking the Reins. Although she didn't have an official title because she and Logan were a partnership, Logan handled the operations side of things while Amber mostly oversaw the business details. A task that she was definitely up for, and her perfectionism instincts kicked into overdrive while she and Charlene made some quick decisions for the rest of the shoot.

Fortunately, it didn't take very long to get the rest of the shots and when they were complete, Logan took Austin for a trail ride as payment for his role in the entire campaign, leaving Drew and Amber alone for a few minutes.

"He's going to talk about this for days," Drew said when they were sitting down in Amber's cabin. "Thank you so much for letting him be a part of it."

"Are you kidding?" Amber handed her a mug of tea. "He did us a huge favor. He's the perfect little boy model. Thank you for letting us pay him in trail rides. The budget is still pretty tight."

"He loves it." Drew smiled over her mug. "And I totally get what you mean about the budget."

"What do you mean?" Amber lifted her own mug and inhaled the spicy chai. "I thought you were in good shape financially?"

After Eric had died, as a favor to Drew, Amber had gone through all their paperwork and helped her friend sort out her financial situation and work through all the details of her husband's death. "The life insurance policy put you in a good spot, from what I can remember."

Drew nodded absentmindedly. "It did, but...I don't feel right living off money I got because my husband died, you know?"

Amber didn't know. Obviously and thankfully, she'd never had to worry about being in that situation, but throughout her career as a lawyer, she'd seen more than her fair share of people who had no qualms at all about living off money they'd earned in a lot less legitimate ways than that. And that's what life insurance was for, after all. She told Drew so.

"I know," Drew said. "But I think I'd really like to get out on my own and do something for myself, too. I mean, don't get me wrong, it's nice to not have to really worry very much. But I also don't want to sit around and blow through everything, forcing us into a situation that I never should have been in. Does that make sense?"

Amber nodded. "Perfect sense. I think that's really smart, actually. So what are you thinking of doing?"

The moment she asked the question, Drew's face lit up. "I have an idea." She leaned forward in her seat. "Tell me what you think."

"Okay."

"You know how I love to cook?"

Amber was positive it was a rhetorical question because not only did everyone know Drew loved to cook, but they also knew how amazing her food was. Still, she nodded.

"In Nevada, before we…well, before Eric got sick and we still went out and did things socially, there was this new thing that was growing in popularity." Amber listened, intrigued. "It was called a cook night," Drew continued. "But I could probably come up with a catchier name. But basically, it was where a chef would come into your home and teach you and your guests how to cook. It was totally hands-on, and each night had a theme."

"Like a cooking class?"

"But better." Drew sat back and nodded. "Way better. Cooking classes are all very formal, in a professional kitchen and really regimented. But this was very casual and relaxed. There was always a few bottles of wine involved and everyone got in on the cooking, together. So the chef would do the instructing and a lot of the preparing, but also get the guests to chop and mix and plate everything. It was really fun and everyone felt like they learned something."

Amber let the idea roll around her head. "That sounds interesting, for sure."

"Really?"

"For sure. I'd totally do it," Amber said. "How much does something like that cost?"

"I think I could charge about one hundred dollars a person and after food costs, make about eighty."

Amber nodded. "That's not bad."

"It's not. But it's not great either. I think I could probably do some catering on the side as well. But the best part is, I have a little wiggle room financially."

"It's true." Amber watched her friend explain everything, and she couldn't help but feel as though it were exactly the right idea for Drew. "It's a fantastic idea," she told her. "I think you'll be amazing at it. You've been thinking a lot about it."

It wasn't a question, but Drew answered anyway. "I have." She took a sip of her tea. "I've been thinking a lot about a lot of things."

All of a sudden, the light-heartedness was gone, and the worry and hurt Amber had seen in Drew's eyes earlier was back. "What's going on?" she asked. "What happened earlier? While Austin was on the horse?"

Drew shrugged. "I don't really know."

"Liar."

Drew shook her head. "I don't know whether I should love that or hate that about you."

"What?"

"The in-your-face approach to everything. And the fact that you know me so well," Drew answered. "I mean, sometimes I think it might be kind of nice to just fly under the radar a little bit, but you would never let that happen."

"You're right," Amber agreed. "Because what kind of friend would I be if I didn't notice all the—"

"I'm scared."

DREW HADN'T INTENDED on talking to Amber about this, at least not today. But once her friend started pressing the issue, the words flowed out of her like water from a broken pipe.

"What?" Amber shook her head. "What are you scared of? Because something tells me this isn't just about the new business idea. What's going on?"

Drew shook her head slightly. "Nothing, just...well...okay, here's the thing. Scared might be the wrong word." Drew put her hands down on the table and looked straight into Amber's eyes. "When I was watching Austin on the horse, I was struck by the fact that Eric would never see his son on horseback and then it kind of snowballed into a lot of other things that Eric would never see." She swallowed. "That happens sometimes. I just get hit with it, like it's fresh again. And I think it's worse right now because when I was going through his things the other day, I found this list that he'd made."

"What kind of list?"

Drew told her friend all about the list of things that Ben had decided to take on and dub the Bro List. She finished her explanation with a rundown of the sidewalk vandalism they'd done a few days earlier.

"That sounds great," Amber said when she was finished explaining. "But why would that make you sad or even scared? It doesn't sound like the list is particularly dangerous. I mean, camping in the middle of the mountains can always be—"

"It's not the list. It's Ben."

The moment she said it out loud, Drew wanted to take it back. It didn't make any sense and she had no business saying anything, especially when she wasn't even sure of all the feelings that had been swirling around her head over the last few weeks. "Never mind," she added quickly. "I shouldn't have said anything at all. I don't know what I was—"

"Why are you scared of Ben?" Amber watched her with narrowed eyes that made Drew nervous, because her friend was smart, and she knew her well. "What's going on, Drew?"

She squeezed her eyes shut, unsure of how much more she should say. But she was already in too deep. There was no way Amber was going to let her off the hook that easily.

"I'm scared of the way I'm feeling."

"About Ben?"

She nodded. "I can't really explain it, but..."

"Well, you guys have been friends forever and he has really been awesome with you and Austin and you guys have been spending a ton of time together, so I'm sure you care about him—"

"It's more than that." She swallowed against the lump that had formed in her throat. "The other night when he was talking to that girl at the Log and Jam, I was..." She glanced down at the table, tracing the wood grain with her eyes before looking up again. "I think I was jealous. How does that make any sense?" She jumped up from the couch. "You know what? It doesn't make any sense and I'm just being ridiculous. Besides, it's not like I have any feelings for him myself. Not like *that.*"

The lie tasted unexpectedly bitter on her tongue.

From the couch, Amber twisted around and watched her carefully. "Drew? What is—"

"Before Eric died, we talked a lot about *after,*" she interrupted her friend.

"After?"

"Right." Drew nodded. "When you know you're going to

lose your husband, and he knows he's leaving you behind, it really forces the issue of talking about *after.* "

"Ahh, I see. So you guys talked about what that would look like? For *you*? And I don't think we're just talking about finances, am I right?"

Drew nodded again.

"And?"

"And he told me he wanted me to open my heart and move on." Amber didn't look surprised at her words. "He told me he didn't want me to be alone and to sit around crying over him and letting time go by when I could be finding new happiness. He told me he wanted me to fall in love again and get married, maybe have more kids, the whole thing."

"That makes so much sense." Amber nodded knowingly, but Drew had to look away from the worry in her friend's eyes.

"But it's strange, don't you think?"

"What's strange?"

Drew turned around again. "To have that kind of conversation with your husband?"

"Not at all. Not in the situation you were in." Amber stood and crossed the small room to her. "You're young and have so much life left. Eric wouldn't want you to spend your life alone. I know that. But why is this coming up now? And what does it have to do with Ben?"

What does *it have to do with Ben?*

That question slammed into her. But she didn't bother to answer it, not even to herself. Ben had always been special to her. Like a best friend, but...

She didn't have time to dwell on that particular point because Amber's next question froze her to the spot. "You're not thinking of moving on already, are you?"

Already.

Is that what it was? *Already?*

The ground spun around her. The pictures on the wall

looked as if they dipped and dropped and for a minute, she thought she was going to fall over.

It had been almost a year since Eric had died, and longer still since he'd gotten sick. They'd had so many conversations about *after* that she'd had to make him stop. They'd talked for hours about her moving on. Or more like, Eric had. For the longest time, it had been easier for Drew to ignore it. Like an ostrich in the sand. If she didn't think about it, it wasn't happening, right?

But it had happened.

And maybe it *was* too soon. They hadn't really talked about *when* Drew would move on. Only that she should. Of course Eric told her to do it right away, but that was *way* easier done than said. But, maybe…was there really a timeline for grief that she wasn't following? That she didn't know about?

"That's not what I meant," Amber said quickly. "You know I didn't mean it like, *already* already. You know that, Drew. Right?"

Drew nodded, but she couldn't find any words. Her brain spun with the idea that if her best friend thought it was too soon, then maybe it was, and what would everyone else think, and Eric—what would *he* think and…

"There's no time limit." Amber was talking, but Drew wasn't listening. "I truly believe that, Drew. I really do."

It was hot. She was sweating and she needed a glass of water. Or fresh air. Or both.

She had to get out of there.

"Hey," she said. "I totally forgot that I had some running around to do. Would you mind bringing Austin home when they're done riding? I don't want to cut it short, but I just remembered that I have some things I need to—"

"Of course I'll bring him home for you." Amber put a hand on her arm in an effort to stop her from fleeing. "But it's okay, you don't have to go. I didn't mean to—"

"Oh, I know." Drew forced a smile. "But I really do need to get going."

"Drew, I—"

"Thanks, Amber." She turned and reached for the door handle before her best friend could say anything else. She'd heard enough for one afternoon.

SHE'D LIED to her best friend.

Drew didn't have any errands to run. At least nothing that couldn't wait. The truth was she couldn't sit there for one more moment and see that look on Amber's face. That look that told her she was a monster and a terrible person for even entertaining the idea that she might want to move on from her dead husband.

But was that even what she was doing?

Yes. The thoughts she'd had...

But no. She hadn't *done* anything. *She...*

She groaned and clutched at her head.

She didn't know. She just knew that things were changing. The constant ache of missing him wasn't there anymore, at least not all the time. She laughed more. She smiled more. She...had started living again.

And that made her feel both fantastic and terrible all at the same time.

The moment she was inside her house, Drew locked the door behind her, and went straight to her bedroom, where she changed into her favorite pajamas and despite the fact that it wasn't even dinner time, crawled into bed.

She didn't cry, because at least for the day, there were no tears left. But she hugged the spare pillow—the one that sat unused on Eric's side of the bed—and curled up tight in a ball.

She'd known she was taking a risk by talking about how she

was feeling when she wasn't even sure herself. But she had to get the feelings out because they were driving her crazy and the person she'd normally talk to about everything was…well…no longer available for a conversation.

"Dammit, Eric." Her words were muffled into the pillow. "Why didn't you tell me exactly what I should do before you left?"

To her surprise, Drew actually laughed at herself the moment she said the words aloud, because Eric *had* told her what to do. She just hadn't wanted to hear it. Not then, and maybe not even now.

Still chuckling a little, Drew sat up and reached for the glass of water she always left on her nightstand. She drank deeply and remembered for the first time in months exactly how that conversation had gone.

It was before Eric had gotten really bad, but after they'd moved to Timber Creek already. They'd just come home from a night out at the Log and Jam. Nothing major, just a few drinks with some friends. After they'd sent his parents home, relieved from babysitting duty, they'd sat on the couch and shared another bottle of wine. She remembered it being the most either of them had had to drink in a long time. They weren't drunk by any means, but their tongues were definitely looser as they dove into some of the tougher subjects that Drew usually liked to ignore.

"I want you to remarry, Drew. You shouldn't be alone."

"I'll be fine." She took a sip, letting the wine coat her tongue before swallowing. On nights like this one, where besides his extra-thin frame and the sickly pallor that always seemed to cling to him, he looked fine. It was so hard to think that in only a few weeks or months, he'd be gone. That is, until they started discussing it. Then it was all too easy to believe.

"Oh, I know you'll be fine." Eric chuckled. "You're a strong woman. I just don't want to think of you being alone. It would be such a..."

"A what?" She tried to smile and keep the tone light. But how did you keep the tone of such a conversation light? "I would be just fine on my own."

He ignored her and answered her first question. "It would be a waste, Drew," Eric said seriously. "You have so much to offer and so much life to live." He slipped his hand on her thigh and squeezed a little. "I don't want your life to end when mine does, okay?"

She shook her head and opened her mouth to insist it wouldn't. But she couldn't bring herself to say the words because she couldn't be sure it wasn't a lie.

"I mean it, Drew. I mean, I know you're going to be sad and—"

"I feel like that's an understatement." She shook her head wryly.

"Okay. Yes. There will be lots of feelings, but I want you to know that no matter what you feel, it's okay. I would never be upset with you for feeling anything, okay? Even if...no, especially if that feeling is for someone else."

"Eric, I—"

"I know you don't want to talk about it, babe. But it's important to me. It'll give me peace to know that you understand this."

"I do."

He tilted his head and laughed. "Do you?"

She'd nodded, although she didn't. Not really. How could she even think about having feelings for anyone else when the man she vowed to love forever sat in front of her? It was insane. "I'm not worried about it." She set her wine down and scooted closer to him on the couch.

"I am."

"Clearly." She took his glass from his hand and crawled up

until she was nose-to-nose with him. "But you shouldn't be." She kissed him then. Soft, sweet, and with a purpose that was clear.

He slipped his arms around her and splayed his hands across her back to hold her to him. "One more thing." His breath came in warm puffs on her mouth. "There will be a day when you remember this conversation vividly. And I hope on that day you can also remember when I tell you that I will always know how much you loved me and will always love me. That will never change, no matter how you feel about someone else. *Anyone* else. There is love enough in your heart for everyone. Do you understand?"

She nodded, although she wasn't sure she did.

"There's no timeline for this, Drew," he continued, although all Drew wanted him to do was stop talking. "The only thing I'd be upset about is if you tortured yourself by being alone and unhappy. I don't want you to be one of those old ladies, alone and bitter because her only son never comes to visit, with only her six cats for company."

She smacked him playfully. "Eric. Seriously. Austin will always visit me." Drew smiled and hoped that was the end of the seriousness.

"I never want you to be unhappy, babe," Eric said, the seriousness returned to his tone. "You deserve everything. Love and happiness and a life well lived."

She nodded again.

"Promise me you'll fall in love again."

She stared at him, her heart breaking in a million pieces.

"Promise me, Drew."

"I promise." She'd finally uttered the words despite the fact that she didn't believe them to be true. Not really.

"I'm going to hold you to that," he teased and she smacked him again.

"Good luck with that, Mister."

He laughed. "Don't you worry," he said. "I'll find a way. One day you'll be feeling something and—"

She cut him off with a kiss. "Right now all I'm feeling is how much I want my husband to take me to bed and make love to me." On some level his words sank in, but Drew was done talking. She wrapped her fingers in his hair and tugged him closer. She kissed him again while he somehow managed to scoop her up from the couch and carry her into their bedroom, where that's exactly what they did.

It felt like a million years ago that they'd held each other in the very bed where Drew now sat alone. She didn't even realize she was crying until a tear landed on her hand. But they weren't sad tears; instead, they were tears of realization. Eric had been right. He'd known her well. Too well.

"Well," she said aloud. "You were right, Eric. But I bet you never thought I'd have those feelings for your brother."`

Chapter Ten

"GOOD JOB, AUSTIN," Ben yelled from the base line. "Keep your arm steady and...yes!" He pumped his arm in the air as Austin nailed the ball off the tee and it flew through the air toward the shortstop. It took Ben a moment to realize that Austin was still standing at home plate, watching the ball he'd just hit. "Run!" he yelled at the boy. "Run to first!"

Ben couldn't help but laugh as Austin finally did as he was told. Fortunately, he had lots of time to get to the base. Ben jogged over and gave him a high five. "Good work, buddy. You nailed it."

"I did it!"

"Of course you did." Ben's heart swelled, watching his nephew take in the moment of his first base hit. "I never doubted you for a second."

"Thanks, Uncle Ben." Austin threw his arms around Ben's waist and hugged him tight. "Oh." He pulled away. "Am I supposed to call you Coach during the game?"

"You can call me whatever you like, kiddo." Ben stepped back. "But you need to pay attention to the game. Conner is up next and when he hits the ball, you need to run to second base, got it?"

Austin nodded seriously and turned his attention to the game.

A few hours later, the game over and the Timber Creek Trout the victors over their rivals, the Bridgetown Bears, Ben and Evan took the team and their parents down to Timber Treats for some ice cream.

"I'm proud of all of you," Evan announced as he lifted his own cone into the air. "They played pretty well, don't you think, Coach Ben?"

"I couldn't be prouder." Ben's eyes landed on his nephew, who looked so much like his brother had when he was young. The only difference being the freckles that were sprinkled over Austin's nose. Those came from his mother. He had to turn away. "Congratulations, Trout! You played a great game."

The kids all let out various whoops and hollers.

"And a big thank-you to the Trout fan club, too," Ben added and raised his cone to the crowd of parents and grandparents. Including his own mom and dad and Drew's parents. "We love our cheer section."

There were more hoots and hollers before everyone turned their attention to devouring their ice cream.

"You're doing a great job, son." Sylvia Ross met him with a smile as soon as he turned around, and Ben pulled his mom into a hug.

"Thanks, Mom." He wished he couldn't, but Ben noticed the gleam of unshed tears in her eyes. As sad as his mom was about Eric's death, Ben also knew it was just who she was. His mom had always been quick to tear up. It didn't mean she wasn't okay. "I know Eric would have been the first to jump in as coach, so I hope Austin likes that I'm helping out."

"Oh, I think everyone likes it." She smiled. "It means a lot and you're a great uncle, Ben."

"Good job, son." His dad joined them with his own ice cream cone. "I think you'll take those Trout all the way to state this year." They all laughed and rolled their eyes.

"Well, maybe at the very least, we'll have a couple of kids who fall in love with the sport."

"That's perfect," Mitch Ross agreed. "We're going to go say hi to Laura and Paul and get out of here. Good job, Ben."

Ben gave his mom one more hug, and watched as they joined Drew's parents to enjoy their ice cream. After a moment, he turned to find his co-coach and eat his own melting cone of double chocolate.

"Wasn't that great?" Evan took a seat on the picnic table next to him. "That's the best part of coaching," he continued. "Watching the kids hit the ball for the first time and run as hard as they can to get to the base."

"It was pretty cool," Ben agreed. "I'm glad you talked me into being a coach. I had no idea it was so much fun."

Evan laughed. "There is a reason I subject myself to crazy baseball parents year after year," he said.

Ben's eyes floated across the crowd to Drew, who sat with Conner's mom and dad, laughing at something they were saying. "Not all the parents are so bad," he said absent-mindedly.

It didn't take long for Evan's eyes to follow where Ben was looking. "Right," he said, drawing out the word. "Not all the parents are so bad at all. Some of them are downright—"

"Don't say anything." Ben whirled on his best friend, who held up his hands protectively.

"Whoa. Stand down. How did you know I was going to say anything at all?"

Ben shrugged. He'd always been defensive where Drew was concerned. And it seemed as if it was only getting more intense as he struggled to sort out his feelings. Evan was only one of very few people who knew how much he'd loved her once.

Once? More like *always.* Those feelings had never gone away. Not in any real sense. Something he realized more and more every day.

"I wasn't going to say...okay, I was going to say something," Evan confessed before turning his attention back to his ice cream.

Ben waited, knowing his best friend wasn't going to be able to stay quiet long.

Just as he predicted, Evan took a big bite of his ice cream and, a second later, said, "I was just going to mention that... well, I know that you've been so supportive to Drew and don't think I don't think it's awesome. I mean, I think we all know that Eric would want you to be there for them."

Ben nodded and looked out across the parking lot. "He asked me to watch over them. I'm just trying to do my best, man."

"I know you are. And honestly, I think it's been just as important for your healing, Ben. I mean, you lost a brother, man. That's not a small thing. And I'm definitely not saying it is." Something in Evan's voice had Ben turn to face him. "I also know how you feel about her," he continued.

And there it was.

Ben shook his head. There was no way he was having this conversation now. "No. It's not about how I feel." It was a lie, but not completely. "We're all healing, and...I just need to make sure they're okay."

"I get that." His friend nodded and for a few moments they went back to eating their ice cream in silence before Evan said, "Cam told me that Drew had found some sort of list and you were helping her with it. What's that all about?"

"It's more like it was a list Eric left for me. Some of the fun things we did when we were kids. I think he probably wanted Austin to be able to experience all of that, too, so I'm just making sure he does and…Drew wanted to come along. That's all."

"That's all, huh?"

Ben turned again and stared at him. "Is there something you wanted to say, Evan? Because I'm not in the mood to play games with you. Just say what you need to say, already."

Evan's face grew serious. "There's nothing I need to say," he said after a moment. "You don't need me telling you that you're playing a dangerous game. She's your brother's widow, and—"

"Dammit." Ben jumped up from the table. "I knew you had something to say." He glanced around, and was once again aware that they were surrounded by little ears. He took a deep breath and looked at his best friend. "I'm not playing any kind of game with Drew and trust me, I know damn well she's Eric's widow. If you think that I can forget that even for one second, then you don't know me at all."

"Ben." Evan held his hand up. "That's not how I meant it. It's just a really complicated situation and—"

"It's not complicated, Evan. Because it's not about anything else except for Austin." *And his mom.* Ben shook his head in an effort to clear it. "Besides, I met a girl. Just like you said I should."

He knew it wasn't fair to talk to Evan about this. Not when he didn't think of Calla as anything more than a friend. Despite the idea he'd had when he'd first met her. It had become clear in a few phone calls and talking to her the night of the patio grand opening that as great as Calla was, there was no romantic connection.

"Really? The girl from Petal Pushers?"

Ben nodded and pushed down the little voice that was screaming at him to stop talking. "Right," he said, ignoring the voice. "Calla. She really helped me out and she's really…well, she's nice."

"*Nice?*"

"Yes." Ben glared at his best friend, already regretting having this conversation. "She's nice. We've talked a few times."

"And when are you going out with this *nice* girl?"

He shrugged. "We're both pretty busy."

That made Evan burst out in laughter. "Right. You're pretty busy with another woman. I guess that is true."

That did it. Ben stepped up to his friend, no longer caring that kids might be watching, and stood right in his face. "I told you. It's not like that," he hissed. "It'll never be like that with Drew. I think of her like a sister. That's it." The lies tasted bitter on his tongue, but maybe if he said it out loud he just might start to believe it himself. "I'm just trying to help her out," he continued. "I feel really sorry for her. That's it. Got it?"

Evan nodded and the smile faded from his face. But Ben could see Evan didn't believe a word that he'd just said. He stepped back, and remembering where he was, looked around. His eyes landed on Conner's parents, but Drew was no longer with them.

"She's over there," Evan said.

Ben turned in the direction his friend pointed without even questioning how Evan knew who he was looking for. Drew was walking quickly, her head down, with Austin's hand tightly in hers, heading away from them and the group.

"Where's she going?" Ben asked aloud. She hadn't been sitting close enough to overhear anything he'd said, and even if she had... "Do you think she heard what I said?"

"What does it matter?" Evan said slowly. Something in his voice made Ben turn to see the knowing look on his best friend's face. "After all," Evan continued, "you said it wasn't like that."

IT WAS ALMOST a week after the Little League triumph for the Timber Creek Trouts and Austin was still insisting on wearing his jersey to school every day. Drew had given up trying to fight that fight. There was no point; she was bound to lose. Besides, the school year was almost over and Austin could have picked worse things to wear. The problem was completely her own because every time she saw the red and black shirt, with the Log and Jam name proudly displayed across Austin's little shoulders, right above his number five, Drew couldn't help but think of Ben.

And more specifically, what she'd heard him say.

It'll never be like that with Drew. I think of her like a sister. That's it.

And then, worse: *I feel really sorry for her. That's it.*

The words had been on repeat in her brain for days. *Is that really what Ben thought of her?*

Of course it was.

She'd been stupid enough to let herself, even for the slightest moment, think that what she was feeling for Ben was something more than just a friendship. That she might be able to feel something for someone again. That all the feelings she was having racing through her whenever she saw him could possibly be her allowing her heart the chance to open up again.

Maybe Amber had been right. It was too soon.

Okay, she hadn't said that. Not in so many words, but she might as well have.

"Besides," Drew said aloud as she dug through her pots and pans, pulling out the tools she was going to need to create her sample menu, "I have more important things to worry about now." She found the saucepan she'd been looking for. "Like perfecting this sauce." She slammed it down on the counter with more force than she'd intended, and got to work.

She'd been so busy avoiding Ben for the last few days that all the time she normally would have spent with him had been filled instead with her digging out all her old cookbooks from the boxes in the garage, and hours upon hours of her poring through the pages in search of the perfect recipes for her tasting menu.

She'd compiled a good list of things she could put into her cooking classes, but she didn't just want to cook her tried-and-true things, but come up with some new creations as well. Which was why she was spending her Friday evening surrounded by ingredients and pages and pages of ideas she'd jotted down. Austin was sleeping over at her parents' house and she had the house to herself. Determined not to go to bed until she'd perfected her menu, Drew connected her phone to the portable speaker she kept in the kitchen, turned on a nineties sing-along playlist and cranked up the tunes while she got to work.

She was so lost in what she was working on that she didn't hear the knock on the door, or the doorbell, or then the front door opening, followed by all her best friends as they used the spare key Drew always kept under the mat, and walked into the house.

With a tray of homemade flax and parmesan crackers in the oven, Drew shook her butt and sang into her spatula, "I like big butts and I can not lie. You other brothers can't deny." She spun around and screamed, dropping her spatula as she jumped. "What the hell?"

"Baby got back!" Christy picked up the tune as she danced into the kitchen. Amber and Cam started laughing and, as soon as Drew recovered from the shock, she joined in and turned down the music.

"What are you guys doing here?" She didn't bother asking how they got in. It had been Christy's idea to have the spare key outside and it was definitely not a secret. "I was just—"

"Singing." Christy laughed.

"Terribly singing," Cam added.

Christy held up her hands. "I wasn't going to say it."

Despite the shock of having her friends show up unannounced, Drew found herself glad they were there. "Seriously, what are you guys doing here? It's Friday night. Don't you all have lives you should be living?"

"That's exactly what we're doing." Amber put two bottles of wine on the kitchen table and helped herself to glasses before pouring everyone except Cam, who was breastfeeding, a glass. "We're spending our Friday night with our best friend, who, by the looks of things..." Amber looked around the mess and back at Drew. "Actually, I have no idea what's happening in here. Are you having a dinner party?"

"No dinner party." She shook her head and checked the timer over the oven. "But I am testing a few things and you guys are just in time. These crackers are almost done and..." On cue, the oven chimed.

"Crackers?" Cam looked over her shoulder as she removed the hot pan. "You *made* crackers? I didn't think you could do that?"

Drew laughed at her friend's incredulousness. Cam wasn't known for her culinary skills. "Of course you can. Give them a few minutes to cool down."

"They smell delicious," Christy said from across the kitchen. "Is this all for your new class that you're working on?"

Drew shot Amber a look but she only shrugged. "What? You didn't say it was a secret."

It wasn't.

"It is for the class," she admitted. "I'm hoping to have a few things that are easy enough that everyone can actually feel like they can pull them off, but fancy enough for people to think that they're really getting value from the class."

"That makes sense." Cam nodded. "But don't forget to account for total kitchen disasters like myself."

Drew laughed. "Don't worry. You are my target audience."

While they all chatted and caught up with each other, Drew pulled out a few condiments that she'd been working on earlier: a roasted red pepper hummus, and a smoked salmon spread, along with a fig jelly. She gathered everything on a tray and once her cracker creations were cool enough, put them on a plate and carried it to the table where the women dug in to the unexpected snack.

"Okay, so we know that I've been trying to juggle a baby and a business," Cam said once they were all settled. "Never mind a teenager and a husband. So my life is pretty boring."

"That hardly sounds boring." Drew raised an eyebrow.

"Well, it's not nearly as exciting as Christy's life."

"Whatever." Christy laughed. "Mine sounds similar to yours. Minus the teenager."

"And plus the singing career that's blowing up," Amber added. "What's the latest on that, anyway? When do we get to see you win a Grammy?"

Christy shook her head, but the smile on her face gave away her excitement. "No Grammy yet," she said. "But we did sign with an agent, and he's pretty sure he can get us a record deal."

"No way!" Cam's mouth fell open. "I mean, not that I'm surprised," she added. "You guys are amazing. But it just seems so surreal. Like, we know a famous musician."

"We do." Amber lifted her glass of wine. "And soon, a famous chef."

Drew laughed so hard she almost choked on the cracker she'd just taken a bite of. "I don't know about famous," she said. "But I'll be more than happy with *successful*. I'm excited about doing this."

"As you should be," Amber said. "It's delicious. And I'm

sure your business will be a huge success, too. In fact, I was hoping you would agree to cater the grand opening of Taking the Reins whenever it finally opens."

"Of course. Do you have a date finally?"

"Not quite." Amber shook her head. "It's so frustrating, but Harry finally made some things happen and we can finally see some real progress. We're all closed in, drywall is up and now it's just a matter of finishing things up. So, hopefully we'll have a final date within a few weeks, but we should be in by the end of July. Hopefully earlier."

"That is so exciting," Drew said. "I know you guys have been working really hard. And I would be absolutely honored to provide some food for the big day." They spent the next few minutes discussing the details of what Amber and Logan were looking for, while Christy and Cam traded baby stories. Drew sketched out a few things in a notebook, and her mind spun with ideas for her very first catering affair.

"Hey." Amber leaned in to whisper. "We're okay, right? I mean…the other day…I didn't mean to say—"

"It's good," Drew cut her off. "I know you didn't…well, it's fine."

It wasn't fine. But Drew wasn't upset with Amber. The truth was, everyone was going to feel the way they were going to feel about things when she did decide to move on, and there was nothing she could do about that. Besides, she *wasn't* moving on and any feelings she thought she might be having weren't real anyway. So none of it mattered.

"It's not fine." Amber put her hand on Drew's arm. "You were trying to tell me something, and if you want to tell me about—"

"Hey," Cam interrupted unknowingly from the other side of the table. "I just remembered that Evan told me about the camping trip that you and Ben are going on with Austin."

Drew stiffened but on the inside, her stomach did a weird flipping thing at the mention of Ben's name.

"*You* are going camping?" Christy added. "Like, you actually agreed to this?"

Drew nodded but didn't say anything.

Next to her, she heard Amber ask, "Are you okay?"

"Not only did she agree to it," Cam continued, "but from what Evan tells me, she actually asked to go."

Drew was aware that all three of her friends were staring at her. After a moment, she managed to push the strange feelings in her stomach down, shake off Amber's hand, and force a smile. "It's true," she said. "I did ask Ben if I could come along, but there's actually more to it." She ended up explaining the Bro List to her girlfriends, and how it was discovered. By the time she was done telling them about it, not only did they all fully understand why she would willingly go along on a camping trip, when she'd always been the only one of them who'd hated doing outdoorsy things when they were young, but she'd also managed to quell the queasiness that had appeared at the mention of Ben's name.

It's for Austin. She needed to remember that. It had nothing to do with her and judging by what she'd overheard Ben say, that's exactly how he felt, too. Which was exactly how it should be.

For Austin. Plain and simple.

Chapter Eleven

IT WAS ALMOST the end of June before Ben and Drew were able to find a weekend that worked for both of them to take Austin camping and hiking so they could cross some more activities off the Bro List. They'd both been so busy, it had been almost impossible to nail down one weekend that didn't have a Little League game, or a function at the Log and Jam, and then there was…well, he couldn't put his finger on it, but if he didn't know better, he would have thought Drew was avoiding him.

Or at least, trying to find reasons why one weekend or another wouldn't work. He couldn't be sure, but he'd finally cornered her after a Little League practice and made her commit to a date. They were leaving for the camping trip in three days, which meant that Ben had a lot of work to do to get ready.

He'd already spent the better part of the day going through his parents' garage, digging up whatever camping and fishing supplies he could find. Sadly, it wasn't much. Most of what they had was so old it was barely usable anymore. He had his own stuff, of course, but he didn't even need to ask to know that Drew didn't have any camping gear. Eric may have had some, but Ben was pretty sure he hadn't done much in the way of outdoorsy stuff after he moved to Nevada. Which meant Ben was going to have to come up with enough supplies for everyone.

And there was one guy Ben knew would have everything he needed: Evan.

He hadn't been able to avoid his best friend because they were both coaching the Trouts, but besides their nights with the kids, Ben had done his best to limit his time with Evan. It was easier than trying to defend himself against whatever crazy ideas Evan had about him and Drew.

And that's what he needed to do—defend himself, because none of what Evan thought he knew was true.

Except it was.

All of it.

For his entire adult life, Ben had done his best to pretend he wasn't desperately in love with Drew. He'd even managed to convince himself at one point that he didn't have any actual feelings for her, but it hadn't lasted long. And ever since they'd moved back to Timber Creek, it hadn't been about his feelings for Drew. Far from it. The focus had been strictly on Eric and then on Drew and Austin and making sure they were going to be okay. That was it.

But now...

He couldn't even think about it.

Ben shook his head, took a deep breath, and rapped on Evan's front door.

A moment later, his best friend answered the door with a grin. "Hey, man."

"I need your help."

"Yeah, you do," Evan teased. "Come in."

They went straight to the kitchen, where Evan got them

each a beer from the fridge. "You're going to tell me that you need help with—"

"Before you say anything." Ben held up a finger to stop Evan from saying anything that would piss him off further. "I don't want to hear anything about my personal life."

Evan opened his mouth, but Ben once again stopped him from talking. "I mean it, Evan. I need a favor from you, and that's it. I'm not looking for advice." Once again, Evan opened his mouth. "I mean it," Ben emphasized. "No advice. Deal?"

He stared at his friend until finally, Evan nodded. "I got it. But for the record, my advice is pretty damn good and it's not going anywhere. You let me know when you want it."

Despite himself, Ben laughed. "Noted, but I don't think that's going to happen."

"Oh, it will." Evan took a deep drink from his beer. "But what can I do for you today?" His tone shifted so quickly, Ben almost laughed.

"I need to borrow some camping gear."

"For your trip with Drew?"

"And Austin."

Evan gave him a look, but true to his word, didn't offer any additional comment.

"I don't have enough sleeping bags or fishing rods. Or… well, I should probably have another tent."

He could see how hard Evan was working to not say anything. Finally, Evan opted for another sip of his drink. "Okay," he said after a moment. "Let's go see what I have. I'm sure I can help you."

A few minutes later, they were in Evan's garage, surrounded by bins of camping and fishing equipment and Ben had a small pile of supplies next to him. "When are you leaving?"

"Friday." Ben leaned against the shelf. "It's Austin's last day of school and I guess Drew's been really busy. It was hard to find a weekend that would work, but I'm glad we did."

Evan nodded. "You're going up to Bizarro?"

"The cave is on the list. Eric and I used to test each other to see how far we could go in without a flashlight."

Evan laughed because no doubt he'd done the same thing. "I can't imagine Drew will be up for that. I can't believe she's going on this trip with you. Cam said she was looking forward to it, though."

"Really?" Something inside him brightened. It was no secret that camping wouldn't have been on the top of Drew's list of things to do, but Ben truly hoped she would enjoy herself.

"Really." Evan nodded slowly. "Cam says she's doing really well and even starting up her catering and cooking class business. I guess she's going to cater Amber and Logan's grand opening."

"That's great." Ben turned away so Evan wouldn't see the surprise and hurt on his face, because he had no idea.

"Yeah," Evan said. "It is great. It's good to see her laughing and smiling again." Something in Evan's voice made Ben turn around.

"You said you'd keep your mouth shut," he warned his friend. "Don't say a word."

Evan shrugged innocently. "You might like what I have to say."

"Not if it has anything to do with Drew, I won't." He gathered up his pile of gear. "Thanks for your help on this. I'll return it next week."

Ben loaded up his Jeep and headed for home, still stewing about what Evan had said or not said. Having a best friend who knew you better than anyone else was a good thing, but sometimes it was a royal pain in the ass.

And to make matters worse, as he drove away, he realized he'd never gotten that second tent.

BY FRIDAY AFTERNOON, Drew couldn't be sure whether Austin was more excited about the last day of school and the festivities they had planned, or the camping trip they'd be going on with Ben when that was all finished. Either way, Drew was pretty sure she was going to have one very tired little boy when the excitement wore off.

She waited for him outside after the little pre-kindergarten graduation ceremony the teacher had held in the classroom. Next year, he'd be off to full kindergarten, and then after that…well, time went quickly. Just like this past school year had, all of the years to follow would go just as fast.

Drew stood on the sidewalk and stared at the school, waiting for the bell to ring. She hadn't been there for the first day. It had been Amber who had to take him, a week after the official first day of classes, because Drew was still so consumed by grief over the loss of Eric she could barely get out of bed some days.

A lot had changed.

She'd changed.

But without a doubt in her mind, she knew Eric would be proud of her and how far she'd come.

He'd also laugh at the idea that she was about to willingly spend a weekend in the woods. The thought of her husband laughing at her made her smile. He'd also be incredibly impressed, Drew thought. Because not only was she going to go on the camping trip, she was going to fully immerse herself in it. She'd spent the last week preparing snacks, as least as much as Ben would let her, insisting he'd take care of the food. She'd raided Cam's closet and found some thermal clothes in case it got cold at night and she'd even gone out and bought a new pair of hiking boots.

She was determined to show everyone that she could be outdoorsy when the situation called for it. She wasn't scared of the bugs, or bears, or anything else that could possibly be out in the woods.

After all, the scary stuff wasn't out there. It was inside her. And those thoughts and feelings were going to be there wherever she went, so she might as well distract herself with a camping trip.

Before she could think any more about what she didn't want to think about, the bell rang and the schoolyard filled with shrieking kids. A smile spread across her face as she scanned the crowd. Her eyes landed on Austin, who made a beeline for her.

"We're going camping!"

"We are." She laughed. "Are you ready?"

"Am I?" He pumped his fist in the air and shoved a handful of artwork into Drew's hands.

"I'm going to guess that it's a yes." She laughed again. "Let's get going then. I betcha Uncle Ben is already waiting for us."

Sure enough, when they pulled up to the house, Ben's Jeep was parked in the driveway. He was leaned up against the door, his arms crossed over his chest.

Drew tried and failed to ignore the flutter in her stomach at the sight of him. But she couldn't help but smile when he bent down to greet Austin with a huge hug.

"Ready for this, buddy?"

"Totally." Austin wiggled out of his grip. "I just need to change. Mom says I can't wear my jersey."

"Go change," she told him. "We're ready when you are." She turned to Ben. "That's the only way I could get him to take it off."

"What can I say? He's a ball player."

She rolled her eyes. "I just have a few things in the kitchen for snacks. I'll go grab them."

He followed her inside. "I hope it's not much. The cooler is all packed and I told you to keep it simple."

She whirled around, not realizing how close he was. "Who says I didn't?"

Ben raised an eyebrow. "It's you we're talking about. Besides, I heard a rumor that you were testing recipes for your new business." There was the slightest question in his voice, and she immediately felt guilty because she hadn't talked to him about it. Which was ridiculous, because there was no rule that she was supposed to talk to him about this stuff.

But they were friends.

Friends.

And just because her feelings were bruised, or hurt, or whatever it was she was feeling since she'd overheard him talking to Evan, that hadn't changed. They'd always been friends. That shouldn't be changing now. "I am," she said. "I was going to tell you about it, but—"

"You've been avoiding me."

Her face flushed and she shook her head. "I haven't." It was a lie and they both knew it. "I've been busy." She stared at him for a minute. He stood so close she could smell his shampoo. *Peppermint.* She inhaled and tried to work up the courage to be honest with him, but how? Finally, she exhaled and turned around. "Let's get packed up. Austin will be ready in a minute and trust me when I say he's not going to want to wait one more minute."

Ben had been right. Drew made too much food and after a quick negotiation, they put some back in the fridge and loaded the rest into the cooler before strapping Austin into his booster seat and pulling out of the driveway.

Drew was thankful she didn't have to make conversation on

the drive out. Austin kept up a steady stream of chatter. He bounced between telling them all the details of the last day of school, to his friend's summer plans, to asking questions about camping and hiking. Drew was exhausted just listening to him, but Ben was incredibly patient. He took his time answering each of the questions and explained the details of what was going to happen when they arrived at the camp site he'd selected. At some point, Drew stopped listening to the two of them and focused her attention out the window, lost in her own thoughts.

She had been camping one other time, but not since their senior year in high school. The only reason she'd agreed to go was because the entire graduating class was going, and she'd been assured by her friends, including Ben, that it would be fun.

And it had been.

They'd gone out to Ghost Lake and turned the beach into a tent city. Their days were spent suntanning and floating on the water while the guys fished and threw a football back and forth. The nights were spent around a roaring bonfire, where the entire graduating class would gather and tell stories, and drink cans of beer they'd snuck from their dads' garages. The couples among them would cuddle and make out. But because Drew was dating Eric back then, and he was older, he'd been away at college. Not that he'd be welcome at the camping trip, anyway, considering he wasn't part of the graduating class. And without Eric there, Drew found herself more than once sitting alone with Ben around the bonfire.

They'd always been so easy together. He'd been one of her best friends almost their entire life. She'd had a few beers on the second night of the camping trip. Not enough to be drunk, but definitely enough to loosen her tongue a little. And although neither of them talked about it after, she still remembered the entire conversation.

"How come you're not over there?" She'd pointed to the other side of the campfire, where most of the couples were wrapped up in each other.

He'd laughed. "No one to be there with."

Drew paused, her can of beer halfway to her lips. "Why not?" She'd always kind of wondered why Ben had never dated through high school. Plenty of girls had been interested. Hell, she herself had always had a crush on him, but that was before. "Why don't you have a girlfriend?"

Ben grinned and shook his head. "It's just one of those things."

"That's not an answer." She laughed and put her hand on his arm. He'd stiffened under her touch, but she'd only barely noticed, because the heat from his skin raced through her, cutting off her laughter. She tilted her head and looked at him. "You're cute and smart. I know you have girls throwing themselves at you all the time."

"You think I'm cute?"

He pinned her with his gaze and for the briefest moment, with her inhibitions lowered, she'd almost told him about her own crush. Instead, she laughed, and said, "And smart. Come on, there must be someone you're interested in." She asked the question seriously, and waited for an answer, but he only stared at her. "Come on, Ben." She pulled on his arm. "There must be someone."

Maybe he'd been a little drunk, too. Or maybe he thought she wouldn't remember the next day, but after a minute, he looked directly in her eyes. "There's only one. But I can't have her."

In that moment, despite the alcohol in her system, she'd heard and felt everything clearly. She didn't even have to ask him who he was talking about. She opened her mouth to say something, but couldn't think of one thing to say. A second later, Amber pushed her way between them and started talking about something Drew could never remember. She'd snuck one more look at him across her friend, but the moment had been lost.

The next morning, they'd all woken up, packed up their gear, and gone home to their lives. They'd never once spoken of that moment, and over the years, Drew had largely forgotten about it.

Until now.

Chapter Twelve

"OKAY, AUSTIN," Ben called across the tent. "Just pull that side tight." A second later, the nylon was pulled from Ben's hand. He tried not to laugh. "Okay," he said. "Not *that* tight." Austin tried again, and the fabric pulled snug so Ben could pound the nail in to hold it in place. "Good work. I think it's almost all set up. We just need to put the beds together."

"I can do that." Drew appeared, holding a sleeping bag. "But I thought that…" She leaned closer so Austin wouldn't hear her. "The list," she said. "I thought it said sleeping under the stars."

"It does." Ben grinned. "And there's only one tent." He'd checked the forecast, and it looked good, but in the mountains you could never be sure. Either way, he'd be outside. There was no way he was going to share such a tight space with Drew. And with only one tent…he'd make it work. "This is backup. Mostly for you two. I'll sleep out by the fire."

"You're not going to…" She looked over the ring of stones where the fire would soon be. "You're going to sleep out here."

He laughed. "You just said yourself that the list said sleeping under the stars. Where did you think I was going to sleep?" He didn't want her to answer that question. Not really. There was some strange tension between them lately, and although he had no idea what it was, at least not as far as Drew was concerned, it definitely wasn't going to be made any better by sleeping in close quarters with her.

"Are you sure?"

"Absolutely. Just leave my stuff in the Jeep. I'll grab it later."

She hesitated for a moment, but nodded and continued to unpack the bedding while Ben took Austin and started gathering kindling for the fire.

"You need to look for dry pieces," he told the boy. "About this size. And any bark and dry moss is really good, too. Got it?" Austin nodded and was already at work, filling his hands with kindling. "When you have a good pile, just put it over here, okay?"

"Got it, Uncle Ben."

He couldn't help but smile at the boy's excitement over the simplest things. Things Ben himself had always taken for granted. Camping and being outdoors was just part of his lifestyle, and had been since he was young. Eric had loved it once, too. But things changed, and circumstances changed. Ben was just glad he had the opportunity to teach Austin these things.

It wasn't long before they had a roaring fire and were finally able to relax and roast some hot dogs. "Go slow," Drew told Austin as he jammed his roasting stick into the flames. "You have to roast it around the edge of the fire or it will burn."

Ben watched as Drew showed Austin the proper way to hold the stick and couldn't help but grin.

"What are you smiling about?"

He shook his head. "Just...well, who would've ever thought that you'd be showing anyone how to roast a hot dog over a fire? I mean..."

"Okay, okay." She laughed. "I know I'm not the most outdoorsy, but I'm not stupid, Ben. I know a few things."

"Really? By all means then, what else can you tell us about camping?"

"Well…I can tell you…" She looked around and Ben tried —very unsuccessfully—not to chuckle. Finally, she nodded triumphantly. "I can tell you that it looks like you might have a wet sleep tonight." She pointed to the sky and the gathering clouds.

"That's where you're wrong." Ben shook his head and tossed another log on the fire. "A little cloud cover is a good thing. It actually keeps the warmth from the day *in*." He used air quotes. "Otherwise it can get a little cool out here at night."

"What about the rain?"

"What rain?" He shrugged. "The forecast looked great. Clear with no real chance of precipitation. Those clouds aren't rain clouds. In fact, I'm willing to bet they clear out completely and we get a great night for stargazing."

"When will the stars come out?" Austin looked up from his hot dog long enough to ask the question.

"Soon," Ben assured him as the boy yawned. Drew gave him a knowing look. It had been a big day for Austin. "But maybe we can save our stargazing for tomorrow night when you're not so tired."

"I'm not—" His words were cut off by a yawn and Ben once again had to hide his laughter.

"It's okay, buddy. You eat your hot dog and get a good night's sleep. Tomorrow is a big day."

Despite his protesting, Austin fell asleep on Drew's lap shortly after consuming his dinner. Ben carried him into the tent and they tucked the boy in for the night. "There's no reason you should go to bed," he told Drew. "After all, it's only barely getting dark. It's the best time to enjoy the fire."

She looked between Austin, cuddled in his sleeping bag,

and Ben at the door of the tent. "I don't know. Maybe I should stay..."

"He'll be fine here," Ben said. "Besides, we'll be right over there." Not for the first time, Ben was struck by the fact that there was something going on with her. She'd been acting strange for weeks. Whatever else happened, he was going to get to the bottom of it. "Come on, Drew," he encouraged. "I miss you." Something flashed on her face, but in the dimming light, he couldn't be sure. "I want to hear all about your business."

"Okay," she said. "But just for a few minutes."

He took her hand and helped her out of the tent. She turned and zipped Austin safely in before standing only inches from Ben. Heat flashed through him and before he could stop himself, he took her hand again and led her to the fire. Everything with Drew just felt natural, despite the fact that it probably shouldn't. No matter what he'd said to Evan before, as far as Ben was concerned, when it came to Drew, it was most certainly *like that*. And it was getting harder and harder to pretend that it wasn't.

DREW PROBABLY SHOULD HAVE GONE to bed with Austin. It would have been easier than sitting around the fire with Ben —and not because she was in the middle of the woods and she didn't even want to think about what kind of critters existed in the shadows that she couldn't quite see.

No. The biggest threat to her was the one right next to her, putting more logs on the fire.

"There." Ben put yet another log into the flames. "That should keep us warm." He sat back in his foldable chair and turned to her with a grin on his face. "This is fun, right?"

She nodded and managed a smile. "So fun."

"Oh, come on, Drew." He laughed. "You don't really hate camping that much, do you?"

She shook her head. "Honestly?"

"Of course."

"I don't think it's fair for me to say if I hate it or not." She shrugged. "I've only actually done it the one time, and that wasn't so bad." Her foot kicked at the dirt. She hadn't meant to bring up the high school camping trip. Not that he would remember it, but still. "Honestly, I just never really got the chance to do a lot of outdoorsy things and then there was that time we went hiking as kids, and I might have been a bit of a wuss."

"A bit?" Judging by his howl of laughter, Ben remembered the elementary school trip well.

She turned to him, her mouth open, ready to protest, but ultimately just shook her head and laughed. When they'd been in elementary school, either grade five or six, the class had gone on a field trip to the woods. It had been part of an outdoor education unit that involved a hike, an outdoor cook-out, and some basic camping skills. Drew had been at a doctor's appointment the day before and had missed the reminder that the teacher had given about proper dress. Both she and her mother had completely forgotten about the field trip the next day and Drew had shown up for school wearing a dress and patent leather shoes. There'd been no time for her to go home and change before the bus left, so she'd been left wearing the dress and totally inappropriate shoes. But despite her unreasonable attire, she'd done her best to keep up with the group. Even if it had meant slipping and falling over roots and rocks until her dress was tattered and stained beyond repair.

"Hey," Drew defended herself. "I didn't dress that way on purpose."

"Sure you didn't." Ben chuckled. It had become an

ongoing joke that Drew was too much of a girly girl to go for a hike, and she'd always taken the ribbing with good spirits. "But I have to say, I completely fell in love with you that day."

"I didn't—" She froze as Ben's words sank in. *Had he just said what she'd thought?* "You what?"

He shook his head and ran his hand roughly over his face. "I just meant...that day..." He took a deep breath and exhaled slowly. "You were so determined not to be left behind. So many girls would have freaked out to see their dress ruined that way, and would have cried and...well, you didn't do any of that. You just...you just did it."

She nodded slowly. "But you just said you—"

"You know what?" He jumped up from his chair and slapped his hands on his thighs. "I totally forgot that I brought a bottle of wine."

"Wine?" Drew blinked. "Ben...what..."

"Wine," he continued, as if she hadn't said anything. "To celebrate the Bro List. I thought maybe a beer would be more appropriate, but I didn't think you were much of a beer drinker, so I—"

"Beer will be fine," she interrupted him quickly. She didn't love beer, but she couldn't help but think that drinking wine with Ben might not be the best idea. At least not while she was so confused by everything she was feeling. *And what the hell had he just said?*

"Okay." Ben opened the cooler. "Beer it is."

He handed her a can and they once again sat in silence around the fire. The carbonated liquid was cold on her throat and bitter on her tongue. But drinking the beer gave her something to do so she didn't have to focus on the awkwardness between them. After a few minutes, Ben got up and fetched two more cans from the cooler. He offered her one and she took it without a word.

The logs cracked and popped in a way that completely

mesmerized her. But despite Drew's focus on the fire, she was acutely aware of the man next to her and the tension in the air. She wasn't the only one who noticed it either because, after a few minutes of uncomfortable silence, Ben cleared his throat awkwardly.

"Why didn't you mention your new business?"

"I wasn't sure if...well...I don't know," she finished lamely.

"I'd like to hear about it."

"You would?"

Ben spun in his seat so quickly, his flimsy camping chair wobbled, but he didn't seem to notice. "Of course I would, Drew. Why would you think any differently?"

This was her chance to clear the air. To tell Ben exactly why she'd been so distant. How her feelings were hurt in a way she couldn't even explain and that definitely didn't make any sense. She'd never kept secrets from him before. Of course, she'd never had a reason to.

She took a breath and considered her situation.

Sitting there with Ben, everything became really clear. She was being completely ridiculous. "You know what?" she said before she could change her mind. "I'm sorry. I've been really silly and that hasn't been fair to you."

"What do you mean? With your business? I don't—"

"No." She stopped him. "With everything." She turned so she faced him, their knees almost touching. The fire danced and lit his face as she spoke. "You're really going to laugh when I tell you this, but..." She took another breath and went for it. "I've been kind of avoiding you."

"Really?" Even in the firelight, Drew could see him roll his eyes. "I noticed, Drew. What's going on?"

"It's so dumb but I think with everything from the last few months..." She waved her arm. "You've just been so good to me and Austin and as everything started to get back to normal, and I started feeling better, I started to think that maybe there was…never mind." Despite the fact that she knew he couldn't see her, she was blushing.

"Drew. What is it? You're worrying me."

"So, here's the thing." She chuckled a little to herself. "I somehow managed to convince myself that I had feelings for you. I know it's so dumb, but somehow I guess I thought…well, it doesn't matter and then I heard you tell Evan that you didn't think of me like that and—"

"But I do."

"So I think for the last few weeks I was just—what?" She blinked and worked hard to focus on him in the firelight. "What did you say?"

Ben reached across the space and took her hand in his. She drew in a gasp at his touch and the heat that fired through her. He squeezed her hand and looked into her eyes. "I do feel that way about you, Drew."

She had the sensation that the world was spinning and her chair was collapsing out from under her but for whatever reason, she hadn't fallen to the ground. Her eyes locked on his hand clasping hers. She focused on it until she steadied. Finally, she gathered the courage to look up at Ben's face. He was watching her intently, cautiously, as if he were worried she would tell him everything she'd just said had been a joke.

But it wasn't.

And now he was telling her… "What are you saying?"

He shook his head slightly and smiled a little. "Drew, I've been in love with you ever since we were kids. Maybe it wasn't exactly the day of that hike in elementary school, but it was close. I have spent my entire life trying to figure out how to love you."

"But…" She was going to protest and say something about how she'd never known, but that wasn't true. Not entirely. On some level, she'd always kind of been aware of his feelings for her. "You never said anything."

"How could I?" He squeezed her hand. "When we were young, I was scared and stupid. Too chicken shit to say anything and then you asked me to tell Eric that you liked him."

"You know what's funny?" She squeezed her eyes and let herself remember that day. "I asked you that to see if *you* liked *me*. I was so sure you liked me but wouldn't say anything." She shook her head and laughed at how mixed their signals had been. She remembered the day well. She'd been so convinced that he liked her, but instead of telling Ben she liked him, too, she panicked and asked him to ask out Eric for her. A few days later, when Ben walked up to her locker, leaned up against it looking all cool, but a little nervous too, the butterflies in her stomach took flight. She'd been so sure he was going to admit his feelings then, but instead he'd said, "My brother wanted to know if you might think about going to the dance with him."

"The dance? With Eric?"

"Yup." He'd looked down and kicked his sneaker against the linoleum floor. "So will you?"

She'd been flustered and caught completely off guard. Up until that moment, despite the fact that *she'd* been the one to say something to Ben about him, Drew would never have guessed that Eric even knew she was alive. It had been stupid, she knew it even at the time, to play such a game, but she'd really expected, or at the very least *hoped* that it would be Ben who would admit his feelings and ask her to the dance. But in that moment, it was clear that he wasn't interested. Not like that. So she really had nothing else to lose. "Okay," she'd said.

"Okay?" He looked up; his face registered shock. "You will? Like, you want to go with him?"

She'd shrugged, trying not to look disappointed. "Sure. Why not?"

It felt like a million years ago that Drew had watched him

walk down the hall, presumably to tell Eric that she'd agreed to go to the dance with him.

"What else was I supposed to do?" Ben said, bringing her back into the moment and out of the past. "I guess in hindsight I should have told him—no, maybe I should have told you that I was in love with you." He chuckled and shook his head. "But I regret nothing. Not really."

She let his words sink in and after a moment, she said, "Neither do I. My life with Eric was…well, it was unexpected," she admitted. "But it was amazing and I wouldn't trade it for anything." It was the truth. She'd never expected to fall in love with Eric, but that's exactly what had happened. They'd spent the next almost eighteen years loving each other completely and totally. "But now…" she continued. "I don't know how to feel about what I'm feeling."

Ben leaned over in his chair and took her other hand in his, forcing her to look him directly in the eye. "I get that. I sure as hell don't know how to feel what I'm feeling. You are my brother's…well… I'll be honest, Drew. I'm not sure I know how to sort that out in my head."

She nodded, letting his words roll around in her head. It was complicated, yes. Messy even. But being with Ben, she couldn't help but feel more at peace than she had in months and that counted for something. Drew bit her bottom lip and squeezed his hand. "Maybe we can figure it out together?"

He was quiet for a second, but when he looked into her eyes and said, "I'd like that. A lot," it was all she needed to hear.

Chapter Thirteen

"DO you ever think about having kids?" Amber asked the question lightly, but she kept an eye on Logan from the corner of her eye. With most of the finishing work done in the lodge, they were finally starting to move furniture in. While the movers they'd hired did all the heavy lifting, Amber and Logan were walking from room to room with a clipboard and a checklist.

Logan looked up from what he was writing. "Pardon me?"

"Kids," she said again. "Have you ever thought about them? I mean, I'm sure you've thought about them, but... having some of your own."

Logan walked across the guest room they were in and stood in front of her. "Is there something you want to tell me?"

Amber shook her head and laughed. "Not at all. It's just something I've been thinking of and I guess I wondered what you thought of the idea. We've never talked about it."

"Well, we've been a little busy."

It was true. They'd been so consumed by Taking the Reins and making the treatment center a reality, they really hadn't discussed any of those things that couples usually talked about early on in their relationship. "I know," she said. "But maybe we should. I mean..." She swallowed. She'd never been one to mince words, or shy away from saying what she really wanted. There was no point starting now. "I love you," she stated.

Logan laughed and wrapped his free arm around her to pull her close. "I know, baby. I love you, too." He pressed his lips to hers and kissed her slowly to demonstrate just how strong his feelings for her were.

"My point is," she said when he finally pulled back, "is that we've never talked about what's next. And because I love you, I obviously want to spend the rest of my life with you, but I guess we've never really talked about what that looks like."

He eyed her out of the corner of his eye and released his arm from her waist. "And what do you think it looks like?"

Amber swallowed and told him exactly what she'd been thinking for the last few months. The ideas floating through her head still shocked her considering it wasn't all that long ago that she'd been certain she'd always be a single woman with nothing but her faithful romance novels to keep her warm at night. Career had been everything and her whole life, she'd focused on it with laser precision. Nothing else mattered as much as making partner at her fancy law firm in San Francisco. Nothing. Not even her health.

Until it did.

A *cardiac event* that exposed her addiction to Adderall had changed everything and brought her home to Timber Creek, where she'd met and fallen in love with Logan. Everything had changed. It hardly even felt real some days, but other days, Amber felt like a completely different person with a whole new set of priorities. Priorities that included making sure Taking the Reins was a huge success so they could help as many people as possible with equine therapy. But also, those priorities included her friends and her family, especially her newly rekindled relationship with her dad, that was stronger than ever. *And maybe those priorities also extended to a family of her own?* It was a thought she'd been having more and more.

"I think maybe it looks like us getting married and having a family." She ran a hand down Logan's chest and pulled him close to her once again, using the front of his jeans. "I mean... I think I might be convinced to be Mrs. Logan Myers and —what?"

He'd stiffened under her touch, and the normally light-hearted smile that was ever present on his face had turned into a frown. "Amber, I..."

"You what?" She took a step back and crossed her arms over her chest. Based on his body language, she was pretty sure she knew what he was going to say, and she was going into full-on defensive lawyer mode, an old habit she'd always used to protect her emotions.

He shook his head and tried to step closer to her. "Don't be like that. Don't close up on me."

"Tell me what you were going to say, Logan." She wasn't going to let him off so easily. She needed to know. It suddenly seemed very important to know at that very moment exactly how Logan felt about moving their relationship forward. "It's important, don't you think?"

"Of course it's important, Amber. But I don't know if this is the right time to talk about it. Why don't we go home tonight and have a glass of wine and—"

"No." Her voice was louder in the empty room than she'd intended it to be. "Tell me now," she said, somewhat softer. "I mean, I already know what you're going to say." She hated herself for sounding so defensive, but she couldn't seem to stop. She'd been so happy a moment ago, so sure of where every-thing was going and now...in an instant, she was unsure. And Amber hated being unsure. About anything.

"Okay, okay." Logan held a hand up. "I don't think this is where we should do this, but I'll tell you." She pulled in a breath. "I never wanted to get married." Her heart stopped, which was ridiculous because the idea was still so new to her, too. "And I've never really thought about kids," he continued. "Except for that I don't think I need to have any of my own to be fulfilled. I mean—"

"Enough." She couldn't hear anymore. She ran a hand through her long, dark hair. "Maybe you're right." She forced herself to be calm. "Maybe we shouldn't talk about this here." She lifted her clipboard and tried to scan the list, in an effort to focus on something, anything else.

"Amber, I—"

"We'll talk later."

But she wasn't sure they would. *How could they, if she wasn't sure what she'd say?*

Somehow over the last few months, Amber had talked herself into having a future she'd never before imagined. And without even knowing she was doing it, she'd fallen in love with the vision of a future with Logan that he didn't see.

And now, in an instant, she had no idea what any of it looked like.

Chapter Fourteen

THE NEXT MORNING, Ben woke up with a sore neck and a crick in his back. They'd stayed up late into the night, talking and holding hands. That was it. It was so innocent, yet at the same time, it wasn't.

A line had been crossed in their relationship to be certain, but it didn't feel wrong. In fact, it was just the opposite.

Ben couldn't remember the last time he'd felt so comfortable and content and just...happy. He could have sat there just like that until the sun came up, but when Drew started trying to stifle her yawns, Ben stood and pulled her to her feet. "I think you should probably get some sleep." He'd held both her hands in his and pulled her close, so they were almost pressed up to each other. "We have a big hike tomorrow."

She hadn't even bothered to protest. "You're right." She smiled. "And I am definitely going to redeem myself from the last time you hiked with me. I even brought hiking boots."

He couldn't help but laugh. "I can't wait."

He led her to the tent, guiding her with a flashlight so she wouldn't trip on any of the roots or stones in their path.

"Are you sure you'll be okay out here tonight?"

He knew she was asking out of concern and not because of anything inappropriate. And as much as the idea of lying in a small tent, curled up next to her, now appealed to him on many levels, instead of scaring him, he needed the space. For his own sanity. "I'll be fine."

She bent to unzip the tent but stood again before disappearing inside. "Thank you for...well, for all of this. It means a lot."

"Of course." More than anything, he wanted to pull her up against him and kiss her.

"And for..." She gestured between them. "Not being weird about—"

"Drew?" Ben put two fingers under her chin and lifted it so she was looking at him. Despite the darkness around them, the glow from the flashlight lit her face enough for him to see the confusion that still remained there. He had no doubt it would be that way for a while. After all, they were navigating some uncharted territory, to be sure. "You don't need to thank me, okay?"

She nodded and then he could no longer resist. He pulled her close to him and wrapped his arms around her in a tight hug. He yearned to kiss her and feel her lips pressed to his, but it wasn't time. He settled for pressing a soft kiss on her forehead. "Get some sleep."

After stoking the fire for the night, and organizing a makeshift bed close to the warmth of the coals, he curled up in his sleeping bag to spend the rest of the night dreaming. Only when he woke, he realized that it hadn't been a dream. He *had* confessed his feelings for Drew. And she for him.

None of that had been a dream.

He stretched out the stiffness from sleeping on the ground and got to work with the supplies from the back of the Jeep. In no time, Ben had the camp stove out, and some hot water boiling for coffee.

He snuck a glance at the tent, but despite a little bit of rustling, there was still no sign of anyone, so he got started on cooking up the big camp breakfast he'd planned. Just as he'd guessed, it wasn't long after the bacon started sizzling that he heard the zipper of the tent and Austin, followed by his mom, appeared.

"Good morning."

"Morning, Uncle Ben. Are you cooking bacon? Mom never lets me have bacon!"

"She doesn't?" He ruffled the boy's hair and feigned surprise.

"She says it isn't healthy." Austin rolled his eyes.

Ben grinned over his head at Drew. "Well," he said to Austin, "we're camping and when we're camping, some of the regular rules don't apply."

Austin pumped his fist and jumped up. "I love camping."

"Me too." Ben poured a cup of coffee for Drew. "Good morning." He handed her the cup and leaned in to kiss her on the cheek.

Her hand came up to her face, and Ben worried he'd overstepped, but she only smiled. "Good morning. Did you sleep okay out here?"

"Surprisingly well."

"You slept out here?" Austin spun around to stare at him. "Like outside? Here?"

Ben laughed. "I did, and maybe tonight you'll join me?" The question was aimed at both of them, but it was Austin who yelled out his request.

A good night of sleep was exactly what the boy needed to reenergize him. After they finished breakfast and cleaned up, he was more than ready to get moving on the hike. Ben gave him a little briefing on safety and animal awareness; however, with all of Austin's excited chattering, he really didn't think that would be a problem. If there were any wild animals around, they would no doubt be scared miles away by all their racket.

"He's loving this," Drew said about twenty minutes into the hike. She'd fallen into step beside him. "I can't believe I've never taken him on a hike like this before."

"Well, I can't imagine there were a lot of forests in Nevada."

She laughed. "Not so much. But still, we should have come home more."

Or at all, Ben thought but didn't say. "Why didn't you come home?" he asked instead. It was a question he'd often wondered about, even though he was pretty sure he knew the answer.

"Honestly?"

"Of course."

"Eric didn't want to." She shook her head. "And I know how ridiculous that sounds because Timber Creek was my home, too. But it never really seemed worth the fight. Besides, our parents all liked coming to visit us and then you know, you get busy having a life and…"

"Time goes by."

"It does." She reached out and grabbed his arm for a moment. "I regret it, though."

They stopped walking and Ben turned to look at her. For a moment, his stomach sank at her words. *What did she regret? Last night? Their confessions?*

"Not coming home more, I mean," she clarified and he released the breath he hadn't realized he was holding. "I should have insisted. It wasn't right staying away like that and I see it now. I see how unfair it was for you not to know Austin better and for…well, for you and Eric. You used to be so close and then—" She put a hand to her mouth, her eyes wide at the thought in her head.

"What?"

"Do you think I was the reason Eric didn't want to come home? I mean, last night you said…" Ben remembered exactly what he'd said. "Did you ever talk about it?" she asked. "With Eric, I mean—did he know how you felt?"

Ben shrugged and considered lying to her. It wasn't something they'd spoken about often, although he was sure Eric always had an idea. Almost everyone else did—how could Eric not? But there was one time when not only had they spoken about it, they'd fought over it. It was right after Eric had proposed, a day that had hurt Ben deeper than he could have imagined. They'd been living away, while both Drew and Eric went to school, that first year. But after he popped the question, the couple had come back to Timber Creek to announce their engagement, and although Ben managed to suffer through the family dinner, later that night everything came to a head. Eric and his buddies had decided to have a guys' night, while Drew and her friends gathered at Christy's house for a sleepover. Because he was trying to be a supportive brother, and there was nothing he could do about it anyway, Ben decided to join the guys at the End of the Road for a drink. The owner at the time didn't care about checking IDs as long as everyone paid their tabs and didn't cause trouble.

He'd arrived late and the other guys had already had a few drinks. They were hooting and cheering at the mostly naked women performing on the stage, an unfortunate side effect of the only bar in town. It wasn't Ben's scene, but judging by the look on Eric's face as he took in the view of the scantily clad woman who was leaning down in front of him to place a drink in front of him, it was his brother's scene.

Ben had taken one look at what was happening in front of him and without thinking, crossed the room to Eric and physically put himself between his brother and the woman. "What the hell are you doing? You just got engaged."

"Exactly." Eric laughed. "We're just taking in a little entertainment. It's a bachelor party."

"His last chance for a little fun," one of his friends hollered. "Relax, Ben."

"I'm not doing anything wrong."

Ben glanced around and could see a variety of Eric's friends engaging in lap dances and tucking dollar bills into the stripper's G-strings, but as he'd said, Eric didn't seem to be doing anything wrong.

Still. It didn't matter. "Get up." He glared at his brother and spoke through gritted teeth.

"I'm not going anywhere, Ben. It's innocent fun."

Ben's fists clenched reflexively. "You don't deserve her."

It might have been the alcohol he'd consumed, or maybe Eric had finally had enough of his little brother mooning over his fiancée, but Ben would never forget the way his brother's lips twisted up in a snarl as he did finally stand up to confront him. "That's what this is about, isn't it? Your stupid schoolboy crush on Drew. Face it, brother—I won. She chose me. For better or for worse. Get used to it."

Ben took a step toward him and cocked his fist.

"You're going to hit me?" Eric egged him on. "Go ahead. If it's going to make you feel better, do it."

So he did. Ben's fist connected with his brother's face. Never as adults had they fought. Not seriously. And the moment the punch landed, Ben regretted it.

Eric put a hand to his face, and stumbled backward but didn't retaliate. Instead, he said, "Did it make you feel better?" He spit out the words. "Did it help you get it through your head that she's mine?" The words hurt, because he *didn't* feel better. Quite the opposite. "Like I said, little brother. This is just innocent fun. No lines are being crossed. And whatever you might think, Ben, I love her more than life itself and I'll never hurt her." He pulled his fingers away from his lip and

Ben spotted the blood. Eric only shook his head. "I hope you can get used to it, Ben. She loves me and she's going to be my wife. That will never change."

Ben remembered the entire scene as if it were yesterday.

He knew in his heart that Eric would never do anything to hurt or disrespect Drew. He'd known it that night. But his emotions were too raw. The next day, Eric and Drew left to go back to school. A few years later, after they'd both graduated, they made it official and got married. Ben had gone to the wedding, but Eric hadn't asked him to stand up for him and nothing had ever been the same since.

To answer Drew's question, he was pretty sure he knew exactly why Eric hadn't wanted to come home. But could he tell her?

"Ben?" she asked. "Do you think—"

"Mom! Uncle Ben!"

Both of them swung their heads in the direction of the voice, Drew's question forgotten as Austin announced from up ahead on the trail, that he'd found Bizarro Cave.

***

"THIS IS where your dad and I carved our initials, buddy. See?"

Drew took a step back so Austin could see what his uncle was pointing at. Her son's enthusiasm made her laugh as he clambered to get a closer look. Austin was a little too short to see clearly, so Ben scooped him up. "E.R. & B.R." Ben traced his finger over the faded initials.

"I see them." Austin put his finger over Ben's and traced the initials with him.

Drew had to swallow the lump in her throat. The immediate and unexpected rush of emotion caught her totally off guard and she had to look away.

Despite growing up so nearby, Drew had never been to

Bizarro Cave. The location was gorgeous. The lush pines and cedars lined the path leading up to the cave and some wildflowers sprouted up among the moss and ferns on the forest floor. The cave opening itself was quite a bit bigger than she'd expected and let out a great deal of cool air. She pulled her fleece out of her backpack and tugged it over her head before turning around again to watch Ben and Austin.

They'd sat down on the rocks and Ben had pulled out a pocketknife. She stepped closer so she could overhear them.

"Let's put you first," Ben said. "Ready? You put your hand over mine and we'll make an *A*."

Drew had to bite her tongue to keep her from stopping them or warning them to be safe. She trusted Ben explicitly. He'd never do anything to put Austin at risk.

But would she?

Not on purpose, of course. But what if confessing her feelings to Ben was the wrong thing to do? What if she was just confused and had made a mistake? Was letting Ben get too close going to hurt Austin if it didn't work out?

Of course it would.

But Ben was Austin's uncle, and that was a bond that would never be broken. He would always have him in his life. Drew knew that in her soul. Ben would never walk away from Austin. No matter what happened between them.

She took a deep breath, letting her lungs fill with the fresh, cool air.

She left the boys to their task, and started walking into the cave. It was quite open, which provided a lot of light, although the farther it went, the dimmer it got.

Drew stepped from rock to rock and let her mind drift as she walked deeper into the cave.

Being with Ben was easy and last night it had felt right, just sitting with him by the fire. In fact, there wasn't a time in recent memory when she'd felt quite so relaxed and just… well…good.

And that could only be a good thing, right?

There was no rule book when it came to this type of thing. No instruction manual she could refer to. She had to go with her heart.

It would all just be so much easier if she could reconcile what her brain was telling her with what her heart was saying, but the reality was, Drew wasn't sure that either her brain or her heart had their own messages straight.

"Drew?"

"Mom?"

She froze in place at the sound of Ben and Austin's voices echoing through the space, but she didn't turn around right away. Instead, she looked around for the first time. She'd gone in quite a distance. The cave had a small stream running through the middle of it, and a few rock formations sticking up from the ground. There were a few places a little farther in, where she could see similar formations coming down from the roof of the cave. It was oddly pretty and the solitude was comforting in a way she couldn't explain.

"Did she really go in there?" She heard Austin say, his voice echoing in the tight space. "My mom would *never* do that. She's totally scared of that stuff."

"I'm pretty sure she did, buddy," Ben replied. "And you know what? Your mom is pretty tough. She can do whatever she puts her mind to. In fact, I don't think she's scared of anything."

"I don't know." Drew strained to hear her son's reply. "She was pretty scared when Dad died." Her heart clenched in her chest.

"I bet she was." Ben's reply was soft. "I bet you were, too, huh? And that's okay."

"I was a little. Just…like…I didn't know what it would be like without him, ya know?"

"I actually do know."

Drew blinked back a tear. She felt a little bad for eaves-dropping, but at the same time, it was nice to hear Austin opening up in such an honest way.

"But it's been okay," Austin said. "I mean, I miss him." His voice shook and the urge to go to her son and hug him was strong. But she stopped herself. He clearly needed to talk. "But it's been nice having you to do things with, Uncle Ben. Dad told me you'd be around a lot and I was supposed to go to you if I needed anything."

"He did, did he?"

"Uh huh."

"Good. I'm glad." Drew could hear the emotion in Ben's voice. "You know I'll always be here for you and your mom, right? No matter what."

"I know. Dad told me that, too."

Ben chuckled a little. "What else did your dad tell you?"

"He told me to take care of Mom and make sure she got happy again." A tear slipped down Drew's cheek. Austin had never told her about any of the many chats he'd had with his dad in those last few months. Obviously Eric had done a good job preparing their son the best way he could. "And you know what?"

"What's that, buddy?"

"I think she's getting happy again." Drew nodded despite the fact that no one could see her, and no one was even talking to her. "But she's not going to be happy if we leave her in that cave. Let's go get her."

Drew smiled and went to meet Ben and Austin so they could begin their hike back down to camp.

Chapter Fifteen

"SO YOU WENT HIKING? YOU?"

Drew nodded but Amber kept staring at her.

"And camping? Like real camping? In a tent?"

"Yes." Drew rolled her eyes and focused her attention on Mya, who was just shy of a year old already and was a very busy baby, grabbing at her necklace and trying to shove it in her mouth. The girls had gathered for a quick lunch at the Riverside Grill and Drew was using the opportunity to get all her baby snuggles in.

"It's not a big deal." Drew focused on the baby so her friends wouldn't see that she was lying. Because it *was* a big deal. Every part of her camping trip with Ben had been a very big deal—and not for the reasons her friends thought.

"Well, I'm impressed." Cam shifted baby Theo in her arms as she tried to dig in her purse for something.

"Let me take him." Amber reached out for the baby and something about the way she looked at the baby grabbed Drew's attention. She watched, the conversation about her forgotten for a moment as her best friend gazed at the baby with something that resembled sadness on her face.

"Did you wear actual hiking boots?" Cam teased beside her, and Drew's attention was drawn away from Amber and the baby and back into the conversation, but not before she made a mental note to ask Amber what was going on.

"Yes," Drew said to Cam. "I wore actual hiking boots." She stuck out her tongue.

"I'm more impressed with Ben," Christy said from across the table. "Especially with Ben. I mean, taking on such a big task? That's pretty impressive."

"You mean, taking on the Bro List?" Amber asked. "That is a huge deal and so sweet."

"It is sweet." Christy laughed. "But I meant, taking on Drew." Her laughter cut off and she put her hand to her mouth. "I meant taking Drew camping. I mean, I didn't—"

"It's okay." Drew had debated on how much to tell her friends, unsure of how they'd react to…well, to *things* with Ben. In the end, she knew she couldn't keep secrets from them. A few months earlier, when they'd all discovered that Amber had been lying to them for years about her addiction, they'd sworn to never again to hide anything from the others. "He kind of… I sort of…" She let herself trail off, unsure of how to actually tell them what was going on. Especially considering she didn't understand it herself.

"What's going on, Drew?" Amber looked up from baby Theo for the moment. "Do you…" She tilted her head in question. "Is this about…"

"What?" Cam demanded. "What are you talking about? I feel like I missed something."

Drew sighed and once again removed her necklace from Mya's chubby fingers. "Did you guys know that Ben has always had feelings for me?"

Christy coughed and choked on the piece of roll she'd just put in her mouth. Amber's mouth fell open and Cam immediately began stuttering. "Wh—what—you—I—"

"Clearly you knew." She rolled her eyes and tried to stifle a giggle. "Nice job keeping that from me all these years." Her voice dripped sarcasm. "So much for not keeping secrets." She was teasing, mostly, but she couldn't help but be a little disappointed that her friends hadn't let her know about something that could have—what? It wouldn't have changed anything. She knew that. She loved Eric. That would never have changed. It just would have made things with Ben even more awkward than they'd turned out to be.

"It wasn't like that," Cam said. "I mean..." She looked to the other women for help.

"She's right," Amber jumped in. "It wasn't like that at all."

Drew raised her free hand for a moment before returning to bouncing the baby. "It's all good. I get it. I'm not mad. Honestly." And she wasn't. It made perfect sense to her and if the roles had been reversed, she probably wouldn't have said anything either.

"I think the bigger question now," Christy said, "is how you've come to find out. I mean, why now?" She tilted her head and examined Drew. "What's changed?"

Drew looked to Amber, the memory of their last conversation on the topic of men and moving on still clear in her head. Would they judge her for being ready to move on? Would they judge her because it was *Ben*? Amber smiled encouragingly and gave her a little nod as if she already knew what Drew was going to say.

Maybe she did.

"It's kind of complicated to explain," Drew started. "But I've been feeling lately like maybe there's more out there for me. Of course I still miss Eric terribly—that will never change."

"Of course." Her friends nodded in sympathy and understanding and Drew continued.

"As you guys all know, Ben has been amazing and has been

there for Austin and me so much that I don't even know what I would have done without him. And I think over the last few months, some of those feelings of friendship turned into something a little bit more." She looked down at the baby, suddenly worried to see her friends' reactions. "I guess on some level there've always been some feelings from both of us. I mean, we were such good friends and—"

"You don't have to explain yourself to us, Drew." It was Amber who spoke. Drew looked up to see her best friend smiling at her. Amber reached out with her free hand and touched her arm. "It's okay. You don't owe anyone an explanation."

Cautiously, Drew turned to look at the others and they both had a similar expression on their faces. One of understanding and love.

"You don't think it's too soon?"

She didn't ask the question to anyone in particular but Christy answered. "Do *you* think it's too soon?"

Drew didn't hesitate with her answer. She shook her head. "No."

"Then that's all that matters," Cam said. "Sweetie, I don't think any one of us can even begin to wrap our heads around what it would be like to lose our husband."

"Especially so young," Christy added. "Only you know how that feels. And more than that," she continued, "only you know what's in your heart. Everyone's journey is different and there is no right or wrong for this."

"But what will people—"

"Don't finish that statement." Amber held up a finger. "It's nobody's business what you do or don't do. And if anyone has an opinion about it, that says more about them than it does about you."

"Exactly." Cam nodded. "I just read this the other day in a book and I think it applies perfectly." She looked straight at

Drew. "What other people think of you is none of your business."

That made them all laugh and baby Mya started to fuss. Drew bounced her a little and then ultimately handed her back to Christy.

"It's true, though," Amber said after a moment. "There are no rules for how you're supposed to live your life after your husband dies."

"No." Drew shook her head and chuckled a little. "There certainly are not."

Drew felt better after talking to the girls. They didn't judge her or have any opinions about her moving on, and she knew deep in her heart that they wouldn't, despite her earlier concern. But others would. It was a small town, and people would talk. Did it matter? Maybe Cam was right. Did anyone else's opinion really matter?

"Okay," Christy said, interrupting her thoughts. "Now that we got all that out of the way, tell us about Ben. Because I, for one, think this is perfect."

"And amazing," Cam said. "I mean...Ben." She raised her eyebrows and Drew couldn't help but chuckle.

She spent the next few minutes telling her friends about how her feelings had grown and then come to a head around the campfire a few days earlier. Of course, they wanted all the juicy details, but there were none to give. Whatever it was that she and Ben were doing, they were doing it slowly, and that was just fine with Drew.

LUNCH with her girlfriends had been just what Amber needed to clear her head after what had been a tense few days with Logan. They hadn't really talked more about children or marriage and truth be told, Amber had done her best to avoid the topic. She couldn't resist holding Theo, though. And maybe she shouldn't have, because just having his sweet, chubby body in her arms made something deep inside her ache.

Hell, maybe she should have talked to her friends about it. Never in her life had she avoided a confrontation of any kind. Hell, in her past life as a lawyer, she'd loved nothing more than diving into a good fight.

But this was different.

If she and Logan really had different views on what the future was going to look like, what would that mean?

She wasn't willing to explore it. Not fully. At least not until she was sure about exactly what it was that she wanted.

She left the restaurant, but, not completely ready to go back to the ranch, she hovered about in the parking lot until it was only Christy left standing by her car.

"What's going on?" Christy unlocked the door to her SUV. "You have a look."

"A look?"

"Yup," Christy said. "A look that says something is going on with you but you don't want to talk about it, so clearly you *really* need to talk about it. What's going on?"

"How did you know you wanted kids?" Amber blurted the question before she could over think it. "I mean, I know you've always wanted kids, that's no secret."

It certainly wasn't. Christy had wanted to be a mother since they were kids themselves. Infertility troubles had plagued her and almost derailed all the plans she'd made for herself and her marriage.

"No." Christy laughed. "It certainly isn't. But I don't really understand your question then."

Amber took a deep breath and tried again. "I think I want kids."

"That's great." Christy shifted her own baby up on her hip.

"Kids are…well, they're wonderful. But honestly, I didn't think you wanted children of your own."

Amber shrugged. She could easily see how Christy and everyone else would think that. After all, she'd never once mentioned it or even discussed anything besides putting her career first. "Things changed."

"Logan." Christy nodded, a small smile on her face. "I could see that," she continued. "Falling in love changes things."

"It does." Amber kicked at a stone while a million things ran through her head.

"But what's the problem then?" Christy asked. "I mean, if you're thinking about wanting kids, that's the first step. Honestly, your heart will tell you what to do and you'll just know when it's right."

Amber looked up. "I will? I'll just *know*?"

"You will." Christy turned around and leaned into the backseat of her car. Amber watched while she fiddled with Mya's car straps and fastened her into her safety seat.

Was it really that simple?

After a moment, she turned and faced Amber again. "It seems like I'm missing something." She crossed her arms over her chest. "You seem…I don't know…unsettled."

"Logan said he doesn't want kids."

Christy's face fell and instantly Amber wished she would have kept her mouth shut.

"I mean, he didn't say it in so many words," she continued quickly. "But I was talking about getting married and maybe having a family one day and…"

"He doesn't want that?"

Amber shrugged. "He didn't come right out and say it. Just that he didn't think it was important. And that he'd never wanted to get married."

"And is it important to you?"

Amber thought about it, but just for a moment. "Yes," she said with certainty. "Very."

"Well then, I think the two of you have a lot of talking to do," Christy said kindly. "And I do think you need to talk to him, Amber. Some things in life aren't negotiable. And if marriage and kids are something that's really important to you, well, personally…I don't think you should have to sacrifice that. You'll always regret it."

"But I…" She didn't bother finishing the statement because they both knew how strongly Amber felt about Logan.

Christy pulled her into a quick hug. "Talk to him," she said again. "And don't make any decisions until you know exactly how both of you feel." She pulled back and smiled at Amber again. "If there's one thing I know, it's that sometimes these things work out just the way they were supposed to. So try not to get yourself too worked up, okay?"

That was easier said than done, and they both knew it. But after Amber drove back to the ranch and had a few minutes to think about it, she realized that Christy was right. The most important thing was to talk to Logan. She couldn't be afraid of what he might say, even if she didn't want to hear it.

Yes. The sooner she had the chance to talk to Logan, the better. After all, it was better to know where you stood than to be left wondering.

There was no sign of him at their little cabin, so Amber checked in the main lodge building next. She walked through the rooms that were almost finished and felt both a sense of pride and a twinge of sadness. *What would happen if Logan truly didn't share her vision for the future? How would that change things for Taking the Reins and everything they were trying to build together?*

It was a thought she couldn't dwell on. At least not yet.

One thing at a time.

With no sign of Logan inside, she went next to the stables,

which should have been her first stop, as it was his favorite place to be. With the horses.

Sure enough, she found him standing next to Peanut's stall, stroking the horse's muzzle. From a distance, Amber could see he was talking to the horse, and it didn't surprise her. After all, that's what his entire business was founded on. *Their* entire business.

She took a step back.

Again, the reality of what she was doing slammed into her. What would happen to Taking the Reins if she told him how she felt and he didn't feel the same? Everything they'd been working for together could be jeopardized. And for what? A passing thought?

Was it really just a passing thought?

She couldn't be sure.

Not yet. And if she wasn't completely sure, she simply couldn't take the risk. Not unless she was one hundred percent sure about what she really wanted.

Amber turned and walked from the stables. She swiped blindly at the tear that threatened to slip down her cheek. The only thing she could be sure of was how much she loved Logan and how she couldn't bear the thought of losing the love she'd only just discovered.

Chapter Sixteen

DREW'S HANDS shook with nerves she hadn't felt for years. It was ridiculous. After all, it was just Ben. But it wasn't *just* Ben. It was *Ben.*

Her mom and dad had offered to watch Austin for the evening so Drew and Ben could go out on an actual date. She'd sat down and talked to her mom, who despite being unsure about Drew moving on, especially with Ben, had declared that she'd be supportive.

And Drew believed her.

Her dad had just hugged her, kissed the top of her head, and told her, "Kiddo, you only have one life. Just be happy."

His support brought tears to her eyes, but it wasn't surprising. Her parents had always just wanted the best for her and watching her go through Eric's illness and ultimate death had taken a toll on them, too.

There was a new movie playing at Timber Theater, and it had been so long since either of them had seen a movie that wasn't on Netflix, it seemed like a good first date. Nothing with too much pressure.

Perfect.

Except even without too much pressure, Drew was feeling it. Her hand shook as she applied eyeliner and a quick swipe of mascara. She'd never been the type of girl to go out without at least a little makeup on her face and on special occasions, she definitely liked to kick it up a level. Not that a movie was a special occasion…

Her hand hovered over her eyeshadow palette. *Was that too much? Would she normally—*

"I'm totally overthinking this." She laughed at her reflection in the mirror, but left the eyeshadow alone, opting for some lip gloss instead.

"You look nice," her mom said as soon as she appeared in the kitchen. "It must be a—"

"It's not a special occasion." She held up a finger to prevent her mother from finishing the sentence. "It's just a movie."

Her mom pressed her lips together in an obvious effort to stifle a smile and nodded, but thankfully, didn't say anything more.

"Mom!" Austin ran into the room and threw his arms around her legs. "You look pretty. Where are you going?"

She crouched down to kiss him on the cheek, a move that caused him to wipe the lip gloss off his cheek in disgust. "I'm going to a movie with Uncle Ben."

"Can I come?" He jumped up and down with the question. Normally, Austin of course would be going with them, but this was not normal.

"Not this time, buddy," she said. "It's an adult movie."

"Besides, you get to hang out with me and Papa," her mom said, steering him away from Drew's legs. "And we're going to make your favorite cookies."

"And eat them all?"

Laura laughed. "Not all of them." She bent down to whisper in his ear. "But some."

Behind them, Drew's dad, Paul, cleared his throat and gave Austin a wink. They all laughed as Austin tried to wink back, but all thoughts of the movie were forgotten in exchange for the promise of home-baked cookies and Austin barely noticed when Drew left. Her mom waved and told her to have fun and not worry about hurrying home and that was it.

She was already outside when Ben pulled up in his Jeep. He quickly hopped out of the driver's seat and came around. "I was going to come to the door," he said. "And pick you up properly. After all, it is our first date."

The butterflies in her stomach returned with a vengeance and started some sort of gymnastics routine in her gut.

"Trust me," she said as she climbed in. "It's easier this way." No doubt her mom, as casual as she was behaving with Drew, would have interrogated Ben in some ridiculous way, and then Austin would start asking questions. Yes. For now, this was definitely better.

Ben waited until she was situated before returning to his seat and reaching into the back. "These are for you."

"You didn't need to do that." She protested even as she inhaled the beautiful blooms.

"I told you." Ben grinned. "It's our first date. I'm going to do it right."

Drew didn't protest further and once the initial nerves wore off and they settled into the conversation that had always been so easy between them, she actually found herself forgetting how ridiculously nervous she'd been.

"You look beautiful." Ben handed her the popcorn as they took their seats in the theater. "I meant to mention it earlier. Also, I'm really glad we're doing this." He took the seat next to her but turned to look at her. "I know it might be—"

"It's fine." She interrupted him before he could say anything that might make her feel weird again. "I'm really glad we're doing this too."

Thankfully the lights went down and the previews started before they could keep awkwardly talking about the fact that they were actually on a date.

The movie was loud and full of action and just enough humor to keep them laughing.

After the credits rolled, and the lights came up, Ben took her hand as they walked outside into the warm summer night. "It's a nice night. Are you up for a little walk down by the river?"

She wasn't ready to go home, and definitely wasn't ready for the night to end. She squeezed his hand. "That sounds perfect."

They walked in silence for a few minutes, when finally Ben stopped suddenly and pulled her arm so she faced him. "Why does this feel so strange?"

"I don't know. It's not like we've never—"

He silenced her with a kiss, his hands coming to either side of her face, and his lips pressed softly on hers. It was a gentle kiss but full of promise, and fire shot through Drew's body. It took a second for the shock to wear off and just as her mind caught up with her body, it was over.

"I needed to get that out of the way." Ben's lips curved up in to a smile, but he didn't release his hands from her face. "I've been wanting to—"

It was her turn to silence *him*. Drew didn't overthink it but let her heart lead her and that was all she needed. The kiss was sweet, with just the right amount of heat and, better than anything else, it felt right. At that moment, nothing could have felt more perfect than standing next to the river, kissing Ben.

DREW'S KISS WAS EVERYTHING.

Her lips were deliciously salty from the popcorn but with a

sweetness that was uniquely hers. Ben's heart soared and flipped and all but danced in his chest at the feel of her lips on his. For years, he'd imagined what it would be like to have her in his arms and kiss her, but it had always been in an abstract way. Nothing real.

And nothing he'd ever imagined could ever have prepared him for what was happening.

Ben didn't know how long they stood there, but as far as he was concerned, it wasn't long enough. It would never be long enough.

When Drew pulled back and brought her fingers up to her mouth, he was lost.

It was official—he was completely and totally in love with this woman and in a way that was so different from the feelings he'd had before. This was real.

Slowly, Drew removed her fingers from her lips and replaced them with a bright smile. A moment later, she was laughing.

Confused, and if he was being honest, a little bit hurt, Ben took a step back while Drew doubled over in a fit of giggles.

"I'm sorry." She straightened, one arm wrapped around her waist while the other went to her mouth in an effort to stop the laughter. "I don't mean to laugh and it's not…"

Another fit of giggles consumed her.

Unsure what to think, Ben looked around for a sign of what might be so funny, but the only thing around was…him. "Drew, did I…was that…hell, I don't even know what to say. Was my kiss that—"

"Oh my God." She dropped her hands and took his in hers. "No, Ben. Oh, no, that's not why I was laughing." Her smile fell and she looked genuinely concerned. "No, your kiss was…well…oh my…no. I was laughing at myself."

"You were laughing at yourself?" He cocked an eyebrow and waited for her to say more.

"Yes. I…oh my…" She started to giggle a little again, but caught herself. "I was so worked up about going out tonight," Drew started to explain. "I mean, I was nervous. Like, teenage girl on her very first date, nervous. I mean, at one point I couldn't even feel my toes and I thought I was going to trip and fall on my face."

She was so cute as she was trying to explain herself, that any minor hurt feelings he had vanished as he listened to her explanation.

"And then when you kissed me, I was so surprised."

"Surprised?"

"Right? I mean I shouldn't have been, but I think part of me was still thinking of you as Ben and now you're *Ben*. And it's all so…" She cleared her throat and ran a hand through her long hair before continuing. "Anyway. It took me a moment, and then you stopped, so I had to kiss you myself."

"And what a kiss it was."

"Right?" she said again, and it was Ben's turn to bite back laughter.

"But I don't get it," he said. "What's so funny?"

"I'm so funny." She grabbed his hands again and squeezed tight. "Because I was nervous about nothing. That kiss…you… this…" She looked up into his eyes but it was okay; she didn't need to finish the thought. He knew exactly what she meant. And to prove it, he pulled her close, wrapped his arms around her and once again, kissed her.

———

"I THINK I OWE YOU A DRINK." Ben slid a pint of beer across the bar to Evan.

After taking Drew home at a very respectable time despite the fact that he would have been happy to stand by the river and kiss her all night, he hadn't been ready to go home to an empty house. Besides that, he owed his best friend an apology.

"You don't owe me anything," Evan said. "But I'll take the beer."

Ben laughed and poured himself one before joining his buddy on the other side of the bar.

"What's going on?" Evan didn't beat around the bush.

"I went out with Drew tonight."

Evan didn't say anything, but raised a brow, no doubt waiting for him to elaborate.

"On a date," Ben said. "A real one."

Evan grinned. "I know."

"You know?" Ben's mouth dropped open, but then he shook his head. "Cam?"

Evan nodded. "Of course. The girls talk, you know?"

He didn't know. Not really, but he should have guessed.

"And how was it?" Evan asked. "Although I still don't know why you think you owe me a beer. Did I lose a bet or something?"

"No." Ben looked seriously at his friend. "I've been a real jackass about the whole thing. At least where you were concerned. I know you were only trying to look out for me and—"

"It's all good, man." Evan cut him off. "Honestly, I'm just glad you're finally being honest about everything. And I know the last few months haven't been easy on you either. You lost your big brother, and I can't even imagine how hard that's been. Especially with all the...well, the history with you guys. I know it's been hard. And I'll tell you, there is no one more pleased to see that smile on your face again."

"Thanks, man. That means a lot." Ben held out his beer for a cheers.

"You know I have your back." Evan took a drink. "Always. And I know this thing with Drew...well, it's been years of this and I know things are a little more complicated now, but maybe…well, maybe this is just how things were supposed to work out for you two."

"You mean Eric dying?" Blood rushed to his head, but Ben knew Evan didn't mean anything by it.

"God no!" Evan shook his head vehemently. "That's not what I meant at all. But I do think that everything has a season and a reason. And when you guys were kids, that wasn't your season. Whatever the reason, maybe it was just meant to be that you and Drew couldn't come together until now. Obviously the circumstances surrounding it are terrible, but there are some things we can't change. And we have to play the cards that are dealt."

Ben thought about it. The circumstances were terrible and if he could, he'd change it all. But Evan was right; there were some things that could never be changed. He nodded slowly and drank deeply from his glass. "I know what you mean. I also know Eric wouldn't want us to live in the past and dwell on the things that can't be changed. That was never his style."

"It certainly was not." Evan raised his glass and they toasted. "So, tell me about the date?"

Chapter Seventeen

IT HAD BEEN three days since their date, and Drew was still smiling. Every time she thought about how awkward she'd felt, she giggled. But then her thoughts would turn to her first kiss with Ben and then their second and later, their third and every single time, her face flushed and electricity ran through her veins. All in all, it had been an amazing evening and the days that followed had been just as great.

Ben had texted her later that night and they'd spoken on the phone a few times, but their schedules hadn't permitted actually seeing each other which, at least for Drew, was turning out to be an exercise in frustration. For as nervous and unsure of dating Ben as she'd been at first, after their date, all of those hesitations were gone. All she felt now was excitement and happiness. And an incredible desire to see him again.

Which was going to happen later that afternoon, because he'd promised he'd be able to sneak away from the bar after the lunch rush. They'd planned to cross another item off the Bro List and were going to take Austin fishing.

That was only a few hours away, and she still needed to finish up her plans for the Taking the Reins grand opening party and go over everything with Amber before lunch so she could get ready.

With Austin spending the morning with Logan and the horses, Drew and Amber were meeting in the kitchen of the brand-new lodge building. Drew was impressed.

"This is amazing," she told Amber, who only grinned in response. "I can't believe all the top-of-the-line equipment you have in here. How many people did you say were going to be able to stay here at one time?"

"Only eight. But we wanted to have the facilities to accommodate anything that might come up and you never know, we might be able to expand in the future." She shrugged. "It's best to be prepared, right?" There was something in her friend's eyes, but Drew couldn't be certain.

"Well, I think it's awesome." She pulled her portfolio out and put it on the shiny stainless-steel counter. "Are you ready to see what I have lined up for you?"

"I can't wait."

They spent the next few minutes going over all of Drew's plans, which were fairly simple. Amber had already tasted most of the items, so there were no major surprises, which was good as far as Drew was concerned because she'd already started preparing everything to keep her work load down to a minimum on Saturday night so she could actually enjoy the party, too. Which meant she still had four days to get everything finished. It would be more than enough time. Especially considering her mom had agreed to help out a bit with some free labor.

"It's going to be great," Drew said when they were done going over the details. "And I heard that Christy and the band agreed to play a few songs, too. I can't wait. Are you excited?"

"Of course." Amber smiled, but it didn't reach her eyes.

The same feeling she'd had the other day at lunch with the ladies returned. Something was going on with her.

"What's up, Amber?" Her friend tried to turn away, but Drew caught her by the arm. "Talk to me. Is everything okay?"

Amber shook her head but followed it quickly with a smile. "I mean, it's just a lot," she said. "The stress of everything. I think it's just getting to me. I'm fine. Honestly."

Drew examined her friend's face for a tell-tale sign that she was lying, but either Amber was a very good liar—which, considering her background as a lawyer, was entirely possible—or there truly wasn't anything wrong. Amber looked tired, and definitely more than a little stressed, and she couldn't quite put her finger on it. But there was something else that didn't sit quite right with Drew. If Amber insisted she was fine, she had to take her word for it, because if it was something serious, Amber would tell her. She had to trust that.

"Okay," Drew said after a moment. "But if there's ever anything you want to talk about…"

"I know." Amber gave her a hug that lasted a moment longer than normal, and once again there was a flicker of worry in Drew's gut. But when she pulled away, Amber's bright smile was in place. "You'd be the first to know if there was ever anything I needed to talk about. Now, don't you have somewhere to be?" She wiggled her eyebrows and Drew laughed.

"We're going fishing." She grinned. "Austin's going to love it."

"And you?"

Drew laughed. "Well, I don't know about the fishing part. But I'm definitely going to enjoy the company."

She'd already filled Amber and the girls in on her date with Ben and although she didn't get into the details of the kiss, they could see from the glow about her how happy she was.

"I think it's awesome," Amber said as they walked outside toward the stables. "Really. I mean, I know you thought maybe I was judging—"

"It's fine." Drew interrupted her. "I know you support me."

"Always." Amber pulled her into a quick hug. "No matter what."

"You know the same stands true for me."

"Of course."

Together they walked to the fenced ring and watched Austin riding Poppy without Logan's assistance.

"He's amazing," Amber said.

Drew laughed. "Do you mean Austin or Logan?"

Amber blushed. "Austin, obviously. He's doing really well with the horses."

"He is." Drew leaned on the fence and watched her son for a moment before turning back to Amber. "Logan's pretty amazing, too. Isn't he? I mean, you guys...you're pretty amazing." She knew she was pushing it, but she couldn't get past the fact that something seemed a little off with her friend.

"Of course," Amber answered quickly. "It's been total chaos around here, but—"

"Amber? Spill it. I know something is going on and if you don't tell—"

"I want to have kids and get married and I don't think Logan does."

She spoke so quickly that Drew wasn't sure she'd heard her properly at first.

"What?"

"I want kids," Amber said again, softer this time. "I don't think Logan does."

"Wow," Drew said after she'd had a moment to digest what her friend had said. "That's a lot."

"It is, and I've been thinking about it. And—well, don't worry about it, okay? I'm going to talk to Logan when the time is right because I need to know either way and—"

"Hey, Mom!" Austin waved to her, pulling Drew's attention away. "Look at me."

"You're doing great, kiddo," she called out. "Good job."

When she turned back to Amber, the moment was over and Amber shook her head when Drew opened her mouth to speak again. But she'd already said enough. Drew's heart went out to her friend. It couldn't be easy for her if she was feeling torn. Especially with everything else going on. She squeezed Amber's hand and hoped it would be enough for her to know that no matter what, Drew supported her.

***

WITH ANNIE OUT SICK, and the brand-new patio bringing in more business than ever before, Ben had no choice but to cover the lunch rush and most nights, the dinner rush as well. It was a good problem to have as the increased business had more than paid off the loan he'd taken out for the patio development. Working in the bar was something he didn't usually mind because he loved his time at the Log and Jam. But that was before he started enjoying his time with Drew a whole lot more. Everything had changed after their date. They hadn't actually been able to spend any time together for the last few days, so Ben was more than ready to get away from the bar and back into Drew's company.

Which was exactly what he did. As soon as the crowd thinned to a manageable level, Ben took off and headed straight to Drew and Austin's, his Jeep full of fishing supplies.

They were waiting on the front lawn, a picnic basket ready to go. At the sight of them, Ben broke out into a huge grin. It made his heart happier than even he could have imagined.

"Are you guys ready to catch some fish?" He hopped out of the Jeep as Austin jumped into the backseat. Ben laughed and met Drew on the sidewalk. He hesitated a moment before leaning in and kissing her on the cheek, when what he really wanted to do was pull her into his arms and show her exactly how much he missed her over the last few days.

"Is that okay?" He glanced behind him to see whether Austin had seen the chaste kiss but Drew only laughed.

"It's okay." Her face lit up. "I don't think anything needs to be a secret. But maybe we should... I don't know...explain things to him when the time is right. I don't want him to be confused."

Ben nodded. It made perfect sense. Austin was not only Drew's priority, but Ben's as well. "Oh," Ben said, taking the moment to let her in on the latest development of the Bro List. "I signed us up for the Timber Creek Challenge. It's on the list."

"The list?" Drew cocked her head. "I don't think a crazy obstacle course is on the Bro List."

He'd been pretty sure that she might not be very excited about the idea. The Timber Creek Challenge wasn't known to be a very easy race, but they had a family friendly option, and Ben thought it would be a lot of fun to do together.

"I thought it would be more fun than a simple running race." He reached for the picnic basket. "Besides, the race Eric and I did when we were kids was just a local car dealership fun run, and they don't have it anymore. This will be way better."

"And harder." She shook her head. "You boys have fun with that."

"No deal." Ben caught her arm and pulled her to him quickly. "You're part of this team." He kissed her quick. "It'll be great. You'll see."

She still didn't seem convinced, but he was pretty confident she'd come around.

"Come on," Austin hollered from the Jeep. "Let's go!"

"I think the only thing he's interested in right now is catching some fish."

"We better get going then."

It was just a short drive to his favorite fishing spot on Ghost Lake, which was a good thing because Austin was bouncing up and down in the backseat, eager to get started. As soon as they got there, Ben left Drew to set up the picnic under a tree, while he started to teach Austin about his fishing rod and all the different types of lures they should use.

"This is for you," he told Austin as he put the fishing rod in the boy's hands. "It used to belong to your dad."

"It did?" Austin's eyes grew wide, but he hesitated before he took it.

"What's wrong?" Ben asked gently. "It's yours. Go ahead and get a feel for it."

"But what if I break it?" Austin's voice was low, his eyes fixed on the rod.

"You're not going to break it."

"But if I do…"

"Then what?" Ben shrugged. "What's the worst that could happen?"

Austin's eyes filled with tears. "Then it will be gone. And there'll be nothing left."

Ben's heart cracked a little. "No, buddy. That's not how it works."

"But if all of Dad's things are gone, then…"

"Your dad is never going anywhere, buddy." Ben lifted Austin's chin with one finger so he was looking into the boy's eyes, so much like his father's. It never failed to strike Ben how much Austin looked like Eric. "He's always going to be with us. Right here." He tapped on Austin's chest and then his own. "He'll be with me, and you. All of us who love him. There's a little bit of him with all of us, but there's a lot of him with you. Did you know that?"

Austin shook his head.

"It's true," Ben continued. "You're so much like your dad was at your age, that I know he's with you all the time. In fact, I think he looks out for you."

"Kind of like a guardian angel?"

"Exactly like that."

"You think he's here right now?"

Ben smiled sadly and nodded. "I'm sure of it. In fact, I bet you he's watching closely to make sure I teach you everything you need to know so that you catch a fish today."

Austin's eyes grew wide. "You think so?"

Ben ruffled Austin's hair. "Absolutely. So what do you say we get started? Because the sooner we get started, the sooner you can catch a fish."

A few minutes later, Austin's hesitation was forgotten as Ben helped him string up a lure. A few quick lessons in casting and reeling, and Austin caught on quickly to the basics. Ben stepped back and left him to it, when he got his own rod ready to go. But before he even had a chance to cast his first line, Austin yelled from the shore.

"I got one! Uncle Ben! Come quick!"

With a laugh, Ben ran down to see what was going on. Drew was right behind him. "Okay, reel it in the way I showed you," he told Austin.

"I can't. You have to do it."

"No can do, buddy. It's your first fish." He tucked his hands in his back pocket. "Just go slow," he coached. "Reel it in. That's right. A little at a time. Okay, now give it some slack. That's right. You're doing great."

"You got one." Drew had her phone out and Ben noticed from the corner of his eye she was videotaping the moment. "You're doing great, Austin."

"I am not!" The boy looked panicked, but Ben knew exactly what was happening; he also knew it would pass.

"Reel it in a bit more," he coached. "Great. Now ease off a little. Here it comes."

"There it is!" Austin almost dropped the rod as the fish came into sight.

"I'll get him for you." Ben knelt down on the rocks and

sand and gently scooped up the fish with his hands. "Okay, hold still. I'll get the hook out." Austin knelt next to him as he gently worked the hook out and Drew took a few pictures.

"Is he okay?" Austin stared at the fish.

"For now." Ben grinned. "But not if you want to have him for lunch."

Austin looked mortified for a moment before pressing his lips together and shaking his head. "No. I think he should be free."

"Works for me." Without hesitation, Ben put the fish back in the water and after a moment, released him and the trout was gone in a flash. "You did great, buddy." He gave Austin a high five, but the boy threw himself into his arms.

"Thanks, Uncle Ben. That was so cool."

"You did great, buddy."

Austin pulled back and looked him in the eye. "You know what? I think you look out for me, too. Just like Dad."

The moment was brief, but it hit Ben in all the feels as he realized just how much he loved this kid. He would happily spend his whole life showing him everything he needed to know. And before Ben could formulate the words, Austin ran off with his fishing rod, eager to try again.

Ben watched for a moment before standing and walking straight over to Drew, who was still watching them. Without a moment's hesitation, he pulled her in for a kiss. It was quick but sweet before she squirmed out of his grasp.

As a reflex, Ben looked over his shoulder, but Austin hadn't seen them. He wasn't sure exactly how they were going to handle things on that end, but it would come. "He didn't see, if that's what you're worried about?"

"No." She giggled. "You smell like fish."

"Do I?" Ben laughed and chased her back to the picnic site, determined to kiss her as many times as she'd let him. Which he hoped would be endless.

Chapter Eighteen

THE AFTERNOON of the Taking the Reins grand opening, Drew was much calmer than she'd expected she would be. She'd done so much of the prep early that everything was coming together nicely. But that didn't mean she wasn't covered in flour, sauce, and various other things. Her kitchen looked as though a bomb had gone off and she was pretty sure there wasn't one surface left untouched.

Not that it mattered. The chaos was fueling her and she couldn't remember the last time she'd felt so energized by something. No matter what, Drew knew she'd found her calling. She was meant to cook.

"Knock knock."

"Come in," Drew called to the voice at the door. "I'm in the kitchen."

"As if I'd expect to find you anywhere else." Ben appeared in the doorway, a bottle of champagne in his hand. "What on earth happened in here?" His eyes widened as he took in the sight. "Are you okay?"

"I'm fine." Drew laughed. "I'm working and I guess I just got a little into it. I haven't had a chance to clean anything up."

"No kidding." Ben tiptoed his way through the kitchen and put the bubbly in the fridge. "I got a little something to celebrate your first job, but maybe I'll help you clean up a little first."

"You don't have to do that." Drew protested, but the truth was, she really could use the help and was glad for it. "But, could you start with the sink?"

Ben shook his head with a smile. But before he headed to the sink, he pulled Drew, messy apron and all, into his arms and kissed her thoroughly before releasing her.

"Austin's in the other room," she said as way of protest, although it was only half-hearted. The last thing she really wanted to do was protest a kiss from Ben. Still, she was a mother and she had to be cognizant of Austin and the fact that they still hadn't explained their relationship to him.

"When are we going to tell him?" The question didn't hold any level of pressure of any kind, but Drew couldn't help but feel guilty. She knew Ben would never try to rush her or the situation at all. The guilt was coming strictly from her and the fact that she didn't have a good explanation as to why she wasn't ready to talk to Austin. Everyone else knew about their relationship. At least, everyone who mattered. Austin should know, too. But for whatever reason, Drew couldn't bring herself to talk to him about it.

"Later," she said as a lame explanation. "Eric's birthday is—"

"Next week," Ben finished for her. He watched her from the sink where he'd started to fill it with warm, soapy water. "I know." He dropped his head a little, and again the guilt in Drew flared up. Of course Ben knew it was Eric's birthday. Ben was his little brother. "So you want to wait until after then?"

Drew nodded and looked back to the tiny puffs she was filling with a smoked trout and cream cheese mixture.

They worked in silence for a few moments, but it wasn't long before Ben was asking questions about what else needed to be done. Once the dishes were done, he started packing up the dishes and pans Drew had already prepared and got them ready to load up in his Jeep to make the trip over to Blackstar Ranch.

"I don't know what I'd do without you," she said when they'd packed up the last of the puffs. "Thank you for all your help." She stood to give him a kiss on the cheek even though she could see the desire in his eyes, and she knew the real reward would be much more than such a chaste kiss.

Ben had been more than patient with her, and extremely respectful as to how slow she wanted to take everything. But she knew he was starting to feel a little impatient, because it wasn't just him who was having those feelings. But she just wasn't ready. Not quite.

"I'm always here," he said. "But you know what?" He wiped his brow with a paper towel. "I think you may have to invest in an air conditioner if you're going to keep using your own kitchen for these jobs. At least the ones at the end of July. This is ridiculous."

Drew laughed and swatted at him with her towel. "We live in the mountains. I'm not getting air conditioning for the two crazy hot weeks we have a year. If you think this is hot, you should have seen our summers in Nevada." She laughed at the memory. "One time our air conditioner died, and we couldn't even sleep. We used to sit in the pool in the middle of the night just to…"

She trailed off as she remembered how she and Eric would skinny-dip in their backyard pool and make love under the stars on those long, hot nights. It wasn't a memory she needed to share.

"Hey."

She looked up from her hands to see Ben in front of her.

He brushed a hair from her face and cupped her cheek. "It's okay," he said, as if he'd read her mind. "You had a whole life together. I know that. Never feel like you can't talk about it or share your memories, okay?"

She nodded slowly.

"I mean it, Drew. I miss him too."

The tears that sprang to her eyes took her off guard, but she let them come. "Thank you."

She wrapped her arms around him, and let him hold her. But only for a moment before she called for Austin. It was time to get him to her parents' house for the night, get the food to the ranch, and get ready. They had a party to attend.

AMBER LOOKED around the crowded room, and her heart swelled. Everyone was there for them and what they'd created. She reached for Logan's hand and squeezed it as they both took in the moment.

The party was in full swing. People were laughing, talking, and eating the amazing food that Drew had put together. The night had gone perfectly.

"Are you ready for this?" she asked Logan.

"More than anything." He tugged on her arm gently so she spun toward him. "But first, I just want to enjoy this moment together. We did this, babe. Together."

She beamed and let the pride of accomplishment fill her. "We did and it's so amazing. I'm so proud of you."

He kissed her softly but thoroughly. "And I am so proud of you."

She smiled against his lips. "Ready to do this?"

He nodded and together they walked to the makeshift stage they'd set up in the corner of the large room. The party was taking place mostly in the main room of the lodge, which had been cleared of the couches and tables that would occupy the space later. The exposed timber beams angled up into a grand, open space that somehow both managed to look spacious and cozy at the same time. It would be the heart of the Taking the Reins treatment center, where clients and guests would gather in the evenings to read, play cards, and talk. They could hold group counseling sessions, or informal movie nights in the space—whatever it was they required.

"Good evening," Logan said into the microphone. The music faded, and the chatter died down as the crowd turned to face the two of them on the stage. "Amber and I just wanted to take a quick moment out of the evening's festivities to say thank you."

Amber lifted her own microphone. "And we really can't thank you all enough. Not only for coming tonight, but for your incredible support of us, Taking the Reins, and what we're trying to do here. Your support really means the world to us."

There was a spattering of applause before Logan continued. "We are so proud of Taking the Reins and what the future holds for equine therapy and the community of Timber Creek." He went on to speak briefly about what equine therapy was for those in attendance who might not understand what they were trying to do, before Amber took over and started listing individuals who required special appreciation. When she was done listing everyone who'd played a role, she turned to Logan. "And a very special thank-you, of course, needs to go directly to Logan Myers, who singlehandedly brought equine therapy into the community. He is truly a remarkable man and I just know that the limits of his talents and care and concern know no bounds."

The audience burst into applause, along with some hoots and hollers. Logan blushed but Amber just beamed, full of pride for the man she loved. Before he could say anything else or protest the attention he'd been given, Amber once again took to the microphone. "Now," she said, "I think that's enough of the speeches. We are so lucky to have Timber Heart to play a few of their new songs, so what do you all say we enjoy the music and dancing? Have a great night, everyone."

She clicked off the microphone, took Logan's from his hand, and handed them both to Christy, who, along with the band, had joined them on stage. Amber took Logan's hand and pulled him off the stage as they struck up the first chord and started playing. She knew exactly what she wanted to do, and that was dance with the man she loved and properly enjoy the night they'd worked so hard for.

The last few weeks and months had been filled with so much emotion and turmoil for Amber as she'd tried to work through things in her head. She was just so glad that the grand opening was finally happening and so much of that stress could be alleviated. Because it was stress that was causing her confusion, of that much she'd decided on. She loved Logan and that would never change. She didn't need anything more than the life they were building in order to be happy.

Amber slipped into his arms as Logan began to lead them around the dance floor in a slow dance.

This was everything. It filled her completely. She closed her eyes and rested her head against his chest so she could soak up the moment and the love she had for him.

"This is perfect," Logan said after a moment. "This entire night...us."

"It is." She murmured her response and nuzzled in closer. It *was* perfect. She'd been shortsighted and likely caught up in the craziness that was the rest of her group of friends, with their new babies and weddings. She didn't need that. Why would she when she finally had *this?* Logan was the happy-ever-after she'd always read about and never even really knew she wanted.

"I love you, Amber."

She opened her eyes and looked into his as he gazed down at her. She could see the love he had for her. Even more, she could *feel* it. "I love you, too." She kissed him quickly on the lips as he took her hand and spun her out onto the dance floor, making her laugh.

The song changed and the beat picked up but Logan didn't miss a step as he led Amber around the floor. As they moved, she was able to take in the scene surrounding them. Her eyes landed on Cam and Evan standing at one of the tables next to the dance floor. Evan was holding baby Theo while Cam doted on them both, fussing with something around the baby's mouth. Even as Amber spun around the room, her eyes kept landing on the little family.

And then it happened.

Her stomach clenched, her breath caught in her throat, and she knew. That's what she wanted. *A family.*

She'd done a good job lying to herself, but that's exactly what it was. A lie.

She may never have wanted any of this in the past, but things changed. Her entire life had been flipped upside-down when she moved back to Timber Creek.

Amber looked up at Logan again and her heart broke a little bit more. She wanted a future with this man more than anything else in the world, but if that future wasn't going to be everything she needed, that wouldn't be fair to either of them.

She needed to know.

It was long past time that they had a real conversation.

"Babe?"

Logan looked down, the smile still on his face.

"We've been so busy lately," she said. "I think we need a little time to catch up and talk."

"Of course." His smile faded a little. "Is everything okay?"

She forced a smile. The last thing she wanted to do was

dampen the festive feel of the night. "Let's talk in the morning, okay?"

"HAVE you tried the smoked trout puffs?" Ben grinned and popped another bite into his mouth, as Drew joined him at the side of the dance floor. "Rumor has it that the caterer takes requests."

"Only from some people." Drew grinned and took a parmesan knot from his plate.

"It's all delicious, Drew," Ben said more seriously. "You did an amazing job and I'm not the only one who thinks so."

"Oh yeah?" She paused before taking a bite. The need for approval for all of her hard work was written on her face, and Ben was more than happy to be the one to tell her how amazing everything was. Not that he would be the only one, because Drew really had done a fantastic job.

"I'm hearing it from everyone," he reported truthfully. "I have a feeling you're going to be very busy. Or at least as busy as you want to be."

She popped the rest of the treat in her mouth and tried to hide her smile but Ben could see how proud she was, and for good reason. She'd worked hard.

"Have you eaten anything yourself?" He watched her finish off the rest of the treats on his plate. "You've been so busy, have you had a chance to even sit down?"

"The last thing I want to do is sit down." She dabbed at her lips with a napkin and took the now empty plate from him. "Besides, I just ate." Drew deposited the plate on a table behind them and took his hand. "Will you dance with me?"

"I thought you'd never ask." He chuckled and led the most beautiful woman in the room to the dance floor area, where he pulled her into his arms. His dance skills were a bit rusty, but

Drew fit so perfectly in the curve of his arms that it was easy to guide her around the floor, and she matched him step for step, as if they'd been dancing together for years.

With every step they took, Ben's happiness grew. Never would he have imagined this moment, but now that it was here, he felt like a little kid on Christmas morning, giddy with the possibility of what could be. Ben was so wrapped up in his own thoughts that it took him a moment to notice that Drew's posture had stiffened.

"Hey." He reached down and lifted her chin so he could look into her eyes. "What's going on?"

"They're looking."

"Who?" Ben instinctively looked around to see what she was talking about, but there was nothing out of the ordinary. "Who is looking?"

"Everyone." Drew ducked her head and tried to pull away, out of his arms. Fortunately for Ben, he had a tight hold so she couldn't make her escape. "They're all looking."

"Drew." He wanted to make light of the situation, but there was a certain level of panic in her eyes that he couldn't quite make sense of. Ben steered her to the corner of the room and stopped moving, using his body as a shield from the rest of the room. "What's going on? No one is looking."

She shook her head, but wouldn't meet his eyes. The shift in her was so immediate and so intense, Ben couldn't ignore her concerns. But that didn't mean he could understand them. "Help me understand what's going on," he pleaded with her.

She tried again to wiggle away from him, but he only held her tighter. Instinctively, he knew that if he let her get away from him, he might not be able to get her back—and he still didn't know why.

"Everyone," she said after a moment. "They're all looking at me."

Ben turned around, his arms still around her, and scanned

the crowd. If anyone was looking at them, it was only because they were causing a very small scene in the corner of the room. But everyone was busy with their own lives, enjoying themselves, and as far as Ben was concerned, no one was paying any attention to them. "I don't know what you're talking about, Drew. No one is looking at us. I promise."

But it didn't matter what he said. She was seeing something, or more likely, feeling something, he couldn't pick up on. Inexplicably, her eyes filled up with tears.

"No, Drew." He wiped at her cheek. "Don't cry. Tonight has been…" He let the statement trail off because it didn't matter what the night had been.

"I'm sorry." She dashed her arm across her face in an effort to clear the tears and sniffed loudly. "I just…we were dancing and…they were looking."

He shook his head, ready to ask one more time, *who* exactly was looking, but she beat him to it.

"Everyone," she said as way of explanation. "They were looking at us dancing and laughing and I know what they were thinking."

The realization of what exactly was going on struck him. "No." Ben shook his head a little. "It's not like that, Drew. No one is looking at us and they—"

"They are." Another tear slipped down her cheek. "And they're all probably thinking about what a terrible person I am."

"Why the hell would they think that? You're amazing."

It didn't matter what he said; she obviously needed to go through the emotions, but that didn't mean he wasn't going to try everything he could think of to make her see the truth.

"I promise you that no one is thinking anything about you or me or whatever it is that we're doing. And you know what else?"

She looked up and blinked at him. Her eyes were wide and

so full of hurt that Ben knew in that instant that he'd do whatever he could to take away any pain that she'd ever felt and give his own life to keep her from feeling any more. "Anyone who would ever think that you're a terrible person is someone I don't want to know and not someone who matters. You know that, right?"

She didn't answer right away, but Ben saw her look past him to the busy room beyond them. He watched as her eyes scanned the crowd before finally coming back to land on him. "I know you're right," she said slowly. "And I don't even know where that came from."

"It's okay." He traced a finger tenderly down her cheek. "You're allowed to feel whatever you need to. There's no right or wrong way to do this." He could see the color return to her cheeks, the light back into her beautiful eyes as whatever panic that had overtaken her receded.

After a moment, Drew shook her head and attempted to laugh. "I really am sorry. I didn't mean to put a damper on our night. It just hit me that this was the first time. I mean, it's our first time out like this and...well, I know people have opinions of what a good widow should look like."

"You're the best widow."

It was such a ridiculous thing to say that they both laughed.

"You know what I mean."

"I do."

"I know this isn't easy," Ben said. "But I would really like to dance with you again, if you're okay with it?"

She took a minute to answer, and Ben couldn't be sure what her response would be. He was fine either way, but having her in his arms, her curves snugged up against him, was just about as close to perfect as he could imagine and he really hoped she would say yes.

The moment she nodded and smiled, he took her hand and

led her to the center of the dance floor. "You're good?" Ben wrapped his arms around her and held her close.

"I'm good." She nodded. "More than good."

"I've got you, Drew." People swirled around them in time to the faster song, but Ben maintained his slow rhythm, focused only on the woman in his arms. "I love you." They'd been three little words he'd wanted to say for so long that they rolled off his tongue naturally. Time didn't matter to him because as far as he was concerned, when you knew, you knew. And more than anything else in the world, at that moment, he knew exactly how he felt about the woman in his arms.

Chapter Nineteen

THE MORNING AFTER THE PARTY, Amber woke up with a sense of dread. The night before had been perfect. Every detail had gone off without a hitch. They'd danced and celebrated and…she'd finally realized her true feelings. She could no longer pretend. She needed to talk with Logan and tell him exactly how she felt. It was the only honest thing to do.

She turned to face Logan's empty side of the bed and trailed her hand over his pillow and the gentle dip where his head had rested. *When had he gotten up?* She hadn't even heard him leave.

Slowly, Amber pulled herself from the safe confines of her bed, dressed in jeans and a t-shirt and went in search of the man she loved. He wasn't in the kitchen of their tiny cabin, which meant there was only one other place he could be.

The stables.

Of course. Logan wasn't stupid; he knew something was up with her. Of course he'd seek out the comfort and company of the horses.

The morning sun was already warm on her bare arms as she crossed the yard toward the stables. It wasn't unusual for

Logan to get up early to spend time with the horses. It was definitely his happy place. And it had become very much a safe space for Amber over the last few months as well.

But this morning her heart was heavy as she pushed the wooden door open. "Logan?" Her voice sounded small in the space so she cleared her throat and tried again. "Logan? Are you in here?"

There was no answer except the whinnying of a horse, so she went into the barn. It was darker inside, but sunlight streamed through high windows and left sunbeam lines marking the floorboards down the center of the space. She blinked to let her eyes adjust to the light, and that's when she saw him.

"Logan?"

Amber stepped farther inside as Logan took a step out of the shadows toward her. "Morning, babe. You slept in. I've been waiting for you."

"You have?"

Even with the distance between them, she could see the smile on his face. "Of course," he said. "You told me last night you wanted to talk."

Her stomach twisted but she nodded. "I did. I mean…I do. I think we should—"

"Before we talk about that," he interrupted her. "There's something I've been meaning to do. Would you mind coming in a little bit and helping me out?" There was something about his voice that she couldn't pinpoint but she did as he asked and walked toward him.

"Logan, whatever it is that you're going to—"

"Babe." He stopped her with a chuckle and the lift of his hand. "Please. I know it's hard for you to give up the control, but just give me a minute, okay?"

She swallowed her protests and nodded as she came to

stand in front of him. Poppy hung her head over the door of her stall and Amber turned to scratch the horse's nose.

When she turned back to Logan, her hand flew to her mouth because he'd dropped to one knee and was holding out...*a ring box?*

"Logan? What the—"

"Amber Monroe, from the moment you walked into my life, you have turned it completely upside-down in all the best ways. I never thought I wanted or needed anything more than what I had and what I was doing with my life, but you have single-handedly changed everything."

Amber opened and closed her mouth but no words came out.

"When I stop to look at what we've accomplished together in only a few short months, I know the future for us is limit-less." He continued as if she wasn't already completely shell-shocked.

Amber couldn't process what was happening. *Why was he doing this? What was he asking?* He'd already told her he didn't want it. He didn't want the same kind of future she did. *What was—*

"I love you so much, and I can't imagine living one minute of this life without you by my side. Together, we can be unstop-pable," Logan continued. "Amber Monroe, will you do me the greatest honor of agreeing to be my wife?"

Every cell in her body screamed at her to say yes. But instead of opening her mouth to utter the simple little word, Amber shook her head. "What are you talking about? I don't understand."

Logan stood and with his free hand cupped her cheek. "What's not to understand, babe? I love you and I—"

"But you told me that you didn't want to get married," she blurted. "You told me you didn't need it or want it and that you didn't want children and I think I do and for a while I thought I'd be okay not having all of that, but now I realize that I won't. As cliché as it all sounds, I can't help it." A tear slipped from her eye, but she ignored it as she rambled. "I can't marry you because I want the whole happy-ever-after ending and everything that comes with it and I know you don't and I have to be——"

"Stop." He pressed his finger gently to her lips in an effort to silence her. "I need you to hear me. I need you, for just a minute, to get out of your head and stop believing everything you think. I never said that I didn't want it, Amber. All I said was that I *had* never wanted it. But now…"

"Now?"

"Now everything is different," he said. "With you, I believe that anything and everything is possible. I want everything." He held out the ring box again. "With *you*."

Amber's thoughts raced through her head so quickly she could barely process what was happening. "You want this?"

Logan laughed. "Babe. More than anything. Now listen to me when I say this, okay?"

She nodded numbly.

"Amber Monroe," he started, "I love you more than I ever thought it was possible to love another person. You are my absolute everything and I can't imagine spending even one moment without you. Now would you please answer the question." He chuckled and lifted the ring from the box. He took her left hand in his and asked again, "Amber, will you please agree to be my wife?"

It didn't happen often, but in that moment, Amber was rendered completely speechless as Logan's words sank in. He wanted to marry her. He wanted all the things that she'd convinced herself he didn't want. He wanted the future she did. With *her*. Of course he did. She'd been ridiculous.

Before she could answer, laughter bubbled up from deep within her. She used her free hand to cover her mouth, but it was too late. Laughter burst from her mouth and somehow at the same time she managed to nod and utter the words that would ultimately answer his question. "Of course I will." Another tear slipped down her cheek and she didn't try to stop it. "Yes," she said finally. "Yes! Of course I'll marry you."

Without a moment's hesitation, Logan slipped the ring onto her finger and wrapped her up in his arms before holding her face in his hands so he could look directly in her eyes. "You really do have quite an imagination," he said. "The fact that you could think even for a second that I don't want to experience every single thing that life has to offer with you is a testament to that. Amber, I plan on spending the rest of my life loving you and together we are going to have it all and that's a promise."

She leaned forward and pressed her lips to his then because there were no words that could have possibly expressed everything that was in her heart.

Chapter Twenty

DREW POURED herself another coffee but she knew that even the strongest coffee in the world wasn't going to be enough to shake her out of the fog she was walking through the morning after the grand opening of Taking the Reins.

The night before had been a roller coaster. She'd ridden high on the success of the food and her very first catering event. There'd been a few hiccups, but all in all, it had gone off perfectly. There'd been no leftovers and everyone she'd spoken with had complimented her on the food. She'd handed out some cards, and had more than one person promise her that they'd be calling to book her for their event. As far as she was concerned, it was a success.

She should be thrilled.

But there'd also been lows during the night as well. Her panic attack on the dance floor being the most notable.

Drew dropped her head into her hands at the memory of the night before and the way she'd freaked out being with Ben. It had been about the worst thing she could have done at that moment. Everything had felt so perfect. Being in his arms.

Dancing around the floor with him. She'd been happy. Laughing even.

And then...Ben had spun her around and her eyes landed on a woman she only vaguely knew from Austin's school. She was the mother of one of his classmates and she'd been looking at Drew. There'd been something in her eyes. Judgment. *Scorn?*

Drew couldn't be sure, but then just like that, a switch flipped and suddenly it had seemed as if everyone were watching her. And they were judging her. They were talking about her and every single person in the room thought she was a terrible person because how on earth could she be laughing and having a good time with another man when her husband had only just died?

Logically, she knew that wasn't what they were really thinking. And even if they were...who cared? She'd never before cared what anyone else thought. Not really. *But...*

"I can't believe I did that." She groaned aloud and took another sip of her coffee. The caffeine would have to work its way through her system sooner or later.

"Did what?"

Drew started at the sound of her mother's voice as Laura walked into the kitchen.

"Sorry." She laughed. "I didn't mean to scare you."

"You didn't scare me," Drew lied. "It's early. Where's Austin? Is everything—"

"Everything's fine," her mother interrupted. "He's with your dad. He said something about wanting to go fishing so he could show him what Uncle Ben taught him about catching fish, so I thought I'd pop by and hear all about how your first job went."

Drew nodded and smiled to herself at the thought of Austin and Ben fishing only a few days before. Just as quickly as the happy memory popped into her head, the memory of the night before and her freak-out returned. She groaned and looked down into her mug.

"Don't tell me it didn't go well." Her mom poured herself a cup of coffee before sitting down across from her.

"No," she said. "It was great. The food was a total success. It's just…"

"What's going on, kiddo?"

That made Drew smile. No matter how old she got, her mom would never stop referring to her as a kid. It made her crazy and made her feel loved at the same time.

"Talk to me," her mom insisted.

And so Drew did just that. She spent the next few minutes telling her mom all the details about the catering event, and finished with a recap of her freak-out on the dance floor. "What do you think that was all about?" she asked her mom. "I've never had a panic attack like that. Not ever. It was insane."

"I don't think it's all that crazy." Her mom shook her head slightly and took a sip of the coffee. "You've been under a huge amount of pressure. It was bound to come to a head sooner or later. It's okay, Drew."

Drew shook off her mom's casual support. "No, Mom. It's really not okay. Ben is—"

"A great man." She interrupted her. "And I know I had my doubts at first because he's Eric's brother, but when I see the two of you together…well, I couldn't ask for anything more for you. He makes you smile, and we can all see how much he cares about you, Drew."

Her mother's words sank in and affirmed everything she'd been feeling. But still she felt on edge. "I know, Mom. But when all those people—"

"I can't believe that you care about those people, Drew. As you told me not all that long ago, there is no timeline for this type of thing. No right or wrong way to do something. So let me ask you, do you really care what anyone else thinks? Really? Or is this about something else?"

She thought about her mother's question as she sipped her coffee. But it didn't take long to come up with the answer. Sure, she'd prefer it if everyone was supportive of her decisions, but that woman at the party who may or may not have been giving her a look, she didn't matter. It only truly mattered what was in her heart.

And Ben's.

That was really the thing. And maybe, if Drew was being really honest with herself, it was the *real* thing that was bothering her. *He loved her.* She knew Ben cared about her; that went without saying. But this was different. He'd looked right in her eyes and told her that he loved her.

And she hadn't said it back.

<hr>

"HAND ME THAT HAMMER, would you, Ben?"

Crouched next to his father's toolbox, Ben did as was requested, and grabbed another handful of nails. He handed it to his dad, who was holding a board in place on the fence before returning to where he had two sawhorses set up. Expertly and efficiently, he cut another board.

"It's looking good," Mitch Ross said. "Thanks for your help, son. Some of the upkeep on this place is getting to be a bit much for me to handle on my own. It's good to have help."

Ben assessed his father, who was almost in his seventies. He'd always been a healthy and active man, but the last year and Eric's sickness had taken a toll on him. He'd aged. "Have you thought of maybe getting a smaller place, Dad? I mean, you and Mom don't really need all this space."

"Don't you get me started." His dad grinned. "I would have happily traded this place in for one of those new condo units on the other side of town, but your mother won't hear of it. This is her home, the one where you boys grew up. There are a lot of memories here."

"There are." Ben nodded. "But I guess that's the thing about memories—they never go away. You don't need a place to remember things." He shrugged. "It was just a thought."

"And a good one, too. But just not for me." His dad chuckled. "Hand me another board, would you?"

They worked side by side for another twenty minutes and finished repairing the fence before Ben pulled two lawn chairs into the shade and handed his father a beer. "The best part of these projects is celebrating when they're finished." He raised his can in a small toast and they drank in companionable silence.

"Drew's doing well," his dad said somewhat randomly.

Ben looked at him sideways. "She is," he said slowly.

"It's good to see." His dad didn't look at him, focused instead on the fence they'd just repaired. "It's good to see you happy, too, son."

Ben had no idea what his dad was trying to say, but whatever it was, he was making it very awkward. "Thanks, Dad. It's good to be happy. What's this all about?"

Mitch looked at him then. "I'm just saying that I know we don't talk about it much. But it's been a rough year."

"Longer," Ben said with a nod.

"Yes," his dad agreed. "Longer. And it's long past time to see everyone smiling again. Eric wouldn't have wanted us moping around."

"No, he wouldn't. I think he'd be pissed if we were all sitting around crying." Ben shook his head quickly and added, "Except maybe Mom. I think he would have expected that."

Mitch laughed. "She is a crier. That's not changing any time soon. But you do know that just because your mom tears up a lot, it doesn't mean she's not okay, right?"

He nodded. They all knew how Sylvia Ross operated. It didn't matter if she was happy, mad, sad, excited, or had just heard a song that hit her in the feels—she cried. "Oh, I know."

"My point is," Mitch continued, "your mother and I, we both think Drew is very lucky to have you. They both are. You've been...well, I think Eric would be really pleased with how you've stepped up to help his family."

Ben turned and looked at his father again and couldn't help but notice the unshed tear in his eye, but he didn't mention it. "I hope so," he said instead. "I know it's not a very normal situation, but..." He trailed off, unsure of how he should tell his father about his increased feelings for Drew. "You know I've always cared for Drew," he said after a moment. "And Austin, well..."

"It's okay, son." His father grinned at him. "I know there are feelings there," he said. "More than just...well, your mother and I, we've long suspected that you cared for Drew and now...well, like I said, I think she's very lucky to have you. And I think Eric would be happy for you, too."

Ben let that sink in. He'd tried not to think of how Eric would feel about any of it, and just as he'd told Drew the night before, no one else's opinion mattered. The only thing that mattered was how they felt.

But that was a lie.

Without even realizing it, Ben had been worried about what his parents would say.

"I love her." He spoke the words slowly, letting each word sit on his tongue for a moment. "I really do."

His father nodded. "Not that you need it," he said. "But you have our blessing. There is no one else who I could imagine would take better care of Drew and Austin. And I mean that."

"Thanks, Dad."

"And how does Drew feel?"

It was the most intimate conversation he could ever remember having with his father. But just as the last year had changed his physical presence, it had also altered him on the inside as well. Which was why Ben answered honestly. "I'm not sure. Everything is still so new and we haven't really had much of a chance to spend much time alone together."

"Well, we should change that." His dad pushed up from the lawn chair. "Your mother and I will take Austin for the night and let the two of you have some alone time. Would that help?"

Ben didn't know whether it would help Drew figure out her feelings, or more accurately, figure out how to be okay with her feelings, but he did know that it would be more than helpful as far as having some quality time alone with her. And although he had no interest in rushing her into feeling anything and definitely not into saying anything she wasn't ready for, he was very interested in having some alone time.

Chapter Twenty-One

THE LAST THING Drew wanted to do on Tuesday night was leave Austin with a babysitter and go to the Log and Jam with her friends. But Amber had insisted. They all needed to be at the Log and Jam, no exceptions. What she really wanted to do was put her sweatpants on, pull her hair up into a ponytail, pour herself a glass of wine and spend some time alone with her thoughts.

More like her memories.

Eric would have been thirty-six years old.

She'd woken up with a deep sense of loss like she hadn't felt in months. If things had been different, she would no doubt have been planning a big party with all of their friends, some sort of embarrassing pictures or a video slide show or something equally mortifying that showcased some of his more ridiculous moments.

Just as she had every year, Drew would have cooked him a huge breakfast of bacon, sausage, eggs, and waffles. All of his breakfast favorites, because, "Why should I have to pick just one on my birthday?" he'd joked with her their first year married when she'd asked what he wanted for his birthday breakfast. Every year since then, she'd made a point to cook them all.

Except today.

Drew had toyed with the idea of cooking the feast anyway, but ultimately she couldn't bring herself to do it and had poured Austin a bowl of cereal instead while she sipped at a cup of strong coffee. They had, however, sang him "Happy Birthday," because Austin had insisted and there was no way she could refuse that request.

The melancholy feeling had weighed heavy on her all day and instead of trying to brush it off, she let herself sit with it. When Austin went out to the backyard to play with a neighbor boy, Drew dug out a photo album and curled up on the couch. She flipped slowly through the pages, looking at the photos of Eric as a baby to a boy, to the teenager she'd fallen in love with and the man who'd been her husband.

She let herself linger on their wedding photo and traced her finger along the edge of the plastic-covered picture. His eyes were so full of life, of the promise of the future. On his arm, she was young and in love, her own head filled with thoughts of everything their life together would contain.

They were going to have it all.

And they had.

"Today is the start of everything." Drew could still remember the way Eric had whispered in her ear only moments after they'd said their vows. "We are going to have the most amazing life."

She'd believed him. With her entire heart and soul, she believed every word he said. Because of course they were going to have an amazing life. And they had. Until everything crashed down around them.

When you're a young bride with your entire life laid out ahead of you, the last thing you would ever expect is that in only a few years, decades shy of what you expected, that perfect life would be gone.

"You should be here," she whispered to the picture.

She gave herself a few minutes to cry and feel the loss of her husband in a different way before she wiped her eyes and put the album away. She could almost hear Eric telling her to stop crying, just the way he had in the months leading up to his death.

"Tears won't bring me back," he'd said to her. "Promise me you won't spend time crying and feeling sad."

She'd smacked his arm and refused. "You can't make me promise that."

"Don't I know it." He'd chuckled. "But I can still try." He'd grown serious then and taken her hand in his. "I mean it, Drew. I know you're going to be sad and some days will be harder than others—I know that. But promise me you won't waste too much time after I'm gone."

It was a promise she'd made, which was why, even though it was the last thing she wanted to do, later that night, Drew arranged a babysitter for Austin, changed out of her sweatpants and as per Amber's request, joined her friends at the pub.

Drew had considered reminding Amber what the day meant because surely then she wouldn't have been mad if Drew stayed home. But in the end, she hadn't bothered. It was probably better for her to go out and be around people.

And Ben. Besides a few texts earlier that day, they hadn't had a chance to discuss how either of them were feeling on Eric's birthday. And she knew she wasn't the only one feeling the loss. After lunch, she'd taken Austin and went down the street to visit Sylvia and Mitch. Mitch and Austin played catch in the yard while Sylvia and Drew drank a glass of lemonade and talked.

"It's such a strange thing to see him sometimes," Sylvia had said.

"Austin?"

She nodded. "He just looks so much like Eric at that age, that sometimes I catch myself thinking it *is* him." She turned quickly and put her hand on Drew's arm. "Don't worry, I'm not going crazy. It's just…"

"It's okay."

Sylvia nodded. "You just never think your son isn't going to be around, you know?"

Did she ever. Drew could never imagine anything happening to Austin. It would be unthinkable. But she didn't say so.

"You're not supposed to outlive your children," Sylvia said thoughtfully. "But I sure am glad to have you, Drew. And Austin, of course." She squeezed Drew's arm and looked her in the eyes. "And Ben, too. To see you all together the way you are. Well…it makes my heart happy, Drew. It really does."

Impulsively, Drew had hugged her mother-in-law. "I'm so glad, Sylvia. I miss Eric so much."

"I know you do, sweetie. We all do. But I think he'd be very pleased to see you all loving again."

Drew hadn't said anything to her then, but she'd thought about Sylvia's words all day.

Loving.

Love.

It had been a few days already since he'd said the L-word and they hadn't discussed it. At all. It's not that she didn't have intense feelings for him. She did. But she still wasn't sure how she was supposed to feel about anything and it was all still new for her. More than that, she'd never said those three words to anyone else. Would she be able to?

Despite her intense desire to stay home, Drew managed to pick out a somewhat dressier top to match with her skinny jeans and even put a little bit of makeup on. She drew the line at doing her hair and opted for a ponytail after all. But the end result wasn't bad, and it was certainly good enough for a pub night. She couldn't do anything about the redness of her eyes except hope no one would notice.

***

"TO THE HAPPY COUPLE." Ben was the first to raise his glass in a toast after Amber and Logan announced their engagement. An announcement that surprised no one, except for maybe Amber, it seemed.

When Drew told him how Amber had confided her worry over their relationship and how she thought Logan hadn't wanted the same things she did, it was everything he could do not to laugh. Maybe he didn't understand women. No, he definitely didn't understand women because from where he was standing, he could see how much Logan loved her and when it came to loving a woman, a man would do anything for her.

He wasn't surprised in the least that just by loving Amber, Logan had changed his mind for everything he wanted in his future. Love could do that.

Just thinking of love had Ben turning his head and searching through the crowd at the Log and Jam for the woman *he* loved.

Drew still hadn't said it back, but he wasn't in a rush. Some things just didn't need to be rushed.

He spotted her on the other side of the patio, sipping her drink in response to the happy couple.

But she didn't look happy.

She looked distracted. Just the way she had all night. And Ben knew exactly why.

He set his glass down and wound his way through the crowd toward her. The moment he was in reach, he slipped his arm around her waist and pulled her close into his body. She smelled of lemons and a touch of rosemary, as if she'd been in the kitchen, cooking something recently. Which was likely. Ben inhaled the scent of her before leaning down and pressing a soft kiss to the base of her neck. "How are you doing today?"

She tensed slightly in his arms before relaxing.

"I'm doing okay." She turned so he could look in her eyes and see the sadness there. But there was something more as well. Hope. Love. And even under it all, happiness. "It's a strangely hard day."

"It is." Ben absolutely agreed with that. His big brother would have been thirty-six and all day he couldn't stop thinking of it and how completely unfair it was that Eric was gone.

Yes, he had Drew in his arms, but he would have given it all up if it meant things could have been different. In a heartbeat.

"He would have been happy that everyone was together tonight, though," Drew said. "Even if it doesn't have anything to do with him."

"Probably more so because it doesn't have anything to do with him." He laughed. "He probably wouldn't have wanted a celebration of his advancing age."

"True." Drew turned and wrapped her arms around his waist. Around them, the party swirled with people and conver-sation, but as far as Ben was concerned, Drew was the only one in the room. "We sang him 'Happy Birthday' this morning," she told him. "Is that strange?"

"Not even a little bit." Ben grinned and kissed her softly on the lips. "There could never be anything strange about you."

They stood that way quietly lost in their own thoughts but after a moment, Drew spoke up. "They look so happy, don't they?"

Ben turned to see where she was looking, because that comment could apply to pretty much all of their friends. It was no surprise, of course, that she was talking about Amber and

Logan, who did indeed look ecstatic. "They really do. I don't think I've ever seen Logan smile so much."

"Amber either." Drew tipped her head against his chest. "They really do have it all," she said wistfully. "It kind of gives me hope, you know?"

"Hope for…"

"For me."

Ben tensed a little.

If it was hope she was looking for, his love would give her all she needed. If only she would allow herself to accept it.

And he had no idea how to make that happen.

Chapter Twenty-Two

THE REST of the week had gone by in a flash with Drew working on her website and sample menus for potential clients, and if it hadn't been for the promise of a real date with Ben, one that involved dinner at a restaurant without a children's menu—or at least one they weren't going to look at—Drew would have already been in her sweatpants and curled up on the couch with a bowl of popcorn.

But the appeal of some actual adult time with Ben, just the two of them, was strong, so after finishing up in the kitchen, she showered and even spent extra time on her hair and makeup before picking out a cute dress she hadn't worn in years. She did a little twirl in front of the mirror and actually laughed at herself moments before the doorbell rang.

"You don't have to ring the doorbell." She laughed as she swung open the door to greet Ben.

"Sure I do. It's a date—" His mouth fell open briefly. "You look..." Ben shook his head and bit his finger as he took her in from head to toe. "Wow," he finally managed. "You look amazing, Drew."

She could feel the heat from the blush, but she didn't try to blow off the compliment. "Thank you." She bit her lip a little and Ben let out a groan.

"I need to kiss you." He reached out and pulled her close to him, as he pressed his lips to hers. She moaned a little against his mouth as the sensations shot through her like an electrical charge. The kiss was different from any they'd shared before.

Barely restrained, it held the promise of more. Much more. And considering Ben had arranged for Austin to spend the night with his parents, it was a promise that could be kept.

"Damn, girl." He pulled back. "I'm not sure I'm even hungry for dinner anymore."

She laughed, feeling emboldened by his obvious attraction to her. "Forget it," she said. "I didn't get dressed up for nothing and I desperately need a night out."

"And you deserve it." He lifted the bouquet of flowers she'd only barely noticed in his other hand. "You also deserve these, although they aren't nearly as beautiful as you."

"Aren't you smooth?"

As she took the flowers to put them in water, Ben winked. "You ain't seen nothing yet."

"Well, I can't wait to see it all then." She laughed a little at her brazen and obvious flirting as she quickly arranged the flowers in a vase. "Hey." She walked back to the door. "I was thinking. Since this is our first real, no kid date in ages, let's turn off our phones. Just for dinner."

"Really?"

Drew nodded. "Really. For sure. Austin is with your parents and it's just for dinner. I don't want to be distracted by anything."

His smile was slow and sexy as he nodded his agreement. "Drew, the only thing I want to be distracted by is you. Let's do it."

Ben had made them reservations at the Riverside Grill, with a window seat overlooking the river. As always, the food was delicious, but it was everything else that was so much better. For the first time in longer than she could remember, she wasn't worried about the million things that had consumed her for the last few years. The only thing she needed to focus on, and did she ever, was the man in front of her. And it was perfect.

She'd been attracted to Ben for months, but somehow things had shifted. The attraction before was one from the heart. A connection that made her stomach flip and gave her butterflies when he was around. She'd felt drawn to him, safe with him, and sure, when he'd kissed her, it was exciting and new and never failed to stir up desire. But this was different.

Sitting across from him at the table, she couldn't keep from touching him. The way he looked at her emboldened her as she reached across the table to take his hand and trace small circles on the top of it. She tried not to giggle as Ben continually lost his train of thought during their conversation, and she was not about to object when he suggested they skip dessert and get some fresh air.

"I'll meet you at the front," she told him as he finished paying for their dinner. "I just want to freshen up a little bit."

Drew slipped away and with a smile still plastered to her face, pushed her way past the swinging door into the ladies' room. She came up short. The smile faded from her face as she almost ran smack into an older woman on the other side of the door.

"Oh," Drew said. "I'm so sorry. I didn't see you there."

"Well, I certainly saw you."

Instinctively, Drew took a step back. "Excuse me?"

The woman pursed her lips together, which gave her the look of someone who'd sucked on a particularly sour pickle.

Drew's face flushed with anger. She crossed her arms over her chest. It wasn't the first time she'd been on the receiving end of someone else's opinion and she was sick and tired of it.

It was exhausting trying to keep up with what everyone else in the world thought she should be doing or saying or how they all thought she should be behaving. And her girlfriends and her mother were right: it didn't matter what anyone else thought, least of all an old sour-faced woman in the ladies' room. Drew took a step forward, challenging the woman to say what was on her mind, but just as she suspected, the woman made some sort of half choking, half coughing noise and slipped past her out of the washroom.

After she left, Drew dropped her arms to her side, the easy, flirty feeling she'd had only moments earlier, gone.

When was it going to get easier?

When was she finally going to be able to just live her life without having someone else second-guessing everything she was doing?

Hell, when was *she* going to stop doing it?

"YOU SHOULD BE ASHAMED OF YOURSELF."

Ben spun around at the sound of the voice he didn't recognize. An older woman, her face a mottled red and purple with her lips pinched together, stood in front of him.

"Excuse me?" He glanced behind him, but it was clear the woman was talking to him.

"Taking advantage of a fragile young widow like that." The woman's words hit him like a blow and Ben took a step back at the force of her words. Before he could formulate a reply, she continued. "You have no business preying on her that way and to think, your own brother's—"

"I think you need to mind your own business." Drew appeared next to the woman, her face a surprising mask of calm as she confronted her. "You have no business speaking about things you don't understand."

"I think I do." The woman shook her head. "I'm a widow myself and I can tell you with absolute certainty that I would never have been caught dead carrying on the way you are right now. It's shameful."

"Is it?" Drew's voice shook a little, but Ben couldn't tell whether it was from anger or another emotion.

"Drew, I don't think—"

"No." She placed a hand on his arm and glanced at him. "This needs to be said. In fact, it's long past time that I said it." Drew turned back to face the woman. "I am so sorry for the loss of your husband," she said, her voice strong, but full of a compassion that was not there a moment ago. "I know how hard it is to lose someone you love so much." Whatever the woman was expecting Drew to say, it was clear by the shock on her face, that was not it. "But I am even more sorry for you," Drew continued, "that you feel so much anger and resentment toward your own situation that you feel you need to place it on the shoulders of a complete stranger."

"Pardon me?"

"The loss of a loved one is terrible. And no matter what the circumstances, it leaves you with a hole that can never quite be filled. But it's even more tragic if you stopped living the day your husband died." The woman moved to speak, but Drew cut her off gently. "I'm not going to pretend to know your situation, just as you don't know mine. So I'm not going to judge you or your choices. Just as you shouldn't be judging me or mine. But all I will say is that they are *mine*. Not anyone else's. And anyone who judges me...well, that's more about them than it is about me. I hope you have a nice night." She nodded her head at the woman and spun on her heel to face Ben.

More than anything at that moment, Ben wanted to grab her beautiful, sweet face and kiss her. She was so strong, so ferociously confident in a way that Ben could see had lit up a part of her—one that she probably didn't even realize was dark.

Instead, he took her hand and winked at her before leading her out into the hot summer night.

They didn't say a word until they'd reached his Jeep in the parking lot. He spun her into his arms and kissed her hard and fast. "You are simply amazing," he said when he was able to pull his mouth away from hers. "You know that, right?"

She shivered in his arms, but he was pretty sure it wasn't because she was cold.

Instead of answering him, Drew stood on her tiptoes, reached up, and pulled his mouth back down to hers. It was her turn to kiss him. A shiver of desire raced through him at the intensity of her mouth against his. Every kiss they'd ever shared had led to this one, and more than anything, he didn't want it to end. Not unless it meant a beginning, and when she pulled away from him, breathless, her eyes glassy and said, "Take me home, Ben," he knew it was exactly that. A new beginning.

DREW WAS sure that nothing would feel more right than the way Ben touched her and kissed her. But she'd been wrong. Curled up next to him in his bed, her head on his bare chest as he drew circles with his finger on her back, was the closest thing to perfection she'd ever felt.

He'd taken her back to his small house and they'd made love with an intensity and sweetness that she hadn't even known was possible. And now she never wanted to leave because everything about being with Ben was like going home.

They'd drifted off to sleep, only to wake at some point again in the night to explore each other all over again. Now, with their bodies and minds completely satisfied and perfectly exhausted, Drew was content to spend the rest of the night, and hopefully the next day, snuggled up to Ben's hard chest.

"Drew?"

"Mmmm." She nestled in closer and tried not to fall asleep.

"That was…you are…"

She giggled and turned a little so she could lift her head and look at him. The curtains were open, and the glow of the moon lit the small room enough that she could see his face. "Perfect?" she answered for him.

"Absolutely perfect." His smile was tired and sexy and completely satisfied.

"I'm exhausted." She dropped her head back to his chest.

"In a good way, of course."

"Obviously." She smiled to herself. "Promise me we can sleep in."

"Baby, I can't make any promises with you curled up next to me like that."

She thrilled at the desire she inspired in him.

"Either way…" She could feel herself drifting into sleep. "I need to sleep."

He stroked her hair and the last thing she remembered before slipping into a deep sleep was hearing him tell her how much he loved her, and thinking that she felt exactly the same way. She'd tell him in the morning. She was ready.

Drew had no idea what time it was when she heard the banging on the door, but the room was darker than she remembered. Next to her, Ben had shot up at the sound, too.

"What is…who…"

"I don't know," Ben said, his voice strong with authority. "Stay here. I'm going to go check it out."

She watched as he tugged on a pair of athletic shorts,

grabbed a baseball bat from next to the door, and his silhouette disappeared into the house. Drew's heart raced and she scrambled in the dark for her purse but for the life of her couldn't remember where she'd left it when they'd come into the house.

From the other room, she could hear another round of banging on the door and then Ben called out, "Who's there?"

Drew wrapped her fingers around the leather strap of her purse on the floor at the same time she heard a muffled response from whomever it was outside. But she couldn't quite make it out.

It only took her a second to find her phone and flip it on. She'd completely forgotten to turn it back on after they'd agreed to turn them off the night before. Instantly, panic raced through her. *Austin.*

The racket at the front door forgotten, Drew quickly opened her messages.

Twenty-five unread texts?

Her heart in her throat, she clicked over to the missed calls.

Ten.

Austin. She knew without looking at any of them.

She thought she was going to throw up as she flipped the quilt aside and found her clothes. The dress was crumpled in a ball, and no doubt completely wrinkled, but it didn't matter. She needed to get to Austin.

From the front room, she could hear Ben's voice. It was no longer raised or agitated, and then…as she stepped into the hall, Evan's.

"What do you—"

"What's wrong with Austin?"

She and Ben spoke at the same time but both men turned to stare at her. It was Evan who spoke first.

"We've been trying to get a hold of you but…"

"Our phones were off. What's wrong?"

"You should get dressed." Evan spoke to Ben, but Drew

was pretty sure she was going to commit some sort of inexcusable act if he didn't just tell her what was wrong already.

"Evan!"

He turned back to her and in what she was sure was his police officer voice, said, "Austin's in the hospital."

Chapter Twenty-Three

THE HOSPITAL WAS ONLY ten minutes across town, but the drive felt like hours. On the way there, Evan explained to her how Ben's parents had tried calling both of them but couldn't get through on either of their phones.

The guilt for turning her phone off was like a knife in her gut, and the knowledge that she'd been too caught up in Ben to remember to turn it back on was the twist of the knife that made her bleed.

"He spiked a fever," Evan explained. "It was over 104 and Sylvia got worried when she couldn't bring it down."

"104? That's high."

"Does he get fevers like that often?" Ben asked from the backseat.

Drew shook her head. He'd never had a fever that high before. He was a really healthy kid. He didn't get sick at all, not really. And as far as she could remember, the only fever he'd ever had was when he was a baby after his immunizations. But that wasn't 104.

104 was too high.

Ben's hand squeezed her shoulder. "He'll be okay, Drew. He's in good hands."

"He is," Evan said. "I called Mark. I thought you'd want him to be there."

"I do," she said with a nod. She couldn't think of anyone she trusted with her son's health more. "Thank you." She sat quiet for a moment as she realized that everyone knew about her son being in the hospital before she did. Guilt flooded her and threatened to paralyze her completely.

She couldn't think about it. She needed to push the guilt away and get to her little boy.

The moment the car pulled up to the emergency room doors, Drew was out and running toward the front desk. The nurse saw her coming and stood with her hand out for her to stop. "Mrs. Ross. I need—"

"I need to see my son." On some level, Drew was aware she was being irrational, and she needed to calm down, but her baby was in the hospital and if something happened...*no*. She could not and would not allow herself to think that way. "Where is he?"

"Mrs. Ross, I just need you to fill out a few—"

"No." She was just about to run through the swinging doors that she, unfortunately, already knew from experience, led to the beds where her son would be, when a strong arm wrapped around her shoulders.

"It's okay, Delores," Mitch Ross said. "We'll get to the paperwork in due time. I'll take her back."

Drew didn't care what Delores had to say about it; she was going with Mitch. Never in her life had she been so grateful for her father-in-law as she was at that moment as he led her through the doors.

"He's okay, Drew. He's going to be just fine." Mitch's voice soothed her in the same power that both of his sons' voices had and she found herself calming down a little bit, as they walked through the emergency room.

Apparently she hadn't calmed down enough, because the moment Mitch gestured to the curtain that was Austin's, she thought she was going to be sick. There were too many memories associated with hospitals and pale-green privacy curtains just like this one over the years. Only instead of her son, it had been her husband.

"Drew?" Mitch's hand squeezed her arm. "It's okay. He's going to be okay."

She nodded, but her head didn't feel attached to her body. "I know." She said the words, even though she didn't know at all. How was she supposed to know everything would be okay? The doctors in Nevada had all told her that, too. *It's going to be okay. We'll try these treatments...this one will work...this is the latest medicine...just one night in the hospital for tests...*

None of it had been okay.

Her pulse raced, sweat beaded along her forehead, and from somewhere beside her, she could hear Mitch's voice, but it was coming through a tunnel and was so far away. The room tilted and for one terrifying moment, she was sure she was going to pass out.

"Drew."

Eric?

She tried to look around, but couldn't focus on anything. But he'd said her name. She was sure of it. *Eric.*

"I've got you."

She closed her eyes and let his support hold her up. Deep breath. Then another. Finally, she nodded slightly. She *could* do this. She had to. And she wasn't alone. Eric was there. He'd said so. He had her.

"Eric." She said his name so softly, she couldn't be sure she'd said it at all.

"You can do this, sweetheart. Let's go see Austin."

Her eyes snapped open. *Eric never called her sweetheart.* "Ben?"

"I'm here, sweetheart. I've got you."

Ben.

Of course.

Her heart both swelled and fractured in the same moment, but she couldn't dwell on that kind of pain. "I need to see Austin."

"Are you okay?"

She nodded even though it was so far from the truth that she didn't know in that moment if she'd ever be okay. The hospital was too much. It was all too much.

Ben took her hand and together they walked toward the curtain. "I'm fine," she said to him and slipped her hand out of his before pushing the thin fabric aside and going to see her son. Alone.

———

BUT SHE WASN'T ALONE.

Sylvia sat next to Austin's bed, his tiny hand in hers. But Drew didn't even look at her. She went straight for her son.

His eyes were closed but he was breathing. Instinctively, it was the first thing she looked for.

Drew picked up his tiny hand and bent to kiss his forehead. It was so hot.

"He's okay, Drew." Sylvia's voice was soft as to not wake Austin. "They have his fever under control now, but..."

Drew looked up for the first time and saw the tears in the older woman's eyes. "What happened, Sylvia?"

She shook her head, and the tears spilled down her cheeks. "He was fine," she said. "Maybe a little slower than usual. But we watched a movie and ordered pizza and then...it was terrible."

"What?" Drew struggled to keep her voice level. "What

happened?"

"Well, I put him to bed." She sniffed loudly and wiped at her face with a crumpled tissue. "But I just had a feeling something wasn't right, so I checked on him a few times. He felt warm, but nothing crazy. Around ten, I gave him some Children's Tylenol, but then...about midnight it must have been, I woke up to a terrible crashing sound. Of course, Mitch and I both ran to his room, and—" She broke away into a quiet sob, but a moment later looked up at Drew. "He was having a seizure."

Drew's body stiffened and the floor tilted again. *No.* She would not let herself have another panic attack. Not now.

"A seizure?" The word felt poisonous on her tongue.

"It's called a febrile seizure." She turned to see Mark, who'd slipped through the curtain and stood next to her. Her friend put his hand on her shoulder and squeezed. "They can be somewhat common in young children who spike a fever. They're more terrifying for the parents than anything else. The fever was likely sparked by an ear infection."

"An ear infection? But he never said anything about a sore ear."

Mark shrugged. "Sometimes they come on quickly and if the child doesn't complain, it would be all but impossible for you to know about it. He's going to be just fine, Drew. I promise."

She believed him. She could see it in his eyes. Mark had always been one of the few doctors who was painfully honest with her about Eric's cancer. Even when Eric himself tried to protect her, Mark would tell her the truth.

"Mom?"

In an instant, all of Drew's attention was focused on her baby boy. "I'm here, kiddo." She both wanted to laugh and cry when his impossibly long eyelashes fluttered open to reveal the eyes that reminded her so much of his father. "I heard you're not feeling very good."

"Where were you, Mom?"

Guilt stabbed her straight in the heart, but she didn't flinch. Instead, she glanced at Sylvia, who offered her a smile and a small shrug.

"I was out with Uncle Ben, kiddo. But I'm here now. I'm so sorry I didn't hear the phone when Grandma called."

"It's okay." His lips twitched up in a tiny smile that broke her heart. "Can we go home now?"

Drew looked to Mark for the answer.

"Not yet, buddy. I think I'll keep you here overnight to make sure your fever is controlled. But in the morning, you should be all set." He turned to Drew. "If you like, I can—"

"I'm not going anywhere." She cut him off before he could suggest anything ridiculous, like sending her home.

But Mark only chuckled. "I didn't think you were. I was going to offer you a more comfortable chair and maybe a cup of coffee."

LETTING Drew go to Austin's bedside alone was one of the hardest things he'd ever done, but Ben had let her go. Drew knew he was there for her and he wasn't going anywhere.

Until the nurse sent him out to the waiting room. "Immediate family only," she'd said.

"But I'm—" He broke off. Because what was he? *The uncle? The brother-in-law? The boyfriend?*

No matter how you looked at it, he wasn't immediate family. That much was certain.

He didn't like it, but along with his dad, they went to the waiting room where his father and Evan, who was still waiting, filled him in on all of the details of the evening.

"Why are you here?" he asked his friend after hearing all of the details. "I mean, if it's only an ear infection, it hardly seems necessary to call in the cavalry."

Evan laughed. "True, but I think everyone got a little concerned when no one answered their phone. Not that there looked like much to be concerned about..." He wiggled his eyebrows and Ben had to hold back from punching him. It was not the time nor the place and he was definitely not in the mood.

Alone, he walked to the end of the room and stared vacantly at the vending machine. He wasn't hungry, but deciding between a chewy bar and a bag of salty chips would at least give him something to do besides think about how terrified he'd been to hear Austin was in the hospital. Never mind the look on Drew's face. He would have done anything to take that pain away from her. The worry, the stress. The woman had been through way too much. She didn't deserve to have one more moment in her life where she ever had to feel that way again.

"He's going to be fine, Ben."

"I know," he answered Evan without taking his focus from the candy bars in front of him.

"Then why do you look so wrung out? What's going on?"

He shook his head but didn't say anything. Because what could he say? How could he explain to his best friend that he'd just had the best night of his life? A night that had been so completely perfect but then, so utterly devastating in one moment?

"Ben? Talk to me."

"She called me Eric." He hadn't realized he'd spoken the words out loud. Hell, he hardly realized he'd noticed when she'd called him by his brother's name early in the ER. But he had.

"She what?"

Ben turned then and looked at his best friend. "She called me Eric," he said again. "She was freaking out before she went in to Austin. Almost like a panic attack. I thought she might actually pass out and then…" He couldn't bring himself to say it again.

"Sounds like it *was* a panic attack," Evan said. "And can you blame her? When was the last time she was even at a hospital?" He didn't wait for Ben to answer. "I would be surprised if she didn't have a panic attack. I've seen it a lot as a police officer, Ben. When people are under extreme stress like that, they say things…they do things…it's like their body is in complete survival mode, and that's all their brain is focused on. If she called you Eric, well…" He rubbed the bridge of his nose before speaking again. "Look, man. You're in the middle of a pretty crazy situation and that woman…she's been through a lot. Your path? It's not going to be an easy one. There's no doubt about that. I know you love her; you always have. And I have no doubt that she loves you right back."

Ben's chest constricted. He felt her love, but she hadn't… well, hearing her say the words was the least of his worries at the moment, but still, it hurt.

He shook his head a little, but Evan kept talking. "Drew has a whole history. One that you're not really part of, and I know you *know* that," he said. "But you really need to *understand* that. Because that's never going to go away."

"I know that." God, did he ever know it. "And yes, I *understand* that. But sometimes, Evan, it's so friggin' hard."

Evan chuckled. "Yes it is. But if you're going to do this, you'll need to decide one thing." He looked straight into his friend's eyes. "Is it worth it?"

He didn't even hesitate in his answer. "Damn right, it's—"

"Ben?"

WHEN DREW WALKED out to the waiting room, she wasn't surprised to see Ben waiting for her. She knew she could count on him.

Because he loved her.

That's what made what she was about to do so much harder.

He was deep in conversation with Evan and he looked about as rough as she felt.

"Ben?"

He turned immediately, his face transforming from the hard lines of whatever intense conversation he was having. In two strides, he was across the room and standing in front of her.

"How's he doing? Dad said it was an ear infection, but he had—"

"He's fine," she said, not wanting to relive the details. "Tired and wants to go home, but he's fine." She wrapped her arms around her waist to keep from shivering. Not so much from the cold, but from stress, exhaustion, all of it. They'd left the house so quickly, she didn't have a chance to grab anything to put over the sundress she'd worn the night before.

Ben must have noticed as well. "Here." He shrugged out of his hoodie and handed it to her. "You look like you're freezing."

She took it with a grateful smile.

"Drew? How are you—"

"I'm going to stay the night here with him."

"Of course you are." He reached for her hand, but she pulled back, tucking her hands under the hoodie in her hands. Ben hesitated a moment, and then said, "I'll go get you whatever you need and I can be—"

"No." She shook her head. "There isn't any need. I'll be fine."

"Are you sure?"

"You should go home, Ben."

She wouldn't meet his eyes. She couldn't. Because she knew the moment she did, she'd be lost. She knew she wasn't being fair, but she also knew that at that moment, she was stretched so thin she couldn't do anything else.

Without another word, she turned and walked away. She could feel him watching her, but she knew he wouldn't call after her. Not in the hospital. The sobs rose up inside her, clamoring for escape, but she wouldn't let them. She couldn't lose control. Not here.

More than anything, she yearned for the feel of his arms around her, holding her and telling her that everything would be okay. Not even two hours ago she'd felt safe in those arms, like nothing could hurt her.

But she'd been wrong.

Because the thing that could hurt her most was beating inside her chest and it threatened to completely shatter her.

Which was why she couldn't turn around.

Chapter Twenty-Four

"I TOLD YOU I FEEL FINE." Austin whined and after a night of barely any sleep in the hospital chair, Drew thought the sound might actually fracture her skull. "Please let me go outside." He tugged on her sweater and more or less hung off her as she tried to make him a sandwich.

They'd been home from the hospital less than an hour and Drew couldn't decide whether he really was feeling better and just wanted to go out and play or whether his near tantrum was the result of very little sleep himself and a raging ear infection that the antibiotics had barely had a chance to touch.

She was opting for the latter due to the increasing urgency of his whining.

Drew put the butter knife down and knelt on the kitchen floor in front of him. "I think today is an inside movie and video game day."

His eyes grew wide at the mention of video games. She never let him play when the sun was shining outside. This was different.

"Really?"

She nodded. "I think after you've spent a night in the

hospital, you've more than earned a little game time, don't you?"

Austin didn't need to be asked twice. He nodded like a bobblehead doll and turned to head into the living room. Before he left, he quickly turned back, catching Drew off guard as she started to stand. Austin wrapped his little arms around her legs and squeezed tight. "I love you, Mom." As soon as she looked down at his little head, he looked up and added, "And not just because you're letting me play video games."

She couldn't help but laugh as he scrambled out of the room to find his remote, his sandwich completely forgotten.

It was a small thing, but it made her life at that moment a thousand times easier. And sometimes parenting was a game of balancing the best thing for the child and the thing that would keep the mother sane. An hour or so of video games wasn't going to make a difference.

A few hours later, her front door opened with a knock that woke Drew from her nap on the couch while Austin, who had moved from his game to a movie, sat next to her, transfixed with some sort of cartoon robots on the screen.

She spun her head around to see her mother with a plate of what looked like cookies and a grin on her face.

"Don't judge me." Drew dropped her head back to the cushion. She couldn't decide whether she was so tired because of her lack of sleep or her complete and total emotional exhaustion.

Every time she closed her eyes, she saw Ben's face and the hurt in his eyes when she'd told him to go home. She knew him. It would have killed him to leave her and Austin there and drive away. But he would have. Because she'd asked.

"I'd never judge you, kiddo. Especially when I brought our little patient cookies."

"Cookies?"

The promise of Grandma's cookies were worth pausing the movie. Drew listened while Austin told her mom all about the hospital and how his mom had let him play video games all day. If her mother hadn't judged her before, for sure she would now. But Drew didn't have the energy to care.

"Come on." Laura squeezed her leg. "Let me make you a cup of tea. It looks like you could use one."

What she really could use was to be left alone, but she knew enough to know her mom wouldn't leave, no matter what she said.

"Okay," her mom said the moment she was able to drag herself to the kitchen table, Austin once again watching his movie. "What's going on? I haven't seen you look so...well...I haven't seen you look like this since the days right after Eric died. And I know it's more than just Austin being in the hospital."

Drew dropped her head to the table and pressed her cheek to the cool wood.

"Drew?"

After a few moments, she took a deep breath and lifted her head again. "He was in the hospital, Mom."

"I know."

"I wasn't there."

"I heard."

"I was with Ben."

"I know that, too."

Drew couldn't bear to look at her mother's kind smile.

"What if...I just couldn't...I can't..."

"Sweetie." Laura pulled out the chair next to her and took Drew's hand in hers. "What is going on? Talk to me. Austin's fine."

"I know." She nodded, more to convince herself than anything else because logically she knew he was fine. Of course he was. It was only an ear infection. People didn't die from ear infections.

But they did die.

She loved them and then they died.

"What if he dies, Mom?"

"Who?" She tilted her head in question. "Austin? Kiddo, he's not going to—"

"Ben." She whispered the word.

"Oh." Laura nodded and pressed her lips together. "Is that what's going on? I wondered."

"You wondered?" Drew pressed both hands to the table and stared at her mother. "You wondered what exactly?"

"Don't get upset." Her mother's voice was so completely calm that it agitated her further. "But I don't think it's unusual after the loss of a loved one to fear losing others who you love and especially when it's—"

"Who said anything about love?" Unable to sit any longer, Drew shot up out of her chair and moved to the sink. "I didn't say anything about love." She turned to face her mom, who still wore that same half sympathetic, half smiling look on her face. "And stop looking at me like that."

"Like what?"

Drew grunted and looked at her feet. She was acting like a teenager and she was completely aware of it. But she couldn't seem to force herself to stop. The last twenty-four hours had been too much. She couldn't put into words what she was feeling, and what seeing Austin in the hospital had felt like. Never mind her freak-out. She brought her hands up to her face and willed herself not to cry. Or scream.

But the second she closed her eyes, Ben's face filled her mind again. Drew shook her head hard and, defeated, dropped her hands to her sides. "Just leave it, Mom." She looked up at her mom's face. "Please."

HE'D TRIED CALLING her at least a dozen times already. She wouldn't pick up.

Maybe she was sleeping?

After all, it would have been a late night for her. No doubt Drew was exhausted. It made sense and he might even have been able to convince himself of it, too, but Ben knew better.

Something had shifted. He'd seen it in her eyes at the hospital. She was scared. But for the life of him, Ben couldn't figure out what the hell she was scared of.

Finally, when he still hadn't heard from her after lunch, Ben filled a to-go container with Austin's favorite chicken fingers and packed up some of Michael's daily soup creation for Drew, and headed to her house.

Laura Frederick's car was parked behind Drew's and the front curtains were open.

She was home.

But it wasn't Drew who answered the door. "Laura. Hi." He greeted her with a huge smile. "I brought lunch."

She smiled, but there was a smidge of—*was it pity?*—in it. "That was really nice of you." She took the packages from him but didn't make any move to step out of the way to let him in.

Ben tried to peek around her, but couldn't see much past the hallway. He did, however, hear the familiar strains of the Transformer theme song. A cartoon he'd introduced Austin to earlier that spring on a day when Little League had been rained out and he'd been disappointed that they couldn't practice.

"Hey, buddy," he called out past Laura's shoulder.

Drew's mom gave him a look, but he saw her smile when Austin came running to the front door. "Uncle Ben!"

Ben bent down and scooped the boy into his arms before

he could crash into his legs. "How's it going, buddy? Feeling better?"

"Yes." Austin groaned. "Mom won't let me go out and play." As they spoke, Ben stepped into the house as Laura gave up guarding the door, and started walking toward the kitchen.

"I think that's probably a good idea."

"I don't."

"Of course you don't." Ben ruffled his hair. "But moms definitely know best when it comes to stuff like this. Besides, watching Transformers doesn't sound so bad."

Austin pulled back from his hug and looked at Ben in the eye. "Will you watch with me?"

Ben's eyes landed on Drew standing in front of the kitchen sink. She had her back turned to him, her head dropped down. His heart clenched at the sight of her. Something was definitely wrong.

"Maybe in a little bit," he said to the boy. "I'd really like to talk to your mom for a second, okay?"

Austin nodded and wriggled out of Ben's arms.

"Come on," Laura said to the boy. "Grandma will let you eat these on the couch." She held up the to-go container Ben had packed and grinned. They both glanced toward Drew to wait for her protest, but it never came.

With a shrug and a slight shake of her head in Ben's direction, Laura ushered Austin into the other room, leaving them alone.

Ben waited a beat and when he couldn't stand it any longer, he stepped closer to Drew and put his hand on her shoulder. "Drew, I—"

She turned around and the emotion on her face took the words from his mouth.

"Sweetheart? What's...what's going on?"

He reached for her, but she stepped to the side. She shook

her head slightly and a tear slipped down her cheek. "I can't do this, Ben. You should go."

"You can't do what?" He looked around. "Austin's fine. You must be exhausted and I—"

"No." She shook her head again and wiped at her face. "You don't understand. This was a mistake."

Her words were a blow to the gut, and Ben struggled not to react physically. "None of this is a mistake, Drew. None of it."

She wrapped her arms around her waist. "It is. It was," she corrected herself. "I can't do it. It's too much."

"What's too much?" He had to force himself to control his voice, but he didn't care. For the life of him, he couldn't figure out what was happening and what she was trying to say to him. Because if Drew was trying to say what he thought she was, he wouldn't be able to handle it. And he didn't believe it. Not for a minute. *She was tired. She was emotional. She didn't know what—*

"All of it."

She turned again and took a step back, but there was no way Ben was just going to stand there and let her push him away. "Talk to me, Drew." He reached for her and reflexively, she softened a little under his touch, but it only lasted a moment before she stiffened again.

"Please, Ben. This is already hard enough. Can you please go?"

"No." He shook his head. "Not until you talk to me. There is no way that after what we shared that—"

She whirled around. "It was a mistake. All of it. I need you to understand that."

Ben stared at her for a moment, wishing he could think of the words that would make her see that she didn't need to push him away. "You don't have to do this, Drew. You don't have to push me away."

Tears streamed unchecked down her cheeks now and it was all he could do not to wipe them for her. His heart ached, watching what she was putting herself through. What she was putting *them* through.

"Drew, I—"

"You don't get it." She raised her voice. "I can't do it again. I can't lose him...and you." Her chest heaved as a sob escaped her. "Being in that hospital...seeing Austin...you...I just can't. I wish I could, but...you have to go."

When he didn't move, she shoved him and practically yelled, "Go! Get out!"

Ben reeled from everything she'd said and more, everything she *hadn't* said.

He opened his mouth, but closed it again when he realized there was nothing more to say. Not until she realized what she was hiding from herself.

He moved to leave, but before he could take a step toward the door, turned back to look at her. He took the chance of touching her again and cupped her chin gently as he spoke from the deepest part of his heart. "I love you, Drew." He spoke the words softly. "More than life itself and I know you know that. But know this, too. I'm not going anywhere. Not ever. You can push me as hard as you can, but you can't move me. You're scared, that's all. But the only thing you really need to be scared of is closing your heart to the love that I know you feel because you're afraid of what *could* happen. You lost Eric, and it was terrible and awful and you didn't think you could survive it, but you did."

He knew he was pushing it, but it all needed to be said, and if he didn't say it right then, he feared he would never have the chance. So he kept going. "You know damn well that Eric wouldn't want you to run from this. You know it, Drew." She closed her eyes, but the tears kept streaming down her face. "Because you know the truth, just as he did. None of us know the future. Not one of us knows what could happen tomorrow or the next day. And every day you waste by running is a day you might as well already be..." Her eyes opened then and all the words vanished. Ben stroked her chin with his thumb, tears filling his own eyes. "Don't do this, Drew."

She closed her eyes and swallowed hard. For a moment, Ben was certain he'd gotten through to her. But then she opened them and whispered, "Please go."

Chapter Twenty-Five

"I DON'T CARE what you say, Drew." Amber opened Drew's bedroom closet and started sifting through the hangers. It had been two weeks since Austin had ended up in the hospital. He'd made a full recovery from his ear infection and with summer winding down, was going to go back to school soon. But before he did, there was the Timber Creek Challenge to complete, and there was no way Amber was going to let Drew sneak her way out of it. "You're doing the race. We all are."

When they'd found out that Ben had signed up Drew and Austin for the race, most of their friend group had signed up as well. It was supposed to have been a fun day. But judging by her friend's reaction to Amber barging into her bedroom, Amber was going to have her work cut out for her if Drew was going to have any fun.

On the bed, where she was hiding from her best friend, Drew let out a groan. "It's not a good idea."

"It's the best idea." Amber gave up looking at the clothes hanging up and started opening drawers of the dresser. "Where are your workout clothes?"

"What workout clothes?"

Amber laughed before she realized Drew wasn't joking. "Seriously? Like you never went to spin class or anything in Nevada?"

"I went for a run a few months ago."

Drew shrugged.

"And you haven't been training for this race?"

The Timber Creek Challenge was designed to be more than a five-kilometer fun run. The organizers also filled it full of obstacles like a wall climb, some sort of mud pit that Amber didn't want to spend too much time thinking about, and other crazy things that would take teamwork to complete. After they'd agreed to it, Logan and Amber had worked in some basic training into their daily schedule, which for them meant a few light runs on the trails around the ranch, coupled with their usual chores with the horses, and maybe just one or two more bedroom workouts than usual.

"No," Drew said. "Because I'm not doing it."

"You are." Amber emerged from the depth of a drawer with a t-shirt that would work. She stood and threw it to Drew. "It's for Austin and you know it. It's on the Bro List."

Again, Drew groaned, but Amber ignored it. She'd had just about enough of her best friend moping around since everything had gone down with Ben. Not that Amber understood it. No one did. And they'd all tried to talk to Drew about it, both together and separately, but still no one was able to understand exactly what had happened between them or why Drew had pushed him away so hard and fast. They'd seemed happy. Really happy, which was all they wanted for their friend—to find happiness again.

But then it was over.

And nobody but Drew seemed to understand why. Even Ben—especially Ben—struggled to understand how everything had gone so sideways. After a night out with the boys, Logan had come home and reported to Amber that Ben was upset, but also strangely calm. "She needs to work through it. But she will," was all Ben had said to the guys.

But whatever it was that Ben thought Drew needed to work through, as far as Amber was concerned, she hadn't been working through much of anything. Instead, she'd thrown herself into her work and when she wasn't working, she moped around. It was almost worse than when Amber had been there for her after Eric died.

No.

It *was* worse than that, because as far as Amber could see, Drew's pain and heartache had been completely preventable and brought on by herself.

"Here." Amber threw a pair of cotton shorts at her. "These will work. Get dressed. We leave in five."

She moved to leave the room when she noticed Drew still hadn't moved. "Drew," Amber said with more force than before. "I'm serious. I'm not letting you get out of this."

Drew shook her head and pulled her knees up to her chest. "I can't do it, Amber. I can't see him."

"You can and you will. Because it's not about you, Drew. This is about Austin. So if you can't get past it yourself, think of him and how all of this has affected him." She felt a little bad trying to guilt Drew with her son, but desperate times… Besides, the poor kid had already lost his dad; she wasn't going to sit by and let him lose another important man in his life just because his mom was being stubborn.

"I know it's about Austin, but…you just don't understand, Amber." She shook her head and dropped it to her knees.

With a sigh, Amber sat on the bed and scooted closer to her friend. "You're right," she said, forcing herself not to get frustrated. "I don't understand, Drew. Not even a little bit. When Eric died, I got it. I mean, I *really* got it. But this…" She took a deep breath. "I don't get it. Ben loves you and if I had to guess, I'd say you loved him, too. A lot."

Drew looked up, her eyes swimming in tears. "I do."

"Okay." Amber raised her eyebrows. "So I'm going to be blunt now." Drew shrugged. "Then what the hell are you doing putting yourself through this hell? Because I know it's not about what other people think. And I know it's not about concern for what Eric would think. We've talked about all of that and I *know* you're at peace with all of that." She shifted so she faced Drew head on. "So *please* tell me what this is all about, Drew."

"I'm so scared," Drew said after a moment. Tears streaked her cheeks as she spoke. "I can't lose someone else. I just can't."

"You're not going to lose anyone else."

"You don't know that." Drew dropped her legs and crossed them so she could sit straight up. "When I saw my baby in the hospital, it all just got really real. I love Austin more than anything else in this world and—"

"You're not going to lose Austin," Amber interrupted. "It was an ear infection."

"But it could be something serious next time," Drew challenged. "When Eric got sick and went to the doctor, we *never* thought it was cancer. And then we just *knew* he'd beat it. But he didn't, Amber. That could happen again."

"Yes," Amber admitted. "It could."

"Well, I can't do it again." Drew crossed her arms like a stubborn child. "I can't love someone that much and lose them again. With Austin, it's different. But with Ben, I can choose."

"Can you?" Amber laughed. "Can you really choose to stop loving him?" Drew was glaring at her, but she didn't care. "How's that working out for you, Drew? Because I don't see anyone around here who has stopped loving anyone else. Nope, what I see is a woman who is torturing herself and everyone else around her because she's too bloody stubborn to admit to herself that sometimes when you love, you get hurt. And sometimes when you open your heart, everything works out beautifully and you get your happy-ever-after and sometimes shitty things happen and the one thing you *can't* do is predict any of it. But you love anyway, because a life without love is pointless."

Amber jumped to her feet. "You can't prevent something bad from happening, Drew. But the one thing you do have the power to prevent is living a half-life. So get your ass out of bed, get dressed and get out there because we have a race to run."

IT HAD BEEN two weeks since Ben had walked out of Drew's house, but he certainly hadn't walked out of her life. Not as far as he was concerned. She was pushing him and testing him, but he'd meant it when he told her he wasn't going to move.

"You're pretty sure she's coming?" Evan and Mark— dressed in their Team New Dad shirts that read *This* IS *my dad bod* on the back—found Ben standing by the race registration desk. With both of their wives busy with their new babies, the two friends decided to team up together for the Timber Creek Challenge. Not that Ben had expected any of them to sign up for the race, but when he told Evan about the Bro List and that he'd signed Drew, Austin, and himself up, news traveled until almost their entire group was registered.

Ben knew they all had their own reasons for racing, but he also knew Eric would have been happy to see them all doing it together. He would have loved competing in an event like this one when they were kids.

"She's coming." Ben wished he was as confident as he sounded because the truth was, as much as Amber had promised she'd get Drew there, he couldn't be sure. He twisted the shirts he was holding tighter in his hands.

"I like the shirts," Mark said with a head nod. "Very cool."

The day he'd registered them for the race, Ben had ordered the t-shirts as well. They were bright green and on the front they had *Team Bro List* emblazoned in black block letters. On the back of his: *For my bro.* On Austin's: *For my dad.* And on Drew's: *For my husband.*

He'd ordered them before he told her he loved her. Before he felt that love from her in return and before she'd pushed him away. But it didn't matter. Ben had never been threatened by what Drew had shared with Eric. It had been and would always be real. But he also knew that what he shared with her was just as real. Love wasn't finite.

"I think she'll like them," Ben said to Mark.

"She'll love them."

"Love what?" Austin flew out of nowhere and as he always did, wrapped his arms around Ben's legs. He was getting bigger and stronger and it wouldn't be long before Austin was able to tackle him completely to the ground.

"Hey, buddy." Ben bent and scooped up his nephew, giving him a big squeeze. "I've missed you. Are you ready for this?" He changed the subject before Austin could ask where he'd been. He was an observant kid and although Ben made sure to see the boy regularly, his visits had definitely dropped in frequency since Drew asked him to leave.

"For sure," Austin answered before wiggling out of Ben's arms. "Cool shirt."

"I got you one, too." Ben held it out for him and read the words to Austin. "Like it?"

"It's great." It was Drew who answered and when Ben stood up, she was standing in front of him. Their friends had pulled a quick and quiet Houdini and were gone.

"Hi," he said to her. What he really wanted to do was pull her into his arms and show her exactly how much he'd missed her every second for the last two weeks. Instead, he handed her the shirt. "Here's yours."

Ben watched as she held it up and read the back. Instead of a tear, she smiled. "It's perfect, Ben. Thank you. Really."

"I'm going to go check out the park," Austin announced.

Ben looked to see him already wearing his bright-green shirt, running toward the playground and the other kids the moment Drew gave him the okay.

"He's going to run out of energy before the race even starts." Ben laughed.

"Somehow I'm pretty sure that would be impossible." Drew chuckled too, but her smile faded and her face grew serious. "Look, Ben, I wanted to—"

He held up a hand to stop her. There was so much he wanted to say to her, and so much he wanted to hear her say, but Ben knew if they started talking they might not stop, or it wouldn't end the way he wanted and needed it to. "We have a race to run," he said. "It's important."

"It is."

"We'll talk after, okay?"

She agreed with a nod.

"Now, get dressed." Ben grinned. "Team Bro List has a race to win. Or at least complete."

SHE SHOULD HAVE TRAINED.

It was hard.

Really hard.

Drew wiggled her way through yet another giant tire before collapsing on the ground on the other side. Already they'd run farther than she'd ever run in her entire life combined, climbed a net of some kind, balanced on beams through mud—thankfully, without getting too muddy— carried buckets of water, shot a bow and arrow, and now these tires.

Yup. She should have trained.

"You got this." Ben stood over her and offered her a hand,

which she took. He hauled her up and she had to fight to keep from collapsing on him. "You're doing great, Drew. Really."

"Come on, Mom!" Austin, who, as she'd predicted, hadn't tired at all, jumped up and down next to her. "Now we can go to the wall."

Drew looked to where he pointed: a giant wooden wall, with ropes dangling down the front.

"You have to be kidding," she said to Ben.

"You can totally do this."

She really didn't think she could. From somewhere deep inside her, Drew felt a sob building. *Was she seriously going to stand in the middle of this race course and burst into tears?*

It was entirely likely.

The emotional toll of the last few weeks had exhausted her, never mind the fact that she was completely and totally out of shape. She shook her head and squeezed her eyes shut.

"Mom!"

"Hey, buddy. Go grab your mom one of those bottles of water from that aid station over there," she heard Ben tell her son. And then his arms were around her, pulling her close and holding her to him. She was way too tired to object.

Nor did she want to.

"You can do this, Drew," Ben said in her ear while he rubbed her back. "It's just one more thing. You're going to flip this tire and then we're going to go together and get over that wall." She shook her head against his shoulder. "Yes," he said. "We're going to do it together. I've got you. I'm here and I'm not leaving. We're going to do this, Drew. Okay?"

He's got me. He's here. I can do this.

"Do you hear me?"

She nodded and he rubbed her back with more vigor before giving it a small pat and pulling her up off his chest. "I'm right here with you," he said, quieter this time. "Always." Before she could even think about what that meant or let his words sink in, Ben planted a kiss on her dirty, sweaty forehead and stepped back.

"Here." Austin shoved a bottle of water at her. "Drink."

She did as her child told her and drank deeply from the bottle before wiping her mouth with the back of her hand, which she was certain left a smear of mud behind. And judging from the grin on Ben's face, it had.

Drew tossed the bottle in a nearby trash can and looked at the boys, who were eagerly watching her. "Let's do this."

As promised, as soon as she crouched down and flipped the tire, they ran the short distance to the wall, where Ben did a quick survey of it before instructing first Austin how to grab the rope and use the wooden steps provided for the children's modified wall to climb to the top. "Just a few steps and you're up there," he told Austin. "Wait for us at the top, okay?"

With a look of determination Drew couldn't remember ever seeing on her son's face, Austin nodded and did as his uncle instructed.

"Good job, Austin!" She cheered as he easily handled the climb.

"Now it's your turn, Mom!" he called down.

Her eyes grew wide as they looked over to the adult wall. It was higher. Much higher. And there were far less little steps or footholds to help her out. She turned to Ben but he was smiling and nodding.

"You've got this, Drew. You are capable of so much more than you think you are."

"I don't know if that's true." She shook her head at the wall.

"You are," Ben insisted. "And I'm right here with you, okay?"

Numbly, she nodded and listened as Ben gave her some basic instructions on the easiest way to tackle the wooden wall. "Just go bit by bit. Only look as far as the next foothold, okay?

Don't look at the whole thing or you'll get overwhelmed. Just step by step."

Drew took in a deep breath that filled every inch of her lungs. "I can do this," she said as she exhaled.

"Damn right you can," Ben said. "You're the strongest woman I know."

She turned and looked at him and saw nothing but truth in his eyes. Truth and love. Despite everything she'd said to him. Done to him, to push him away. There he was. And he believed in her. More, he *loved* her. And she—

"Come on." He interrupted her thoughts. "Let's do this. I'll be right next to you."

And he was. Ben took the rope next to her and just as he'd promised, he stayed with her step for step, coaching and motivating her as she somehow made her way up the wall.

She'd done it.

Drew took a moment to look around and there it was—the finish line only a few yards away.

She could have cried with relief if it hadn't been for Austin tugging on her hand. "Now we get to slide, Mom."

"Now *that* I can handle."

Together, they slid down the rubber slide that took them back to the ground.

"Let's go!" Austin was bouncing with his endless amount of energy, eager to get to the finish line.

"Almost there," Ben said, much quieter. "Are you ready to do this?"

She looked from her son to Ben and almost cried. This time, not because she was exhausted and spent, but because of the way he was still looking at her, for the love she'd felt coming from him moments before as he got her up the wall, for the love she felt for him no matter what she'd been trying to tell herself.

"Absolutely." Drew took Austin's hand and Ben's in the other. "Let's do this."

There was so much more she wanted to say, but that would have to do for the moment because Austin was already dragging them to the finish line, where, a few moments later, they crossed, hands still joined, arms in the air, cheering and laughing before they collapsed together on the ground, still laughing.

"That was awesome," Austin said. "Dad would have loved it."

Drew smiled through the familiar dull ache in her chest, but she nodded. "He would have loved it. Especially watching you work so hard. You did awesome."

"Let's do it again!"

Drew groaned. "No way." She twisted from where she was still laying on the grass and spotted the playground full of children. "Why don't you go play and as soon as I can move again, we'll come find you?"

Austin didn't have to be asked twice. With limitless energy, he jumped up and took off running.

"You did great, too." She turned to see Ben watching her with a smile of his own on his face. "He would have been so proud of you, Drew."

She wished that was entirely true. Eric *would* have been proud of her in the race, especially after he got over the shock of her actually doing it. But Drew knew without a doubt that he wouldn't have been proud of her at all for the way she'd been acting when it came to Ben. He wouldn't have wanted that for her at all. And she knew it in her soul.

"Thank you."

"You don't have to thank me."

She laughed a little. "Oh yes, I do. I don't think I could have gotten through that without you." She pressed her lips together and nodded a little. "I don't think I could have gotten through a lot of things lately without you."

He pushed himself up off the ground with one arm and looked her straight in the eyes. "I meant what I said back there, Drew. You are capable of so much more than you think you are. You are the strongest, most amazing person I know."

She reached out, knowing she no longer had the right to touch him after the way she'd acted, but unable to stop herself. "You should come by for dinner." She touched his cheek lightly and he closed his eyes. "To celebrate," she continued. "I guess we've completed the Bro List."

"I'll absolutely come over." When he opened his eyes again, they sparkled with mischief. "But there's still one more thing on the list."

Chapter Twenty-Six

EVEN HOURS LATER, after a shower, a quick bite to eat, stopping by the bar to solve a small supplier crisis, *and* picking up everything he needed to finish off the Bro List, Ben still couldn't stop smiling. The Timber Creek Challenge had been the best morning of his life. Watching Austin, and especially Drew, push through each challenge to cross the finish line, at the risk of sounding like a complete and total sap, had been almost magical.

It was as if he'd watched Drew transform in front of his eyes. And although he would happily have taken at least some of the credit for his encouragement, she'd done it all herself. Whatever it was she'd been going through, maybe she'd finally come out the other side.

He didn't want to get his hopes up, but Ben couldn't get the sight of her big beautiful eyes looking at him as they laid on the grass together out of his mind. And the way she'd touched his face. Maybe it didn't mean anything. But *maybe* it did. And he sure as hell hoped it did. He'd been patient with her, and he would continue to do so if need be, but damn, he hoped he wouldn't have to.

His arms were full as he stood on Drew's porch, so instead of knocking, he hollered through the open window. "Hello. I'm here. Can someone grab the door for me? Austin?"

But it wasn't Austin who answered the door; it was Drew, looking gorgeous in her cut-off shorts and a flowery top that slipped off one shoulder to reveal her creamy skin. Ben had to look away from the sight before he became fixated.

"Ben, hi. What is...what are you..." Her mouth fell open when she saw what he held in his arms. "No." She shook her head and backed up. "No way."

But Ben only laughed and offered what he hoped was a fairly innocent shrug. "Hey, we have to finish the Bro List."

"Nope. It's finished," she protested, but Ben could see her melting as she took another step forward.

"It's not finished and you know it." Ben readjusted his bundle as he spoke and scratched it behind the ear. "Austin needs to teach his first dog how to play fetch."

"Oh my God. I could kill you." But Drew was smiling as she reached out to pet the golden retriever puppy. "He's so cute. Austin is going to freak out."

"He is pretty damn cute, isn't he? And so sweet."

"For now." Drew took a step back and put her hands on her hips. Ben could see she was trying really hard to act mad, but she was failing miserably. "But look at those paws. He's going to be huge, Ben."

"He's going to be Austin's best friend. Where is he?" Ben had been dying to give Austin the puppy since he'd secured the little guy's adoption three weeks earlier. It had been torture keeping it a secret, but the timing had worked out perfectly as he was ready to be separated from the rest of his litter earlier that morning.

Drew led the way through the house to the backyard, where Austin sat on the lawn, his back to them, playing with some trucks in the grass. He hadn't heard them come outside, and Ben quieted Drew before she could get his attention. Instead, he crouched and put the puppy down. The little ball of yellow fluff took a few moments to sniff around, before he spotted Austin and pounced his way over to the boy.

Austin jumped a little as the dog snuck up on him, but when he turned and saw the puppy, he let out a noise that could only be described as a combination between a cry and a laugh.

"A puppy?" He immediately reached for the dog, who scrambled into Austin's lap. "Hi, puppy. What's your name?"

"I love that he's not even questioning where the dog came from," Ben whispered to Drew.

She smiled and put her hand to her mouth as she watched her son and his new best friend. "It's almost like he just knows the dog is his. And I think they like each other."

Sure enough, Austin was holding the puppy up as he wiggled in his hands and licked the boy's face madly, causing an outburst of giggles.

After a few minutes of playing, Austin finally turned around to see Drew and Ben watching him. "Is he mine?"

"He's all yours, buddy." Ben felt a twinge of guilt for springing the dog on Drew, but judging by the look on her face at the moment, she didn't seem too troubled by it. "Do you like him?"

"I love him!" Austin put the dog down on the grass and they watched as he climbed right back up into Austin's lap. "I think he likes me, too."

"I think he does."

"What's his name?"

Ben looked at Drew and then back at the boy. "What do you think it should be? After all, he's yours to name."

Austin examined the dog for a minute and finally looked up. "I think I'm going to call him Buddy. Because he's going to be my best buddy."

"I think that's a great name."

Together, Drew and Ben joined the boy on the lawn and the puppy entertained them by running between all of them, chewing on their fingers and licking their faces.

"I don't know if you're going to be able to teach him to play fetch for a little while," Drew said. "He might have to get a little bigger before you can finish off the Bro List."

"He's pretty smart," Austin declared. "I bet he could learn soon. But I might need help teaching him."

"Don't worry," Ben said. "Whenever he's ready, I'll be here to help. I'm not going anywhere." He added the last bit and looked right at Drew when he said it. "If that's okay with you?"

"Ben, I…can I talk to you for a second?" She hopped to her feet before even waiting for him to answer and walked into the house.

HE CAUGHT up with her in the kitchen. Her back was to him, as she looked down at the counter.

"Drew, I—"

She spun around and threw herself into his arms. By instinct, his body knew what to do. She kissed him while his arms wrapped around her, holding her tight to him. *Damn, she fit just right.*

The kiss was fast and hot and there was so much more behind it than could ever be conveyed with words. But that didn't mean he wasn't going to try. He could have kissed her all day, but he also knew there was a lot that needed to be said between them, so, regretfully, he pulled back.

"Drew. I don't know what to say about that."

"Say that it's okay."

"Of course it's okay." He still held her close, unwilling to let her go. "But you…" He shook his head. "Talk to me."

She laughed nervously and dropped her head to his chest. Ben breathed in her scent. "I'm so scared," she said when she looked up again.

"Of what?"

"Of all of it." She shook her head. "Of moving on and forgetting him. Of not moving on and losing you. Of disappointing him." She took a step back so she could look in his eyes properly. "But mostly I'm terrified of letting myself love you because I couldn't bear it if I lost you, too." She smiled a little but unshed tears shone in her eyes. "I'm absolutely terrified, Ben."

"I could tell you not to be scared." He intertwined his fingers with hers. "But I think I've figured out by now that I'll never be able to tell you what to do."

That got a laugh out of her and she shook her head with a smile. "That being said," he continued. "Let me tell you this." Ben's eyes locked onto hers while he spoke directly from the heart. "We don't know what tomorrow will bring, and even if we did, there's nothing we can do about it. But the one thing I do know is that you can't spend your life wondering what *might* happen and hiding from your life and your feelings. Because that's not living. It's time to stop hiding, Drew." With his free hand, he reached out and cupped her cheek. "You don't have to be scared."

SHE WANTED to close her eyes. Not so she could hide from the way he was looking at her, but so she could keep his tender look in her mind forever. But she didn't.

Drew forced herself to look straight ahead into his bright-green eyes, and all the love that was there for her, because it gave her strength.

Not that she needed it. Not for what she needed to say. Not anymore.

"I can't promise you that I won't be scared again," she said after a moment. "This whole thing…it's terrifying." She shook as she spoke, but it was too late to turn back. Besides that, it was the last thing she wanted. She'd finally started moving again; nothing was going to stop her.

"But just because I might get scared, doesn't mean I'll run," she said after a moment. "I'm sorry, Ben. For…" A sob choked her momentarily, but it didn't matter because Ben pulled her close to his chest and held her until the moment passed.

"It's okay, sweetheart." He kissed her forehead and just held her. No expectations, no demands. Just love that she could feel flowing from him into her. "I'm not going anywhere. I told you that once, and I'll tell you that again. Over and over again until you believe it."

"I do believe it." She pulled back to once again look into his eyes. "Ben, I need to tell you—"

"You don't have to."

He was trying to make it easy on her. Protect her. Help her. It's what he did and she appreciated it more than anything, but she didn't need protecting. And definitely not when it came to this.

"No," she insisted. "I *do* need to tell you something." She took a step back out of his arms, not because she needed the distance from him, but because it was something she needed to do on her own. She was strong enough to know her heart, and that included the love *and* the pain that resided there. "Losing Eric was the hardest thing I ever had to face," she started. "As you know, even though he did his best to prepare me, there is no amount of preparation that can help you be ready for the day you lose your husband." Her voice shook, but she swallowed hard and kept going. If she stopped, she was afraid she might never get the words out. "There were times I didn't think I'd survive it. Days when I thought my heart would explode from the loss of him. The last thing I ever expected was to feel anything again. Not like that." She smiled a little to herself. "In fact, if someone would have told me that I'd be able to have feelings for someone else, I would have told them just how wrong they were." She paused and took another deep breath. "But you know what?"

"What's that?"

"I've learned something very important in the last year." He raised his eyebrow in question, and Drew continued. "I've learned that there's no limit on love. I loved Eric and I'll never stop loving him." She could feel the tear slip down her cheek. "But that doesn't mean I don't have room in my heart for someone else. Or that the love I can feel for others is any less. But it *is* different. Does that make sense?" She wiped at her face while Ben nodded slowly. "I guess what I'm trying to say is"—she squeezed her eyes for a moment—"it's different and amazing and scary and exciting and...did I say, so very different, but...Ben, I love you."

She'd never said those words to anyone but Eric, not in a romantic way, and the idea of saying them out loud had terrified her. Was it a betrayal to Eric if she had feelings for someone else? *No.* She knew in her heart that it wasn't and it would never be. But still, she'd half expected the words to feel strange on her tongue. Foreign or wrong in some way. But they didn't. It was the exact opposite. A smile stretched across her face and she said it again with a laugh. "I love you." She laughed again. "I do. I love you."

"Oh, sweetheart." He smiled and shook his head a little. "I already knew that."

Her smile dipped a little as she tilted her head to examine him. "You knew?"

"Of course I knew. He chuckled. "But it still feels damn good to hear you say it. I love you, too. So much." He took her face in his hands and kissed her with a tenderness that made her want to melt completely into his arms.

"Hey! Buddy just—eww!"

Drew jumped back out of Ben's arms and turned to see Austin in the door with the wiggling puppy in his arms.

"What are you…ewww….were you *kissing?*"

"Yes." Ben wrapped his arm around her waist and pulled Drew close to his side. "We were. Because that's what people do when they're in love. Are you okay with that?"

Austin shook his head. But after a moment, nodded slowly. "I mean, I guess. Conner says his parents do that all the time. But it's still weird."

Drew glanced at Ben and moved to crouch in front of her son. "I need you to know that just because I love Uncle Ben doesn't mean I don't…well, it doesn't mean that I don't still miss and love your dad, okay?"

"I know, Mom." Austin put Buddy down on the floor. The puppy immediately started sniffing around under the table. "Dad told me that."

Drew almost fell over. She glanced over her shoulder at Ben, who looked just as surprised. "He did?"

Austin nodded enthusiastically. "Well, kind of. He mostly said that you were going to be really sad and then you'd be happy again one day and that would be good."

"It is good." She tried to fight it, but she couldn't stop the flow of tears as she thought about the very grown-up conversation her husband must have had with her son.

She pulled him into her arms and onto her lap the way she used to and held him tight. A moment later, Ben joined them and Drew's tears flowed in earnest.

"You *are* happy, right, Mom?" Austin looked at her with the concern of a child.

Through her tears, Drew laughed because it looked so different than she would have imagined, and as much as her heart still ached for all that they'd lost, she was, in fact, happy. "More than I could have thought," she answered her son honestly.

Chapter Twenty-Seven

TWO WEEKS LATER, on the last week in August, Drew woke up in the bed she now, more often than not, shared with Ben. Only this morning, she was alone. She stretched her arm into the space where he should have been and reached for his pillow. She inhaled the scent of him before rolling onto her back and staring at the ceiling, the pillow still in her arms.

They'd fallen into an easy rhythm over the last few weeks. If Ben had stayed over, he'd often get up early with the puppy and make breakfast for Austin before Drew got out of bed. They'd usually both walk Austin to school together, unless Ben had to accept an order at the bar, and then after a quiet coffee together, they'd go about their days.

It felt natural and oh so good.

But this morning felt different somehow.

She sat up, flipped her legs off the side of the bed and stretched her arms over her head. That's when it hit her.

August 30.

The anniversary of Eric's death.

The blow of realization almost knocked her back to the mattress.

Had it really been a year?

How much had changed in only twelve months?

Drew squeezed her eyes shut. *How had she let herself forget today was coming?* Obviously she knew when the anniversary was, but somehow it never seemed real. Was she supposed to feel differently? Was she somehow supposed to instantly be *cured* of any lingering pain or hurt?

Even though it was ridiculous, Drew gently patted down the length of her body, feeling for any physical differences. Of course, there were none. Her hands, first one, and then the other, lingered over her heart.

It still beat.

Just as it had every day since he'd died. And just the way it would continue to beat. Maybe even stronger now than before.

Because life went on.

"Knock knock."

Drew didn't get up, but turned her head to see Ben in the door, holding a mug of coffee.

"Good morning." She smiled a little, but still didn't move to get up.

"I thought you might want this in bed this morning." He lifted the steaming mug and walked into the room. He put it on the nightstand and sat next to her. "How are you feeling?" His eyes landed on her hands that still rested on her chest. "Are you…"

Drew nodded.

Ben helped her up to sitting and pressed a kiss to her forehead. "It might be kind of a rough day."

She nodded again. "Definitely."

"Why don't you grab a quick shower?" Ben suggested. "I just got a kind of strange text from Mark. He said he wanted to come by this morning to give you something."

"What? Why?"

"I'm not sure. He didn't say. Just that he didn't want to impose on our day but he had something to give you."

Drew groaned. The last thing she wanted to do was see any of her friends this morning.

"It can't wait?"

Ben shook his head. "I guess not." He squeezed her hand in his. "Don't worry, I'll make sure he doesn't stay. I won't even offer him coffee."

That made her laugh. She leaned forward to give him a kiss and reluctantly got out of bed. "Don't worry. You don't have to be rude to your friend."

"I'd do it for you."

"I know you would," she said from the doorway to the attached bathroom. "And that's why I love you."

WHEN DREW GOT out of the shower, Ben had an easy breakfast of bacon and eggs ready for her, and a fresh pot of coffee. He hadn't been sure what to expect today, on the anniversary of his brother's death. For him, it was kind of an ache in his gut. A realization that he really was gone. Not that he needed it, but after twelve months passed, it just felt a little more absolute somehow and final.

"Feeling better?" He greeted Drew with a proper kiss good morning and was rewarded with a sweet smile.

"I actually feel pretty good." She sat at the table. "It's kind of strange, isn't it?"

"Very." Ben nodded and poured her a fresh cup of coffee. "But also, it feels kind of good in a strange way to know that it's been a year and not only have we, mostly you, survived it, but it's okay. Does that makes sense?"

She grinned, just a little, and nodded. "In a strange way, yes." She turned her attention to her coffee and Ben watched her carefully from the counter. "I still miss him," she said, with a shake in her voice. "And you know I still love him."

"I wouldn't have it any other way," Ben said with sincerity. He'd accepted a long time ago that Drew loved his brother, and he also knew that it would never change. Nor did he want it to. Eric was an important part of all their lives. He'd left a hole that could never be filled, and he would never try to fill it.

Ben also knew that Drew loved him. And as far as he was concerned, there was room enough in her heart for both of them.

He put a plate of toast on the table, but neither of them moved to eat anything. Instead, he took her hands in his. "I miss him, too. Every day."

They sat that way for a few moments, just holding each other and feeling the love between them and around them before Austin and Buddy crashed into the kitchen.

"What's for breakfast?" He leapt up onto his chair and reached for a handful of bacon. Before either Ben or Drew could protest, Austin dropped a piece of the bacon on the floor and Buddy gobbled it up. Drew shot her son a look, but Ben had to hide his grin when Austin said, "What? You told me Buddy wasn't allowed to sit at the table. He has to eat, too."

"He has dog food, kiddo. I don't want to see that again." She chastised him, but Ben knew that at least for today, Austin would get away with it. He'd done really well with the dog, and although Buddy was still young and needed a lot of training, he was a smart puppy and was picking up things really quickly. It wouldn't be long before he'd be able to play fetch, too.

"Can I go outside and play?" Austin grabbed a piece of toast and was already sliding off his chair. "I want to show Buddy his new toy before we go to the lake. Please?"

Drew nodded and Austin took off. They'd planned on spending most of the day, just the three of them at Ghost Lake, doing a little fishing in Eric's memory, but mostly just being together.

"He'll be hungry in five minutes." Drew laughed, but the sound was cut off by the ringing of the doorbell.

Mark.

"Don't worry, I told you I'd be super rude and make sure he doesn't stay."

"You know you can't be rude to Mark." Drew laughed. "It's fine. Let him in."

Two minutes later, their friend stood in the kitchen and refused the coffee that despite his vow not to, Ben couldn't help but offer.

"I won't stay," Mark said. "I know today might be a hard one." He nodded once to both of them, but his eyes landed again on Drew. "But I promised Eric something before he died and I don't break promises."

"What on earth could you have promised?"

It was Ben who asked, but Mark addressed Drew. "He gave me this and asked me to give it to you exactly one year after he passed." He pulled a simple white envelope out of his breast pocket and handed it to Drew.

"What is it?"

Mark shook his head and looked at Ben. "I don't know. But he asked, so…"

"Of course," Drew said, still staring at the envelope in her hand. "Thank you."

"He was a great man," Mark said.

Ben nodded, but focused his attention on Drew. "Do you want to open it now, or…"

She didn't hesitate. "I think I'll go…" She got up from her chair and looked at Ben. There was no need to finish the sentence. He nodded and without saying anything more, Drew disappeared to the bedroom.

"Maybe I'll take that coffee after all."

Ben nodded, happy for the distraction. Obviously she would need a minute to be alone to read whatever was in the envelope, but he wasn't about to pretend it wasn't hard for him too.

"Thanks." Mark nodded and took a sip as soon as Ben handed him the mug. "How's she doing with all of this?"

"Good. Mostly." Ben shrugged and looked to the door Drew had just disappeared through. "Today is hard. But that's to be expected." He looked back to Mark. "She's the strongest woman I know. Everything she's been through…" He shook his head. "And she still has the capacity to open her heart and love."

His friend grinned over his coffee mug. "Of course she does. She has you, Ben. Don't underestimate that."

Ben was about to object, but Mark put his hand into his jacket pocket and drew out a tightly folded piece of paper. "I have this for you, too."

"From Eric?"

"He gave it to me later. Right before…well, you know."

Ben nodded.

"I know it's not in an envelope, but he didn't have one and…well, I promise I didn't read it."

Ben stared at the piece of paper but didn't open it.

"Do you want to be alone?" Mark put his mug down. "I'll go."

"No." He shook his head. "It's fine."

Slowly, Ben unfolded the paper. He recognized it as a piece that had been torn from Eric's notebook where Drew had discovered the Bro List. And there, in his brother's familiar scrawl:

Thank you. For Drew.

Ben read the note twice before looking up. "I don't understand."

He handed it to Mark, who read it and smiled.

"What's he thanking me for?" Ben's thoughts spun. "For when we were kids and... Or..."

No.

He knew instinctively what Eric was thanking him for.

"For taking care of her now," he said to his friend. "For loving her."

"That would be my bet."

"I know I promised him I'd look out for them, but..." Ben ran a hand through his hair in an effort to process. "How could he know that..." He waved his arm around to encompass everything that he couldn't put into words.

Mark reached out and squeezed Ben's arm before giving it a pat. "How could he not, Ben? How could he not?"

Chapter Twenty-Eight

THERE WAS nothing remarkable about the envelope that lay in the middle of the bed in front of Drew.

Except it was far from ordinary.

Drew spent a few minutes simply staring at it. She had to open it. That wasn't an option. But at the same time…what if she didn't? She went back and forth with her internal arguments before finally she snatched it up and unceremoniously tore it open.

It was only one piece of paper, but the simple sight of Eric's handwriting brought tears to her eyes.

No.

She wouldn't cry. Not yet.

First she had to know.

Drew,

Can you believe it's been a year since I've been gone? I mean, I'm sure you can. You had to live with it. And I know, I know—I got to take the easy way out.

She could almost hear the teasing in his voice as she read his words. She shook her head, a small smile on her face, and kept reading.

But it wasn't easy, Drew. Nothing about leaving you and Austin was easy. It broke my heart every day, thinking about how I wouldn't be there for the two of you. I'm sorry, Drew. I never told you that. But I'm so sorry. You never deserved this and I know…you're sitting there thinking that it wasn't my fault. It was cancer. And you're right.

You're always right.

But some nights, when I can't sleep, I think about how maybe I should have fought harder. Maybe I should have listened to you and gone to the doctor right away. Maybe…dammit. The maybes will kill you.

If the cancer doesn't.

She rolled her eyes at his attempt at humor, but it didn't stop the tear from sliding down her cheek. She didn't bother to wipe it away.

Anyway, that's not the purpose of this letter. Do you remember what I made you promise me? I know you do.

She did.

I made you promise not to die when I did. I made you promise to fall in love again and live. Remember?

Drew nodded. She could remember the moment he'd held her hand and forced her to look in his eyes, dulled with pain, and make that exact promise.

I know you, Drew. The only way I could be at peace with leaving you was knowing that you would be okay. And not just with the daily stuff. Of course you'll be okay with that. You've always been so much more capable at all of that stuff then I ever was.

Through her tears, Drew's lips curled up into a smile.

But I needed to know you'd be okay where it really counted.

Now that it's been a year, I thought you might need a reminder of that promise. Maybe you don't. I hope to God you don't, and that you've already found it in yourself to love again. But just in case you haven't… what exactly are you waiting for?

"Don't worry, Eric." She murmured the words aloud. "I have."

Always remember how much I love you, Drew. That will never change. I'll always be with you, watching over you and Austin and loving the hell out of you.

A sob escaped her throat and she bit down on her lower lip.

Please don't be sad for me today. It's just another day. But I know you, and you're probably shaking your head right now.

She laughed through her tears. He'd known her so well.

So, since I know you won't listen to me, raise a glass for me today instead. And then go and open your heart fully and completely and live your life because it's yours to live, baby.

All of my love always, Eric.

Drew finished reading the letter and simply held the paper in her hands. His words were a gift she'd never expected. She allowed herself the time to enjoy it before she lifted the paper to her lips and pressed a gentle kiss on his words before folding the letter and tucking it into the top drawer of her nightstand.

She took a moment to compose herself and wipe her eyes before going out to do exactly what Eric had always wanted her to do. And what more importantly, what she was more than ready to do.

Live.

It had been a long, hard year, harder than she ever could have imagined. But there had been good, too. A lot of good.

Besides, a promise was a promise, after all.

Chapter Twenty-Nine

THE LOG and Jam was packed.

When Drew and Ben started texting and phoning their friends, and of course Sylvia and Mitch, and Drew's parents, too, to ask them to join them in a toast to Eric, neither of them had expected the crowd that had dropped everything to join them to celebrate Eric at the last minute. It was important to have Austin there, too, because Drew wouldn't think of celebrating Eric's life without one of his greatest achievements present.

Thankfully Ben had been able to add family friendly hours at the Log and Jam, which meant everyone they loved would be able to attend.

They'd decided to use the patio space, as it might be one of the last times they'd be able to take advantage of the warm weather. Soon it would be too cold, even with the heaters Ben had installed. But for now, it was perfect and as Drew looked around the space, her heart had never felt more full.

These people were not only her friends, they were her family. And if the last year had taught her anything at all, it was that there was nothing more important than family.

"Eric would have loved this," Sylvia said as she wrapped Drew in a tight hug. "It's perfect."

Drew smiled at her mother-in-law. "I think so, too. How are you doing today?"

Sylvia smiled, but there was an ever present tear in her eye. "Honestly? I'm doing better than I thought I would. I still miss him terribly, as I'm sure you do." Drew nodded. "But it gets a little, well, not easier, but more manageable every day. Does that make sense?"

"Perfect sense."

Mitch and Ben joined them with Austin, who'd been carrying around his dad's baseball bat all day. "How are you doing, kiddo?" Drew ruffled her son's hair. They'd talked a lot about Eric earlier in the day, which had been good for Austin to share his favorite memories of his dad, memories she'd continue to work hard to keep alive for her son.

"I'm good, Mom."

His words were tough, but Drew could see his lower lip tremble a little. She knelt and pulled her son into a tight hug. "It's okay to be sad," she said in his ear. "And no matter what, always remember how proud of you your dad would be. I love you, kiddo."

When she stood, Austin wiped his eyes quickly and gave her a thumbs-up.

"How about you come with me and Grandma over to that bar to see what they have for soda pop, Austin?" Mitch winked at Drew, who only shook her head and a moment later, with his free hand in his grandfather's, they were gone.

"How are you doing, sweetheart?" As soon as they were alone, Ben wrapped his arm around her and held her close as he pressed a gentle kiss to the top of her head.

"I can't imagine feeling any better," she answered honestly. "To have everyone here." She turned so she faced him. "To have you here. And...Eric. I know he's here, too." She smiled, but there was no sadness in it. Not anymore.

"He is." Ben took her hand and pressed it to first his chest and then her own, so it rested over her heart. "He's always been here, Drew. And he always will be."

She used her free hand to run a finger down Ben's cheek before standing on her tiptoes to kiss him. "I love you."

"Are we interrupting something?" Amber tapped Drew on the shoulder.

"Of course we are." Cam laughed.

"Not that it's going to stop us." It was Christy who took Drew's hand and after an apology tossed in Ben's direction, led Drew away with the others.

"Sorry to break that up," Cam said when they had Drew alone in a semi private corner of the patio. "But we just thought we should take a minute."

"It's okay." Drew laughed. "He's not going anywhere." She smiled a little to herself at her choice of words.

Amber pulled out a bottle of wine and poured them all a small glass. "I wanted to propose a toast."

"Good idea." Christy tossed her hair back over her shoulder and raised her glass.

"It's been quite a year," Amber started. She looked to Cam, and added, "I guess it's been a little bit longer than a year, since...well..."

"Since our second chances started," Cam finished for her and they all nodded.

"Yes, I like that," Amber said. "Second chances. That's definitely what these last eighteen months or so have been about. I can't believe how much we've all been through," she continued. "Cam, your divorce." She shook her head, but Cam shrugged.

"The hardest thing I ever had to do," she said. "But it led me back home and back to Evan."

"And your second chance together," Drew said.

"Exactly." Cam smiled. "And thank goodness for that. And Christy, your struggles with infertility and everything you and Mark went through…"

Christy closed her eyes for a moment before speaking. "I wouldn't change it. All of that, it made us stronger and it brought us Mya. That was our second chance."

"And a beautiful one it is," Amber agreed. She looked at each of them in turn. "We all know my second chance was with myself."

Drew took her best friend's hand and squeezed. "I'm so glad you took that chance on yourself. Fighting a drug addiction." She shook her head. "You are incredible, Amber."

"I don't know about that," she protested. "But I'll tell you what *is* incredible, is life with Logan. If I hadn't given myself that chance—well, I don't know what would have happened."

"You don't even have to think about it," Cam said. "I'm so happy for you both."

All four women were silent for a moment before turning their attention to Drew.

"Don't say it," Drew said in an effort to brush away their comments before they could make her cry. She'd done enough crying for one day. Hell, maybe even for years. "We all know why we're here."

"It doesn't change anything," Christy said. "I just want to say one thing about it all, okay?" Drew nodded, because Christy would say whatever it was she wanted to say no matter what. "It's nice to see you smile."

Drew burst out laughing, because whatever it was that she thought Christy was going to say, that wasn't it.

"I think so, too," Amber said.

"Me too." Cam grinned. "Watching your second chance is especially special."

Drew couldn't disagree with her friends, because she felt it, too. Her relationship with Ben *was* special and for so many reasons. But at the same time, it wasn't any more special than what they'd all been through. It was just different.

Just as her love for Ben was different than what she had with Eric. No less special, just *different.*

And she wouldn't trade one moment of any of it.

———

I hope you enjoyed Drew and Ben's story of love and second chances. I loved all of the Timber Creek stories, but something about Drew's really hit me in the heart.

If you loved the friends of Timber Creek, you will absolutely fall for the McCormick brothers of Cedar Springs! You can one click Love in the Moment NOW! And read a special excerpt right after this———>

For more love and happily ever afters, I have an exclusive sweet novella that's not for sale anywhere. You can read it HERE!

Love in the Moment

Please enjoy this excerpt from the first in The McCormicks Series—Love in the Moment

Ian McCormick stole a glance at the woman sitting next to him. He'd picked her up only ten minutes earlier from the bus station and already he'd run out of things to talk about. In fact, beyond the general introductions they'd exchanged, they really hadn't spoken at all. He felt as if he should say something to break the silence, but every time he opened his mouth, he drew a blank. What was he supposed to say to the younger half-sister he'd never met?

The sister that he'd never had any desire to meet, not since finding out about her existence almost ten years ago. As far as he was concerned, Ian could have gone the rest of his life without knowing about Chelsea or her sister, Amber's existence. And he really didn't see any need to get to know either of them. After all, they were the reason his entire life had imploded all those years ago.

Okay, that wasn't entirely fair. It wasn't their fault that their father had led a secret life, with a completely different family. A family he'd finally left his *other* family for, leaving Ian, his brothers, and his mother all alone. *No. It wasn't the girls' fault.* But all of the reasoning in the world hadn't made it any easier for Ian to wrap his head around it. Despite the fact that it had been almost a decade ago.

He snuck another look at the girl who had barely looked up from her phone since she'd sat down in the jeep. There was definitely a family resemblance. She had their father's green eyes, just like he did. And the dark, thick hair. He hated to admit it, but there was no denying she was his sister. And it wasn't as if he could spend the whole summer not talking to her. He'd made a promise to Declan, his second youngest brother.

"It's not her fault," Declan had said on the phone. *"Chelsea and Amber aren't to blame, Ian. You need to get over it."*

Dec was right. He did need to get over it, especially since she was going to be staying with him all summer. He took a breath and opened his mouth to say something, but didn't have a chance.

"I know you hate me."

Ian shut his mouth dumbly.

"And I suppose you think you have a reason to," Chelsea continued. "But it wasn't my idea to come here, you know? Declan pretty much insisted that it would be *good for me* or something, and...well...I kinda trust Dec. Besides, I didn't really have anywhere else to go."

He swallowed hard, giving himself a moment. "I don't hate you." As he spoke the words, he realized they were true. "I just don't know you. And Declan's right. It will be good for you here."

"You don't even know why he said that."

"I don't need to." Ian slowed the jeep to take the turn that would lead them out of town, toward the cottages. His house sat at the end of a row of other log cabins that were used primarily by summer people. Most of the houses were built by families who came from the city for the summer months, and they were still locked up tight because the season wouldn't start for another month or so. It was quiet, but Ian liked it. At least for now, while he was getting settled. And it was true, he didn't know why Declan thought it was a good idea for Chelsea to get out of the city for the summer, but he had a few guesses, and there was no doubt that a little bit of quiet would be good for her, too. "I trust Declan, too," he said as the jeep bumped over the dirt road. It was impossible not to trust Declan. Out of all of his siblings, Dec was definitely the most trustworthy, and the most compassionate and caring and…he was pretty much everything good in the world. "If he thinks it'll be good for you out here, he's probably right."

She shrugged and turned back to her cell phone, looking up a moment later in horror. "The service is terrible here."

"One of my favorite features." He smiled.

"Why would that be a good thing?"

He ignored the question. "It's not that bad, really. Just a little spotty sometimes. Besides, you'll be able to get Wi-Fi at the Dockside as soon as I get it hooked up."

"The Dockside?"

"The new marina." Ian couldn't help but smile. "Cool name, right?" The main reason he'd returned to Cedar Springs was because the economy was starting to pick up, and there were business opportunities to be had. One of the first he'd found was the old marina. It was just next to the Grizzly Paw on the beach in town and Ian remembered it as *the* meeting place for summer fun. He picked it up for a bargain basement price, probably because it needed so much work. By the looks of things, it had sat empty for years and it would definitely take a little elbow grease to get it up and running again. Not that Ian was afraid of hard work. In fact, that had always been his favorite part of a new business: turning nothing into something. "I just closed on it yesterday. And with any luck, it will be open and ready for business in time for the season to start. But if that's going to happen, I'm going to need a little help."

She looked at him sideways. "And I suppose you want me to help."

"You got it. Call it…the price of admission."

She rolled her eyes and shoved her phone into her duffel bag. "Why not? I guess a summer job won't hurt."

"Oh no." Ian braced himself for her response to what he was about to tell her. "Helping at the marina isn't a summer job—it's just an expectation. I got you a job, too. You'll be starting at the Grizzly Paw right away. Sam's an old friend of mine, and she's doing me a favor by giving you this job, so I know you won't let me down."

"Two jobs?"

"No." He shook his head. "Just one. And a family project."

"But I'm never going to have any time to have fun," she wailed.

That was the point, at least as far as Ian was concerned. He didn't know much about twenty-two-year-old girls, but from what Declan had told him, Chelsea was making far too many poor choices. And as the big brother—whether he wanted to be or not—it was going to be his job to help her make good ones. Or keep her too busy to make anything but.

When Gwen Henderson had dreamed of her triumphant return to Cedar Springs after years of hard work and sacrifice, she'd dreamed of driving an expensive convertible down Main Street, her dark hair floating in the breeze as all the men's heads turned to see the beautiful and famous celebrity she'd turned out to be as they kicked themselves for not dating her when they had their chance.

Yes, in her fantasies, it was perfect. In reality, however, she had not imagined that on the eve of her summer visit to Cedar Springs, her secondhand Mustang would have some random, and likely expensive, engine problem that would require her taking the bus into town. And she most certainly did not expect that the one man who'd not only turned her down as a teenager, but had publicly humiliated her ten years earlier at the Summer Equinox Festival, would be there when she got off the bus.

Ian McCormick.

He didn't even *live* in Cedar Springs. What were the odds the one man who still haunted—no, not haunted...*visited*—her dreams would not only be standing there when she got off the stupid, humiliating bus, but would also look her square in the eye and not even recognize her?

If she was honest with herself, and she'd made that a habit over the last few years, that was the part that hurt the most. Ian McCormick had been her biggest teenage crush. No, her *only* teenage crush. Every summer for four years, she had lusted after him. Practically threw herself at him that final summer. But he'd barely even noticed her and when she thought she'd finally had a date with him at the festival, he'd stood her up. Left her there all alone. She knew now he'd only said yes to the date out of pity. After all, it didn't make sense for someone as handsome and smart as Ian McCormick to go out with fat, pimple-faced, four-eyed, frizzy-haired *Giant Gigi*. At the time, she'd been heartbroken—totally destroyed, really. But time and distance had taught her social order. The other thing time and distance had taught her was the impact that health, fitness, contacts, clear skin, a new hair-do, and a name change could do for social order.

It had been five years since she'd dropped the stupid child-hood nickname, adopted a fitness regime and lost seventy-five pounds, finding herself and a new career in the process. Early

on in her transformation, Gwen decided to document everything on social media, using a blog and then a Facebook and
Instagram account to chronicle her progress. The result was
not only a whole new body, but also a very loyal following,
commercial and marketing deals, and the potential for a book
and maybe even a reality television show. She was a very
different person than the sad, overweight teenager she'd been
on her summer visits to see her grandma in Cedar Springs. *Very*
different. And with women looking up to her and men lining
up to date her, she no longer needed Ian McCormick to vali-
date her worth.

*But if that was true, why had her heart done a stupid little flip when
he'd grabbed her bag at the bus stop? And why had her pulse raced out of
control when he looked at her? How was it even possible that he could still
have that effect on her after all these years?*

"Gwen!"

Deanna Gordon shot out of the building across the street
and without even looking, raced across the street and pulled
her into a hug. "Oh my goodness, you look amazing." Deanna
held her out at arm's length for a fraction of a second before
she pulled her back into a hug. "I'm so glad you're finally here.
I was going to meet you at the bus stop—that's crazy that your
car broke down—but I got caught up with a patient and—"

"It's okay." Gwen finally cut her off with a laugh. "I liter-
ally only walked half a block. Don't worry about it."

Deanna bent down and scooped up her bag. "Is this all you
have? One duffel bag? I don't think I could travel that light if I
tried."

Gwen laughed again. "Are you kidding? The rest of my
bags are coming later. I may have sweet-talked the guy at the
depot to deliver them personally."

"You did not?"

She only smiled in response. It wasn't often that Gwen used
her curves and killer smile to get her way, but sometimes she

couldn't seem to help herself. Besides, it's not as though she did it very often.

Deanna shook her head, but her friend smiled. "Hey, if you can get away with it…why not, right?"

"Exactly. And heaven knows I haven't always had this skill. I might as well take advantage sometimes. But don't tell anyone, okay?"

Deanna stared at her. "Who would I tell?"

She forgot sometimes that not everyone lived their whole life online. For Gwen, it was normal to record everything, and censor anything she didn't want getting out. It was a carefully constructed existence, one that was almost entirely public, because she'd built her following by *not* keeping very much private. Her readers liked to hear everything about her, including her workouts, what she had for dinner, her dates, and even more personal things about her dating habits. Not that she'd had much to report lately. She may get a lot of attention from men, but that attention disappeared pretty quickly when they found out who she was and what she did for a living.

"Forget it." Gwen shrugged it off. "I didn't really mean it like that. I mean…"

"I keep forgetting what you do for a living," Deanna said. "I mean, it's crazy to me that you can do that for a *job.* Oh, but I didn't mean it like that. I'm sorry, Gwen. It's just—"

"It's fine. I totally get it. It is crazy. I'm not offended." She decided to change tact and confide in the one person who would totally understand. "But you know what *did* offend me?"

Her friend froze on the sidewalk and waited.

"Ian McCormick." She pronounced every syllable of his name with an edge.

"Ian? You saw him?"

"You know he's here?"

Deanna blinked at her mildly before she put a smile back on her face and ushered Gwen down the sidewalk. "You know what? Let's drop your bag off and then you can tell me all about it over a cup of coffee."

Gwen eyed her friend and shook her head. "How about a *drink*?"

"Why didn't you tell me Ian McCormick was here?" Gwen sat across from Deanna at her kitchen table, a glass of soda water in her hand. She'd gone for the soda, deciding against alcohol. It was her default drink, but now that she had it, she wished she'd gone for something stronger after all. *Ian McCormick was in Cedar Springs.* That had not been part of the plan. Not at all. Sure, whenever she thought of her summers in Cedar Springs visiting her grandma, Ian figured largely in her memory. Whether he knew it or not, his attention—or lack thereof, as was the case—had figured largely in her teenage life. She couldn't remember a summer she hadn't spent lusting after him. As one of the *summer* kids, he was kind of a celebrity among the local kids. Not that she'd been a local kid. But she also wasn't a summer kid. Gwen had definitely floated and never really had any friends except for Deanna.

Ian had no shortage of girls after him, but he'd never wanted to date any of them.

No. That wasn't true. He just hadn't wanted to date *her*. Not that she could blame him. If she'd been a teenage boy back then, *she* wouldn't have wanted to date her. Almost a hundred pounds overweight, with bad hair and glasses, she was a walking cliché. Hell, she was even more of a cliché now that she'd lost all the weight, turned her life around and was returning to her past childhood haunts. She was a made-for-TV movie, for goodness sake.

"I honestly didn't think it mattered." Deanna joined her at the table. "He's a summer kid."

"A…he's not a kid anymore. And, B…you know he's way more than that. He's *way more*."

Deanna almost spat out her water. "No."

"No what?"

"No way you still have a thing for Ian McCormick."

Gwen didn't even have to answer that question, because the woman she'd always considered to be her best friend knew her well enough to know the answer. Or, she should have known her better than that, anyway. She narrowed her eyes and tilted her head.

"No way." Deanna shook her head. "Gwen, how can you possibly still be hung up on him? Honestly, I thought maybe after…well…"

"We said we'd never talk about that, remember?"

The situation they were never to discuss was a moment that could have broken up their friendship forever, but the girls made a decision not to let it affect them. Even though it had been hard, very hard for Gwen. The last summer she'd come to visit, Ian had arrived earlier than he usually had and somehow, Deanna and Ian ended up together at a party where they drank too much and…Gwen didn't like to think about it, but Deanna lost her virginity to Ian McCormick. She could have let it destroy their friendship, but Deanna felt terribly about it and she swore she'd never been more than just a friend with Ian and that's all it would ever be.

"Still," Deanna said. "I honestly didn't think you'd still be thinking of him at all."

How could she not? When they were kids, he'd actually been nice to her. He even talked to her and the conversations they had were real. Not about stupid stuff where she had to pretend to be interested in whatever football team was going to the playoffs or who got drunk at whatever party. But real stuff like what they hoped to achieve with their lives, what the future looked like and where they wanted to go to college. And besides that, he'd been so gorgeous. Correction, he *was* gorgeous. Maybe even more so, if that was possible.

But he still doesn't know you're alive, Gwen, the little voice in her head reminded her. She wasn't more than a townie friend back then, and she was even less now.

"So, he didn't recognize you?" Deanna changed tack. "Not that I'm surprised. You look like a totally different person. Seriously, if I didn't know better, I wouldn't even recognize you and we've been friends since...well, forever. You look crazy good."

Gwen blushed and waved away the compliment. She couldn't seem to get used to the attention she got from people who knew her *when.* It was almost easier for people to think she was just naturally thin and fit. Except when it came to her blog. But talking about her experiences online was a totally different thing. It was safe to hide behind the screen.

In fact, throughout her transformation, it had been a sort of therapy almost. Her website was the place she went to decompress and work through all the feelings that went along with her journey.

She should blog about Ian. Why hadn't she thought of that earlier? It made perfect sense. She could have a chance to process her feelings about seeing him again. *And still being invisible.* And she'd already made her summer vacation into an *event.* When she'd announced her plans to return to Cedar Springs, her readers had gone wild. They wrote in, offering suggestions as to how she should present her transformed self to her old friends, what she should do for a part-time job, and pretty much everything in between. It never ceased to amaze her how invested her readers were in her life and her weight loss journey. In fact, the whole *returning home* thing had garnered so much attention that a talent agent, Jade Johnson, had contacted Gwen about representation, a book deal, and a possible television deal. It was all too crazy to comprehend, but Gwen wasn't about to say no.

She swallowed the rest of her water quickly. "The next one needs alcohol."

"Really?"

Gwen nodded. "Yes. There are only sixty-four calories in vodka. And I'll just run a few extra miles tomorrow. It'll be worth it."

Deanna laughed. "Sounds good. Well, not the running part. I'll leave that up to you. But I don't have any patients tomorrow, so I'll have a few drinks to toast your return. I'll get Marcus to meet us at the Grizzly Paw when he's done up at the hill. He'll want to meet you. I have trouble remembering that you never knew him."

"Nope." Gwen shook her head. "He moved here after my last summer. But it sounds like a good plan to me." Gwen leaned down to retrieve her laptop from the bag at her feet. "But first I need to post an entry."

"Seriously? You just got here."

"I know." She smiled and tried not to take offense to her friend's expression. Ever since her blog started to get real attention and had actually started to make her money, most people had the same reaction. She'd definitely discovered that people struggled with the idea that you could actually make a living writing about your life. Hell, when the advertising offers had first started coming in, Gwen had trouble believing anyone would actually want to give her money to tell her story. "But it pays the bills, Dee. So as long as people want to read it, I'm going to write it."

She flipped open her laptop, signed onto Deanna's Wi-Fi and logged into her account before her fingers froze over the keys. "What do you think?" she asked her friend. "How should I write about Ian?"

"Ian?" Deanna shook her head. "You can't. I mean, you can't use his name or anything."

"Oh my God. Of course not! I don't use anyone's real name. I don't even say what town I'm in. That part is all anonymous. It has to be. But part of the success of everything is how real it all is. So…"

"You're going to blog about Ian?"

Gwen nodded. There really wasn't a question about it. In fact, she'd already kind of alluded to him in past posts as one of her catalysts for starting her weight loss journey. There was no doubt in her mind that if she'd been thin all those years ago, Ian would never have stood her up at the Summer Equinox festival. Not a chance.

"Wait." Deanna got that look in her eye that meant she'd just figured out the connection. "You've already blogged about him, haven't you?"

"You read my blog?"

Deanna gave her a look. "Of course I do. Since the beginning. And that's when you mentioned…Ian is Mr. Summer. How did I not see that until right now?"

Gwen laughed. "I have no idea. It's not like my feelings for him were a big secret or anything. Doesn't everyone remember my public humiliation?"

Deanna grabbed her hand and squeezed. "Gwen, no one remembers that. I promise."

"I remember."

Her friend laughed a little and moved away. "You're the only one. It wasn't even a big deal. He just didn't show up. It's not important. Let it go."

But as Deanna moved about the kitchen, cleaning up dishes and leaving Gwen to write her blog post, all she could think of was that it *was* important and there was no way she could let it go.

Dear Reader,

Sometimes things don't turn out quite the way you plan…

If you're anything like me, you've spent some time thinking about and maybe even daydreaming about how certain people from your past will react to seeing the new and healthier version of you after wronging you. Not to say that I've spent a lot of time thinking on this, but I'd be lying if I said I never thought of it. Of course, as I was planning my return to the town I'd spent all my summers, there was one person in particular that came to mind. Mr. Summer. Long-time readers will remember me mentioning Mr. Summer before. Every young woman—particularly those of us who've struggled with our body image…who hasn't—has at least one encounter with a boy or man that has stuck with them. An encounter for better or worse that somehow shaped or defined how they thought of members of the opposite sex, and sadly, how they thought of themselves.

That was Mr. Summer. I was desperately in love with him from the summers of fourteen to eighteen. Four years of my life in which he barely knew I was alive. When he finally did notice me, he humiliated me and broke my heart.

For years, he was the star of my fantasies when I thought about returning with my new and improved self. How would he react? Would his jaw drop? Would he stumble over his words as he apologized for standing me up all those years ago? Would he beg me to give him another chance?

Well, readers, I can tell you that now, all these years later I finally have my answer.

None of those things happened. In fact, he didn't even recognize me. We came eye to eye and there wasn't even a flicker of acknowledgment in his eyes. (Which are still as dreamy as I remember.)

And now I'm here, on the eve of my first night back in town and already I'm filled with a strong sense of dissatisfaction in regards to Mr.

Summer. So, obviously I cannot let a homecoming come and go without doing something about it. Or can I?

What do you think? Should I confront Mr. Summer and thank him for being at least one of the catalysts that spurred my life change? Or should I let it go and move on? Or maybe something different....

Read the rest of Love in the Moment NOW and fall in love with the rest of the McCormick brothers!

Don't forget to join my mailing list where you'll be the first to hear about new stories, sales and promotions and giveaways!
You can join me here —>
https://elenaaitken.com/newsletter/

About the Author

Elena Aitken is a USA Today Bestselling Author of more than forty romance and women's fiction novels. The mother of 'grown up' twins, Elena now lives with her very own mountain man in the heart of the very mountains she writes about. She can often be found with her toes in the lake and a glass of wine in her hand, dreaming up her next book and working on her own happily ever after.

To learn more about Elena:
www.elenaaitken.com
elena@elenaaitken.com